Early Praise for

THE SILVERSMITH'S SECRET

"*The Silversmith's Secret* plunges the reader into a fast-paced tale of intrigue and mystery that begins with a little-known chapter of Yemen's past, the echoes of which reverberate six decades later as a pair of American journalists confront present-day dangers."

—Eric Schmitt, senior correspondent for *The New York Times* and coauthor of *Counterstrike: The Untold Story of America's Secret Campaign Against Al Qaeda*

"Stephen Seche's powerful novel bridges the decades with a captivating mixture of geopolitics, adventure, and the very human quest for legacy. Taut and engaging, *The Silversmith's Secret* focuses on the tempests of the Middle East, but its themes speak to the commonality of identity and honor. This is a compelling read, and one which shines with the artistry of a new writer who knows his subject and his characters, bringing them to us with precision and grace."

—Greg Fields, author of *The Bright Freight of Memory*

"Drawing on the saga of the mass exodus of Yemeni Jews, Seche weaves a dazzling tale that transports readers to the narrow streets and market stalls of Yemen's ancient capital, where some very modern evils threaten to upend a traditional way of life."

—Edward "Skip" Gnehm, former US ambassador to Jordan

"Seche's debut novel brought me back to the Middle East I remember, populated by intrepid journalists, wily CIA case officers, and cunning rulers. The story races along, pulsing with the sights, sounds, and smells of a mysterious and complicated region."

—Marc Polymeropoulos, former CIA senior intelligence officer, author of *Clarity in Crisis: Leadership Lessons from the CIA*

The Silversmith's Secret
by Stephen A. Seche

© Copyright 2025 Stephen A. Seche
ISBN 979-8-88824-614-6

All rights reserved. No part of this publication may be reproduced, stored in a retrieval system, or transmitted in any form or by any means—electronic, mechanical, photocopy, recording, or any other—except for brief quotations in printed reviews, without the prior written permission of the author.

This is a work of fiction. All the characters in this book are fictitious, and any resemblance to actual persons, living or dead, is purely coincidental. The names, incidents, dialogue, and opinions expressed are products of the author's imagination and are not to be construed as real.

Published by

3705 Shore Drive
Virginia Beach, VA 23455
800-435-4811
www.koehlerbooks.com

THE SILVERSMITH'S SECRET

A Novel

STEPHEN A. SECHE

VIRGINIA BEACH
CAPE CHARLES

For Susan, Kate, Lucy, and Ariel

LUCIDITY INFORMATION DESIGN, LLC

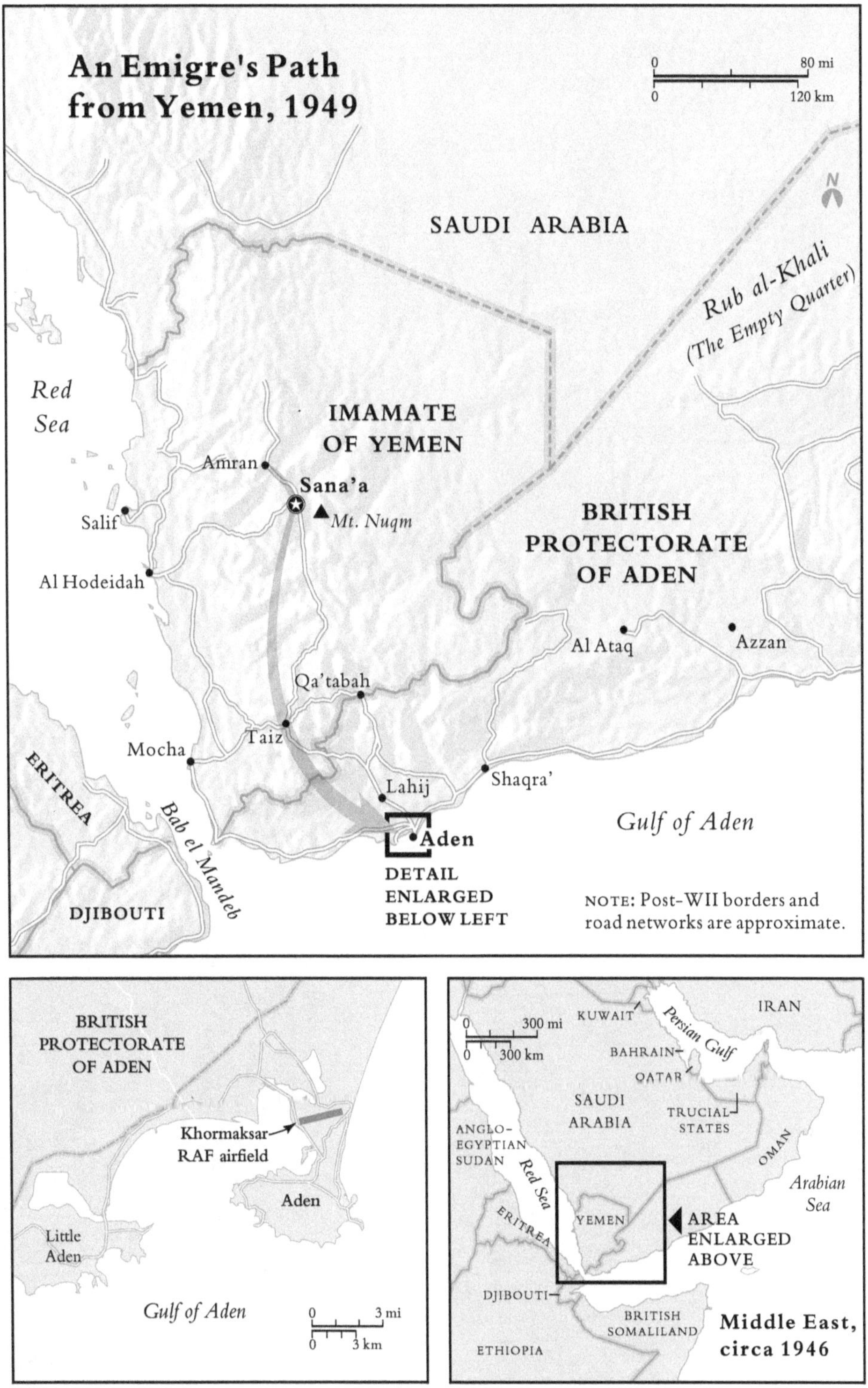

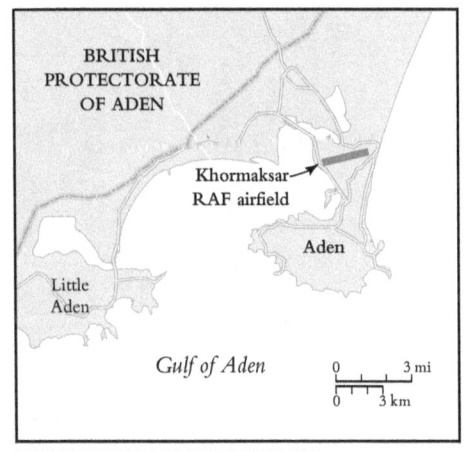

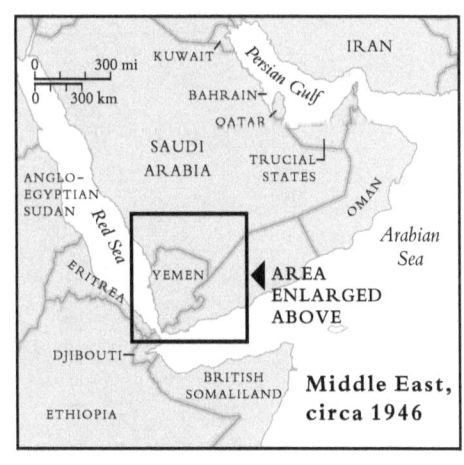

PROLOGUE

I am Moishe Azani, a Jew, a silversmith, a Yemeni. But I can no longer live in my own country, and with God's blessing, will soon begin a new life with my family in the Promised Land of Israel. To make this journey, I have left behind everything, including treasured pieces of handmade jewelry I could not bring myself to sell. I wanted to believe I would return to claim them one day, but now I know that my wife, Shamaa, is right. I will never come back to Yemen.

I have given this note to you because I believe you will be able to go to Sana'a where the jewelry is hidden and retrieve it. Each piece is special in its own way, a contribution made to Yemen's culture by Jews like me. My fear is that as we leave, these traditions will be lost, and the world will slowly forget that generations of Yemeni Jews created beautiful art with our hands. I make no claim that my work is of extraordinary value, although it has allowed me to earn a living and provide for my family. I hope to continue my craft when I am settled in Israel, but I am prepared to do whatever the Lord asks of me. I have watched you and believe you are a trustworthy man, so I am placing my life's work in your care and ask only that you find a way to share it with the world.

Part One

THE NOTE

CHAPTER ONE

Fort Dodge, Iowa
2010

"Sir, I know you can hear me. I need you to stop walking away."

Hank Amato was trying his best to ignore the voice behind him, but it was impossible. It sliced through the thick summer air like a straight razor, sharp and insistent.

For a split second he considered running, but he was on an Air Force base in north central Iowa that was locked up tighter than a drum. Early that morning, he had been bused in along with a dozen other journalists to cover remarks by Iowa's senior senator marking the deployment of the 23rd Tactical Fighter Wing. The ceremony included a flyover by a squadron of fighter planes and remarks by more dignitaries than Hank ever imagined existed in and around the city of Fort Dodge.

"Sir, you might as well stop. You can't get nowhere anyway."

The double negative was like fingernails on a chalkboard to Hank, a self-professed guardian of the English language. So serious was he in his mission that he maintained a file of malapropisms and other notable linguistic gaffes. Just that morning he'd acquired another gem for his collection, courtesy of the base public affairs officer, who assured the visiting press during an introductory briefing that his goal was to "make sure we're all shooting from the same hip."

Hank looked to his right and saw his colleagues slowly returning to the press bus, which was idling quietly at the far end of a large parking lot. It dawned on him that he couldn't afford to have whatever was about to happen take place within view of a bunch of snoopy reporters, any one of whom might see what was going on and decide it was too delicious a scandal to keep to himself.

So he stopped and slowly turned around. Behind him, a beefy security guard, a loss prevention officer in retail nomenclature, was closing in. He was almost a head taller than Hank, who was just shy of six feet. He wore a bright fluorescent vest over a black Iowa Hawkeyes hoodie. His sheer size and the incongruity of the outfit only added to the sense of vertigo that Hank could feel creeping over him.

"I'm sorry, were you speaking to me?" Hank willed his voice to be steady.

The fluorescent vest didn't respond. He simply held out his hand, waiting for Hank to surrender his shopping bag, which contained a paperback novel and a boxed set of four stag horn handle steak knives. He'd only paid for one of the items.

"Before you ask, I'm afraid I don't have a receipt for the knives," Hank said. "I must have dropped it inside the store."

The vest looked at him. Hank thought he detected a smirk. "You'll have to come with me, sir."

Hank glanced again across the large expanse of parking lot. The young Air Force public affairs officer in gray fatigues, their minder for the day, was standing next to the door of the bus, patiently waiting for the rest of her charges to return.

Thirty minutes earlier, she had released them with the following admonition: "As you know, you've all been given guest privileges at the base exchange located in the building directly behind me. You have half an hour to shop before we load the bus. Please don't be late. I am responsible for your sorry butts, so don't make me come looking for you."

Hank thought thirty minutes was plenty of time for him to poke around the PX, given that poking around was something at which he excelled. He couldn't remember a time growing up when he wasn't rummaging through his house, examining the contents of bureaus and closets or musty boxes stacked in the attic. He wasn't looking for anything special, mostly he was just nosy. He liked to see what people didn't necessarily want you to see. And a lot of times, if he liked what he saw, he kept it, a reward for being so enterprising.

He discovered a stash of Franklin half-dollars squirreled away in a cigar box beneath a pile of sweaters in his father's bureau, and sample boxes of amphetamines in the upstairs linen closet, the "not for resale" variety pharmaceutical reps left behind when they visited his mother's office. Slowly, over the next several months, Hank dipped into each, taking care to stop the pilferage before he exhausted the supply of either. If his parents noticed a diminished inventory, they never saw fit to mention it. Hank wondered if that meant he was forgiven.

This fondness for pocketing things that weren't his both entertained and perplexed him. After careful thought, he concluded he was the victim of a rare biological anomaly: the larceny gene. Sadly, he was unable to find any evidence to support his theory, leaving him to ponder his condition without a scientific leg to stand on.

His sticky fingers made for a complicated relationship with stores and store merchandise. He knew the smart play was to stay away from the PX. He was twenty-nine years old and a staff writer for *The Des Moines Register*, Iowa's biggest newspaper, well past the point in his life when he should be entertaining thoughts of petty larceny. But Hank was no more likely to sit quietly on the press bus than he was to walk away from a big pot at a poker game because the odds were long that he would draw the inside straight. Hank was an optimist. He always thought the cards would fall his way. So, in he went.

The PX looked like a compact version of his local Walmart. He wandered past the greeting cards, the school supplies, and the kitchen utensils. He turned a corner and found himself in the book section, staring at rows of hardcover books with colorful dust jackets. Paperbacks were stacked next to each other with military precision.

The display was a far cry from the revolving book racks at Babbitt's Pharmacy which, for a time, had been a regular stop for

Hank growing up in Cedar Rapids. According to the sign on the front window, Babbitt's had been *proudly serving our community from the same location on Broadway for 80 years*. Hank had a paper route back then, and every Saturday after collecting his pay, he'd make his way to Babbitt's. He would park his bike out front and go straight to the paperback books, stacked in a pair of carousels that stood side by side directly across from the shelves that held the magazines and newspapers.

He was twelve, and a voracious reader. He'd choose a book and a candy bar, usually a Nestlé Crunch or a Sky Bar. Some Saturdays he would buy the book and steal the candy, and some weeks it was the other way around. He was such a regular that on the weeks he walked up to the counter with just a paperback in hand, old man Babbitt would invite him to choose a candy bar, not imagining that Hank had already tucked one into his jacket pocket on the way to the register.

Now, in the PX, Hank purchased a paperback promising a gripping account of the 1900 hurricane that devastated Galveston, Texas. The very accommodating young woman behind the counter handed it to him in a paper sack with convenient handles, and he strolled into the housewares section. Fifteen minutes later he was making his way across the parking lot headed for the press bus, smugly confident he had outsmarted whatever security measures Fort Dodge Air Force Base had deployed inside its PX.

CHAPTER TWO

British Protectorate of Aden
1949

Moishe Azani looked hard into the bright blue sky, searching for a sign of what the man pacing nervously in front of them said was an airplane. Moishe had only recently seen an airplane for the first time in his life, but he couldn't see this one, and he couldn't hear it, either. But then, his hearing hadn't been good ever since he was slapped on the side of his head by the police officer back home for not stepping aside quickly enough to let two Muslim women pass without fear of physical contact. That had been quite a few years ago, when being a Jew in his Yemeni village was hard but still manageable. Things had gotten worse in the last year. Much worse. Ever since news began to circulate in early 1947 that Jews were going to get their own homeland, and that thousands of Palestinian Muslims were going to be displaced to make room for it. Overnight, it seemed to Moishe that the only thing the couple dozen Jews in his village spoke about was the need to flee Yemen and make their way south to the coastal city of Aden, the seat of the British Protectorate.

The first imperial acquisition of Queen Victoria's reign, Aden came under British rule in 1839, when a Royal Marines contingent seized control from a local sultan and his allies. London valued Aden as a base that would facilitate access to and from India, its most important colony. Blessed with one of the finest harbors between London and Bombay, Aden had slowly declined into little more than a pirate village preying on Indian Ocean maritime traffic. That changed under British control; piracy came to an end and a thriving civilian and military infrastructure grew around the port, which eventually became a British Crown colony.

Surrounding it all was Aden Protectorate, a vast hinterland of desert and mountains. Indigenous tribal leaders continued to exercise sovereignty over the territory in exchange for protection by the British, with the understanding that the local sheikhs wouldn't enter any treaties with other nations. Looming over the protectorate, to its north and west, was Yemen, a predominantly Muslim nation of nearly 4.5 million people ruled by a Shi'a imam. Yemen also was home to a historically vibrant Jewish community, although as World War II ended, only fifty thousand or so remained, a number that had dwindled dramatically over the years as many grew weary of living as second-class citizens in a majority Muslim society.

In December 1947, the United Nations voted formally to partition Palestine and establish a Jewish state, prompting a spate of attacks by Muslim gangs on Jewish neighborhoods.

"Shamaa," Moishe pleaded with his wife after one particularly difficult day, "I don't know how much longer I can stay here. People come to my shop and get angry because I ask a fair price for the jewelry I make. If I can't sell my jewelry, we will starve. Better we starve on our way to the Holy Land than here, unwelcome in our own village."

His wife of twelve years, a small, modest woman with dark eyes and long brown hair that she concealed under a headscarf, looked carefully at her husband. She knew he was right. Living as a Jew in Yemen was like being a rabbit in the forest. You were always wary, always sniffing the air hoping you'd be able to detect where the next danger was coming from.

Nevertheless, it was hard for her to imagine leaving. "Moishe, this is the only home we have ever known. And not everyone mistreats us. Yasser has always been kind." Yasser al-Alimi was a devout Muslim who ran the village bakery where people lined up each morning to buy flatbread hot from the oven. Each day he put some aside for

Moishe and his family so they wouldn't have to face the harassment that awaited them as they stood in line.

Shamaa continued. "And Mahmoud helps the boys with their lessons when he can. He would like to be able to have them in school. He has told us so."

"Yes, Shamaa," Moishe said, an air of resignation in his voice. "They are good men. But Yasser is a baker and Mahmoud is a teacher. They didn't make the laws that weigh so heavily on us, and they can't change them. We are Jews, living in a Muslim world. We are dhimmis. We are the others. I cannot even ride a horse in my own village. I must ride our donkey, and even then, I must ride sidesaddle, so everyone will know a Jew is coming. I am expected to clean the streets. I am a silversmith. I am not a street cleaner. But the law says otherwise." He sighed. They'd had this conversation before, and it never ended well.

"Shamaa, I know you don't want to leave. I don't either. But this village no longer feels like my home."

"I understand, Moishe. I'll think about it. But for today, let's talk of something else."

They did—the quiet, familiar conversation of two people whose lives were woven together in a thousand small ways. Then Moishe left the house and walked the short distance to his workshop. Business for his fine, handcrafted silver jewelry was often brisk this time of year, as spring made its way to the highlands of Yemen and families began to prepare for long-awaited weddings.

As he turned onto the hard-packed street that led to his workshop, he was surprised to see his friend Shlomo, who ran a small woodworking shop nearby, sitting on the curb waiting for him.

"We need to talk," Shlomo said as he stood and waited impatiently behind Moishe, who was fumbling with the lock on the roughly hewn door of his shop.

"So talk, Shlomo."

"Inside," he said, and he nearly pushed Moishe over the threshold into the darkened shop.

"What is so urgent?" Moishe asked.

"Imam Ahmed has authorized exit permits for Jews to depart Yemen, Moishe. We are free to leave."

"But where do we go, Shlomo?"

"To Israel," he said excitedly. "The British in Aden are preparing to take us on airplanes. The Aliyah is about to begin. Our ascent to the Promised Land."

"And how do you know all this?"

"Because Miriam's uncle traveled to Sana'a to meet with a Yemeni Jew whose own family made the trip to Jerusalem years ago." Miriam was Shlomo's wife; her uncle was the village rabbi. "The man who has returned to help us depart is Yosef Halevi. He said that Israel and Great Britain agree: the Jews of Yemen should be free."

CHAPTER THREE

British Protectorate of Aden
1949

Dewey Poe looked down from the cockpit of his DC-4, startled to see people crowding onto the runway he had just been cleared to use for landing. So startled, he decided to abort his descent and make another run at it—after checking with ground control at Royal Air Force Station Khormaksar to see what exactly was going on.

Dewey pulled out of his landing pattern, banked to the right, and began a long, slow loop that would return him to his original approach while he awaited a reply. Beneath him, the Gulf of Aden shimmered in the midday sun. Small fishing craft bobbed on the gentle swells. The Horn of Africa lay to the south, thrusting itself defiantly into the Indian Ocean.

In addition to Dewey, the DC-4 he was piloting carried a crew of six: copilot Ed Burdette, navigator Steve Reeder, radio operator Jimmy Vargas, flight mechanic Joe Worsley, and two flight attendants he'd met for the first time earlier that morning. They began their day at the Acropol Hotel in Nicosia, Cyprus, the usual overnight destination after an evening flight into Tel Aviv. The state of war between the newly established nation of Israel and its Arab neighbors made spending any more time than necessary on the ground at Lod Airport too risky, so the island of Cyprus, a short hop to the north and west, became the preferred layover location.

Dewey climbed out of bed that morning expecting to fly to Rotterdam, where he was to pick up eight members of the crew of a

Liberian-flagged freighter who had failed to show up when it sailed earlier in the week. His instructions were to deliver them to Tangier, where they would board their ship as it made its way into the Strait of Gibraltar.

That all changed with an early morning phone call as Dewey shaved in front of a comically small mirror hung over the sink in his room. He wiped the soap from his face with a towel, walked to the nightstand, and brought the handset to his ear. The phone line crackled as an international connection was made. Before he could speak, a voice at the other end of the line jumped in.

"Dewey, are you there?" It was Harry Janssen, shouting as he most often did, even though the line was unusually clear. Harry ran the Flagstaff Airlines office in Amsterdam. Dewey had been flying for Flagstaff since he mustered out of the Navy at the end of World War II. The company needed pilots for the surplus DC-4s and C-46s it was busy acquiring, planes the United States no longer needed and didn't care to maintain. Dewey knew the DC-4 nose to tail, or at least its military cousin, the C-54 Skymaster, which he had flown for most of the war, ferrying men and matériel across the Atlantic and back. His job description hadn't changed much with Flagstaff Air; he was still hauling cargo, although recently the company's charter business had picked up and instead of freight, they were ferrying passengers.

"Yes, I'm here, Harry. You're up early, aren't you?"

"I wanted to catch you before you got into the air. Change of plans, Dewey. Rotterdam's off. You're to head directly back to Aden. There will be a cable from HQ waiting for you there with instructions."

"You're being mysterious, Harry."

"That's because I don't have any more information. Except for this. You're adding two flight attendants to your crew. They're both Israelis. They're laying over in Nicosia and they'll meet you at the airport. Sorry for the last-minute change. But look on the bright side. You can go for a swim when you get to Aden. Ciao, Dewey."

Dewey informed his flight crew of the change in their itinerary at breakfast. Steve Reeder said he would go to the airport ahead of the others and file a new flight plan. Twelve hours later, Dewey was making virtually the same approach into Aden he had made three days earlier.

That flight, however, had been full: five crew and fifty-three passengers, all of whom were stateless Jewish refugees fleeing Shanghai as Mao Tse-tung's Communist army approached. RAF Khormaksar in Aden had quickly become Dewey's preferred final refueling stop en route to Israel, a nation barely a year old and eager to welcome Jews from around the world.

The need to avoid the airspace of hostile Arab states while flying a planeload of Jewish refugees from Shanghai to Tel Aviv required a circuitous route designed to make sure a friendly airport was within reach, in case a mechanical problem or other emergency required an unscheduled landing.

Pilots were already telling the story of Charlie Mercer, who was flying a planeload of Jews from Eritrea to Tel Aviv when he ran short of fuel and had to make an emergency landing in Khartoum. As the story went, the Sudanese authorities balked at refueling Charlie's plane without having all the passengers disembark, something he desperately wanted to avoid. So, he told the airport authorities that he would need a fleet of ambulances to take his passengers immediately to the hospital because they were all infected with smallpox. The Sudanese refueled his plane without further discussion, and he was on his way.

The route from Shanghai took Dewey and his crew to Bangkok, Calcutta, Bombay, and finally Aden before reaching their destination, Lod Airport in Tel Aviv. It was becoming a familiar journey after nearly four months and a half dozen trips, each time dropping off a planeload of refugees, most of whom had fled to China from Europe as anti-Semitism grew in the run-up to World War II. Now, once more facing an uncertain future, and with Israel beckoning, they had chosen to move yet again.

Dewey and his crew had developed a familiar routine on earlier flights from Shanghai. They would depart Bombay at night, landing in Aden around nine o'clock in the morning. Their passengers would be taken to a local hotel while Dewey and his crew conducted necessary maintenance, refueled, and prepared the plane for departure the following day.

RAF Khormaksar had seemed a relatively sleepy place on those earlier layovers, and the crew had come to enjoy their sojourns at the Apollo Hotel. Backing onto a small cove, it managed most days to capture a gentle sea breeze blowing in from the Gulf of Aden, particularly welcome during the summer months, when the southwesterly monsoons pushed daily temperatures to well over one hundred degrees, with high humidity and frequent, hot sandstorms.

For the moment, Dewey pushed thoughts of a clean bed and a cold beer at the Apollo Hotel from his mind as he brought the plane around and returned to his original flight path into Aden. He could see vehicles moving briskly below, as the British military responded to his request for a clear runway.

With nothing more than a gentle tailwind to contend with, he set the DC-4 down easily and taxied to a stop. The people who'd been pushed from the runway minutes before began to press forward once again. Dewey and his crew went through their checklist quickly. He signed the logbook and handed it to Worsley, his flight mechanic, who would oversee any work needed before they took off again.

Dewey walked to the rear of the aircraft, past the rows of empty seats, to where the two flight attendants were poised and ready to make their way down the ladder that unfolded from the rear hatch.

"Well, ladies, someone must have told them this was your first trip to Aden, because it looks like they've arranged a special welcome." Dewey poked his head out of the plane and squinted as his eyes adjusted to the unforgiving midday sun. Waves of heat rose from the runway, enveloping the hundreds of people congregating on the concrete apron.

He pulled his sunglasses from the breast pocket of his shirt and put them on. He descended the ladder and surveyed the crowd. They were poorly clothed, and many were without shoes. They looked bewildered, as if they were unsure they had come to the right place. Women held small babies in their arms while other children huddled close. Dewey couldn't remember the last time he had seen such a bedraggled assembly of humanity.

If they were Jewish refugees, they certainly didn't look like those he had been ferrying from Shanghai. He remembered the first group, which emerged from the terminal at Lunghwa Airport wearing multiple layers of clothing because they could bring only a single suitcase and needed the luggage space to pack personal items they didn't want to leave behind. In comparison, these folks looked as if they'd been wearing the same clothes for weeks.

Off to his right, two men were arguing. He recognized one of the men as Group Captain Walcott, the commander of the RAF station. The other man was shorter and thinner, a colorful cloth wrapped turban-style around his head. He was wearing a white short-sleeved shirt and a pair of blue trousers rolled up to just below his knees. Around his waist was a thick, braided cloth belt that supported a scabbard into which a large knife with a curved blade and an intricately carved handle had been inserted. In previous stops, Dewey had learned it was called a jambiya, a ceremonial knife carried by virtually all men in neighboring Yemen. Suddenly, the man bolted toward Dewey.

"Captain, it is such a relief to see you and your aircraft. As you can see for yourself, we are in desperate need to move these people out of here." His English was heavily accented, but clear.

Walcott was right on the man's tail. "No more from you, Yosef. I'll have you physically removed from the base if you continue to obstruct its operations." He looked at Dewey and extended his hand. "Captain Poe. Good to see you again." They shook hands.

"Commander Walcott. Seems like you've got something of a situation on your hands."

Walcott gently steered Dewey away from the other man and they walked toward the front of the plane. "Indeed, we do." He handed

Dewey a cable. "I was told to give this to you as soon as you landed." It was from Flagstaff Airlines headquarters. Dewey unfolded the cable and began to read:

URGENT
TO Captain Dewey Poe
FROM Director of Global Operations

Upon receipt of this message, you are to provide full cooperation with British and Israeli authorities in Aden to support the evacuation to Tel Aviv of Jewish refugees departing Yemen. All other routes are canceled until further notice. Advise Office of Global Operations once flights have begun. Godspeed.

The cable was signed by Charles Springer, the Flagstaff Airlines VP who served as global operations director. Most flight crews had taken to referring to his cables as messages from God, a nod to his position's acronym and his penchant for peremptory instructions that invited no discussion.

Dewey folded the cable and tucked it into his shirt pocket. "Looks like I am at your disposal, Commander," he said to Walcott as he glanced over at the hundreds of people on the runway. "I presume these are the folks we're going to take off your hands." Walcott nodded. "Well, we can get started, but it's going to be a while before we even make a dent in this crowd."

Walcott raised his hands in a display of surrender to the reality of having a single DC-4 available for duty. "I understand, Captain Poe. I assure you these people are not even supposed to be here right now. Our friend," he cocked his head in the direction of the man with whom he had been arguing, "got wind of the cable from your HQ through his own channels in New York and took it upon himself to deliver them, as if they would just magically make their way onto your plane and be on their way. We'll have them returned to their camp, such as it is." Walcott paused for a moment. "But as you've already observed, Captain, we're dealing with a bit of an emergency. The group here is just the tip of the iceberg, if you will, although I realize that is a bit of an odd metaphor for the southern Arabian desert." A weak smile played across his mouth briefly, then disappeared.

He continued. "At last count, over two thousand Jews have made their way from Yemen and are camping all over Aden. Most of them have walked here. They have no shelter, and they're sleeping on the ground with little food or water. We've had to close the border to prevent more from arriving, but I'm afraid that's done very little to stem the flow of traffic. The Israelis have promised to build a proper camp, and my friend there has been sent to oversee that project. His sense of urgency is not misplaced, even if his lack of adherence to procedure is appalling."

Walcott looked over at the crowd still sitting on the tarmac. "As far as they're concerned, Captain Poe, you are the instrument of their deliverance to the Promised Land. I'm told they even have a word for it in Hebrew: Aliyah."

CHAPTER FOUR

Des Moines, Iowa
2010

Hank was the kind of guy who wanted his favorite clothes to last forever, so he never wore them. But today was different. He needed an outfit that would convey sincerity and reliability. Something that would persuade his boss to keep the man wearing these clothes on the payroll, despite the fact that he was recently collared for shoplifting.

He opted for charcoal gray slacks, a white Oxford shirt, a subdued burgundy print tie, and a navy-blue blazer. Now, sitting in the small waiting area outside the office of *The Des Moines Register*'s managing editor, he was sure he had overdressed. He also felt a little lightheaded, a condition he attributed to the tie knotted around his neck.

The last time he'd spoken in person with Mort Connolly was over a year ago, under decidedly happier circumstances. Hank had just won the 2009 George Polk Award for a series he'd written on the work of an attorney who, for the past six years, had been providing legal counsel to one of the prisoners at the Guantanamo Bay Naval Base in Cuba.

Her name was Carole Ann McAfee, and she had earned her law degree at Iowa. She owned a home overlooking Lake Macbride, just a stone's throw from Iowa City. She returned for a couple of weeks each summer, and every year she would host a fundraiser for a local charity.

Hank attended his first one courtesy of a newsroom colleague who flipped an invitation onto Hank's desk one afternoon as he walked by with the day's mail. "You should check this out. I've gone a couple of times and it's been very entertaining. She has a great house, beautiful views of the lake and it's always a good place to meet people who might be helpful someday."

Hank went. He did the requisite internet search beforehand and found out that Carole Ann McAfee had graduated from UI Law in 1979, the year before he was born. She went directly to work for the US Attorney's office in Chicago, where she gained a reputation as a meticulously prepared prosecutor. After eight years she made the jump to private practice, joining Laver and Reynolds, a DC firm with a long and illustrious pedigree, but also a place where she would be free to do the pro bono work that was so dear to her heart.

"I never married," she told Hank in their very first conversation, as they watched the boats moving up and down Lake Macbride and a warm July day drew to a close. "I have no children of my own, so the causes I believe in have become like my children, and I devote as much time as I can to each of them. Does that sound peculiar?" Hank thought the question was designed to disarm him, so he mulled it over for a minute before replying.

"It sounds to me like you've been fortunate to land in a place where you don't have to choose between your job and the pursuits you're most passionate about," Hank said.

"And not just once," Carole Ann added. "In 2004 my firm merged with an old Boston practice, and I was anxious that we were about to become one of those insufferable white-shoe law firms full of privileged Ivy League graduates. But they made it easy for me, and others, to make time for cases that mattered to us. Like my representation of Ashraf al-Akli, the young Yemeni at Guantanamo. My only regret is that I haven't been able to do more to win his release." She paused for a moment and looked back out over the lake. "I can't shake the sensation that I've failed him. He shouldn't be there. No one should. That place violates every principle of justice on which this great country of ours was founded. But I'm not done yet. Not even close," she said, smiling quickly.

"I'm sure you're not," Hank replied." And then, so quickly he even surprised himself, he added, "I'd like to write about the work you're doing at Guantanamo. It's like another planet to most of us around here, and you've got a foot in both worlds."

She took some convincing but, in the end, agreed with Hank that shining a light on what happened inside Guantanamo could hardly make things worse for her client, and might even prove to be helpful. Just as important, Mort Connolly also agreed, allowing Hank to devote most of the next two months to researching and writing the piece, which ran in three installments in the spring of 2008. In February of the following year, the winners of the Polk Awards were announced, and Hank's profile of Carole Ann won in the category of justice reporting.

To celebrate, Connolly invited Hank to his office for a chat, then walked him to the newsroom where the editorial staff had gathered. He said nice things about Hank, how proud the *Register* was to be able to feature the work of young journalists like him, and everyone had a paper cupful of champagne before going back to work.

The voice of Connolly's secretary shook Hank from his reverie. "You can go in now, Hank. Mort's ready for you."

The office was as Hank remembered it, surprisingly small, dominated by a desk shoehorned into a corner so that windows flanked it on either side. The blinds were drawn to keep the late-afternoon sun at bay. Mort Connolly sat behind the desk facing the door, his own necktie loosened and the top button of his shirt undone, which seemed eminently sensible to Hank, who was still experiencing some shortness of breath.

"Sit," said Mort, gesturing to a chair directly in front of his desk. He closed his laptop, removed his glasses, and nodded his head approvingly. "You look nice."

"Not too much?" Hank asked.

"Maybe a little, but I appreciate the gesture."

Hank had decided to dive right into the reason for the meeting, rather than beat around the bush. "Mort, I am truly sorry that this mess of mine has landed on your desk. You've got plenty to worry about, I know."

Mort ran a hand through his hair. "Hank, you've been with us for what now, eight years, right? You're a good journalist. Well liked, best I can tell. And now you've gone off and torched your career. You committed the cardinal sin of journalism: instead of covering the story, you just became the story. Shoplifting? Don't we pay you enough?"

Hank could feel the heat rising in his face. "Mort, this was a huge misunderstanding, and I am absolutely to blame. I dropped that set of steak knives into the bag with the book I had bought because I needed both hands to look at something else. I just forgot they were there when I left the store."

"That's not what the folks at Fort Dodge think, Hank. They think you're a criminal mastermind who rolled onto the base under the guise of covering Senator Price's visit and thought he'd walk out with some new cutlery, that nobody'd be the wiser. They're expecting to have medals pinned on their chests."

"Mort, you gotta know how humiliating this is. I honestly just made a mistake. I would never jeopardize my standing at the paper or put you or the *Register* in an awkward position for the sake of four stupid steak knives. I don't even eat steak." Hank wished he hadn't added that last bit, because Mort shot him a look that made it clear he wasn't going to tolerate cute.

He also realized that he had just invited Mort to do what any self-respecting journalist would do with his disclaimer: ask a follow-up. Which, of course, Mort did. "So why are you walking around with steak knives in your bag if you don't eat steak?"

"They were for my brother Dominic. His birthday is at the end of the month. He eats nothing but meat."

Mort moved on. "Look, Hank. There's only so much I can do here. I spoke with the base commander. He's a good guy—I've known him for years, and he's not interested in embarrassing the paper. And if he felt differently, I couldn't blame him. They welcomed you onto the base, treated you with respect, allowed you to cover the senator's visit, and even extended the extra courtesy of letting you shop at the base PX before getting back onto the bus. And your thank you is to steal shit."

Hank started to protest, but Mort held up the index finger on his right hand, signaling he wasn't done. "I know, I know, you didn't mean to steal anything. But Hank, wake up. They could really bust your balls on this. Yours and mine. But the general's agreed not to. He's agreed to keep this all between us." Hank could feel the tension start to leave his body. Maybe his luck was going to hold, after all. "He did make it clear, however, that in exchange he expects you to resign from the paper."

Mort's words hit Hank like a two-by-four. "Resign? And you agreed?"

"I'm sorry, Hank, did I make the wrong call? Would you rather have your day in court? That's entirely up to you. I can undo this if you want."

"No, Mort, that's not what I'm saying. But losing my job? I've worked so hard."

"You didn't leave me much choice, Hank. If they press charges, this whole episode goes public, and we have to cover it. Imagine that headline: '*Register* staffer charged with theft during Senator's visit to air base.' Your career couldn't survive that kind of attention, Hank. At least this way you get to avoid the spectacle and walk out of here with no one the wiser." He paused, his tone softening. "Listen, for what it's worth, I hate to lose you. You've done really good work. That series you did on the lady lawyer who represents the kid at Guantanamo—what was her name again?"

"Carole Ann McAfee."

"Yeah, McAfee. How'd you ever come across her anyway?"

"She went to UI Law. She has a summer place up at Red Rock. She hosted a fundraiser at her house for the Boys and Girls Club a couple of summers ago. Avery gave me his invitation."

"Well, that was a damn fine piece of work, Hank."

"Thanks, Mort."

"But you fucked up, son. You say you didn't mean to take those steak knives, and I want to believe you. But what I believe doesn't matter. You've put your future in the hands of people who don't know you and who have no investment in you. And right now they're willing to cut you a break. My advice? Swallow hard and accept their offer. Tell folks you need to get away from the daily grind, recharge. All that shit. It's a cliché but it's familiar. Nobody will give it a second thought. Go and travel and find yourself, or whatever the hell one does with free time. Take a year and then find another job. I'll give you a recommendation. This will go away, and you'll be back on your feet."

"Jesus, Mort."

"Yeah, it sucks, Hank. But you know what also sucks? I owe the base commander a favor now, and he's going to call it in one day when one of his airmen fucks up, and he's going to expect me to sit on that story, and I don't know how exactly I'm going to handle that."

"Sorry, Mort."

"Look, Hank, you're young. You need to sort out whatever is going on in your life. Maybe you're forgetful. Maybe you're deceitful. It's really not my business. My business is caring for this newspaper. Right now the best way to do that is to keep this episode from exploding in my face. For that to happen, we need to go our separate ways." Mort reached for his glasses. "Now get out of here and figure out how you're going to break the news to everybody. By the end of the month, you need to be on your way."

CHAPTER FIVE

Des Moines, Iowa
2010

Hank walked out of the *Register* and joined the crowd of office workers spilling out of the surrounding buildings to enjoy lunch outdoors on a mild August afternoon. He headed east on Locust Street and walked onto the grounds of the State Capitol. It was the same route he had taken seven years ago after his job interview at the *Register*. The conversation had gone well and he was elated, even allowing himself the luxury of believing that he would soon begin his career as a full-time, honest-to-God journalist.

Today, though, all he could feel was an overwhelming sense of despair. He sat on a bench and leaned back, welcoming the warmth of the sun on his face, hoping it would deliver some sort of enlightenment, something to clutch onto. Instead, what came to mind was the irony of having just lost his job because of yet another larcenous episode in his life, which was precisely the behavior that had gotten him thinking about journalism as a career in the first place.

It was August 1997, the summer before Hank's senior year in high school. He was sitting on his porch with Charlie Coates and Ray Pinto watching fireflies dance across the front yard. All three had spent the summer caddying at Five Oaks Country Club in Cedar Rapids. With nothing better to do, Hank suggested they walk up to the club and search for stray golf balls. By now, they knew where all the hackers shanked their tee shots into the woods and, because they were too lazy or too embarrassed to search for them, took a mulligan, or maybe two, until they hit a playable ball.

They walked up Cameron Street, took a left onto a familiar path that cut through the woods, and made their way to the golf course. As they walked past the clubhouse, Hank spotted an open window above a sink in the basement.

"Charlie," he said, "I'll bet you can squeeze through there." They popped the screen out of the window frame and Charlie Coates, the smallest of the three, worked his way through the opening and dropped to the floor.

"Close the window behind you and go upstairs to the bar to let us in," Hank said, as he snapped the screen back into place. Satisfied it was secure, he and Ray walked around to the back of the clubhouse and climbed the outdoor stairs to an elevated patio. When they got there, Charlie had opened the door leading inside and thrown on all the lights.

"Jesus Christ, Charlie, it's like fucking Times Square in here," Ray said as he made a beeline for the light switch.

"Let's have a drink," suggested Hank. He went behind the bar, poured each of them a Crown Royal and soda, and carried the bottle out to the patio, where they sat and acted like club big shots, describing their golf game in exaggerated terms. That's when Ray saw the flashing lights of the police car coming up the long driveway that led from Route 22 onto the golf course.

"Fuck, one of the neighbors must have spotted the lights," Ray said.

Hank grabbed the bottle. "Shut the door and bring your glasses." They quickly made their way down the stairs and across the practice green, melting into the woods behind the pro shop. On the way back to Hank's house, they passed the bottle of Crown Royal around like it was the Lombardi Trophy and they'd just won the Super Bowl of petty crime.

The next day Hank checked the police blotter that appeared every day on page two of *The Cedar Rapids Gazette*. There were three items. The second one read:

> *11:45 pm: Officers responded to a report of suspicious activity at Five Oaks Country Club. A thorough search of the premises was conducted but yielded no signs of forced entry. Club authorities were notified.*

Hank smiled. He'd made the papers. He almost wanted to call the *Gazette* and tell them what really happened. He figured a good reporter would be grateful. They must all be as nosy as he was. Hank liked that about the newspaper: it satisfied his curiosity about people. What they did, who they married, their little—or not so little—secrets. He was particularly fond of the obituaries—so much revealed about a person's life at its end, as if death obviated any desire for privacy that person might have had.

The more Hank thought about it, the more convinced he became that a career as a newspaper reporter was tailor made for someone like himself, who couldn't resist sticking his nose into other people's business. Besides, he was still the avid reader he'd always been and was intrigued by the idea that he could become a writer himself. He decided to major in journalism at the University of Iowa and joined the staff of *The Daily Iowan* within days of arriving on campus. Initially, he wrote for the sports page, did some feature stuff, and worked on the copy desk. He liked it all, and he was good at it.

So good the paper's editor agreed at the beginning of his junior year to let him try his hand at a weekly column about campus life, which Hank called "Scattershot."

The column premiered just as students were returning to school the following August, with a graphic designed by a young woman who was the paper's resident artist. In the drawing, a male figure sat slumped over a desk, his most prominent feature a mop of unruly black hair. In his right hand was an exaggerated version of an old-time blunderbuss, its flared muzzle hanging limp over the edge of the desk, spilling a jumble of words and punctuation marks onto the floor.

Hank loved the drawing and, for a moment, thought he loved the artist too. Her name was June, and she had a nose ring and carried a backpack full of pencils and charcoals and sketchbooks. Hank could sit for hours and watch her draw, fascinated by the way she seemed to make sense of the world through pictures, much as he aimed to do with his words. The flip side of that was the difficulty June had expressing herself other than through her drawings, while Hank was hyperverbal. Consequently, it came as a surprise to no one when the relationship fizzled before the Christmas holiday, shortly after June surprised Hank with a special gift: her original artwork for the "Scattershot" column, signed and framed.

When Hank returned to school in January, he looked for June in the newsroom, but she was nowhere to be found. He wanted to talk to her, to make sure there would be no awkwardness between them, so he went by her dorm. One of her roommates, clearly still shaken by the experience, told him that the two of them were among a handful of girls who had stayed in the dorm for a few days after classes ended. According to her, that was when June fell apart.

"Hank, it was terrible. She was like a zombie. She wandered up and down the halls muttering to herself, like she was inside a bubble that none of us could penetrate. When we tried, she would just start ranting. I was so worried I called the campus police, and they sent an ambulance and an emergency team from the county psych hospital. She really flipped when they walked into her room. She even threw a dish or a vase or something at them. But they were good with her. I was in the corridor and I could hear everything. It seemed like they let her vent until she just got too tired to go on, and then they took her to the hospital."

Hank decided to call June and speak with her if he could. He looked up the Johnson County residential mental health facility, which appeared to be about twelve miles from campus. He called the hospital, and after nearly ten minutes of being bounced from an operator to a unit administrator to a nurse, June finally came on the line.

"June, it's me. Hank. I saw Vivian. She told me what happened. I wanted to call to see how you're doing." There was silence on the line. Hank waited.

After a long pause, June replied. Her voice was flat and she sounded tired, as if she was just waking up from a nap. "Hi, Hank," she said. "It's nice of you to call."

What ensued was less a conversation than a series of awkward silences, while Hank searched for something to say that might animate June, and she seemed to search for words to respond. Finally, Hank decided a phone call was not going to work, so he asked if he could visit.

"That would be nice," June said, her voice still a monotone. Hank waited for her to continue, but nothing followed.

"How about tomorrow?" he asked. "Are there visiting hours?"

"Umm . . ." June seemed to be trying to decide. Finally, she said, "Yes, people can come by after lunch. My mom and my sister came the other day. Yesterday, I think. No, it wasn't yesterday. It must have been the day before." Another long pause. "I'll have to give the nurses your name. Thank you, Hank. Goodbye." And June hung up the phone.

A deep sadness settled over Hank. Whomever he had just spoken with, it wasn't the June he knew. No doubt she was heavily medicated, but it occurred to him how fragile a vessel is the human mind. One big wave swamps the boat and you're knocked completely off course. How do you find your way back? He had no clue, but he wanted to believe that if he and June were on good terms it would help. At least it would help him.

The next day he drove to 8466 Somerset Highway, where the Johnson County psychiatric facility was located. As it turned out, that was just one of the many agencies housed on what looked like a low-rent community college campus. Two and three-story brick buildings dotted the grounds, and a large sign directed visitors to the Youth Correctional Facility, the Special Education Hub, and even the Department of Public Works. Hank followed the arrows to the psychiatric clinic and parked in front. He was prepared for a drab, soulless institutional setting, but was surprised to walk into a bright, almost cheery environment. While the door locked behind him and the windows had wire mesh embedded between panes of glass, there was nothing dreary about the place. Staff wore street clothes, and except for the lanyards they wore around their necks with their badges, it was hard to distinguish them from some of the patients.

A nurse directed Hank to a table across the room, where June sat alone, a small set of drawing pencils and a pad of paper in front of her. Hank didn't want to sneak up on her, so he announced himself as he approached.

"Hi, June. It's me, Hank." He didn't know why he felt the need to identify himself, but June didn't seem to notice.

She looked up and smiled lazily. "Hi, Hank."

"Can I sit?"

"Oh, sure," she said.

He did, and the two looked at each other briefly before June turned her gaze back to the drawing pad.

Hank was thinking of what to say next when a tall, baby-faced man walked into the room dressed in pajamas and what appeared to be a velour bathrobe. He made a beeline for Hank.

"Peace, brother," he said as he approached, extending his right hand as if to bestow a blessing.

From across the room came a slender Black man wearing a navy-blue watch cap, a sweatshirt, jeans, and a lanyard. "C'mon, Jeffrey, let's you and I head over in this direction," he said, gently steering the bathrobed man away from Hank and June.

"Thou shalt not manhandle the Lord," the bathrobed man said, as he struggled to redirect his attention back to Hank.

The employee nodded. "Understood, Jeffrey, but you're supposed to be cooling your heels in your room. Remember?"

"Cool thy heels, sayeth the Lord," Jeffrey replied.

"Amen to that." The staffer then led Jeffrey back toward the corridor from which he had emerged.

Hank turned back to June. "Guess you meet all kinds of people here, huh?"

"I haven't met him yet," said June. "He's very loud. All the time. And he pesters people." She sighed. "It's nice to see you, Hank. Thank you for coming. I know I'm not quite myself yet, but the doctor says I'm getting better at putting my feelings into words. He says if I keep at it, I should be able to start classes again, maybe next semester."

"You've had a pretty hard time of it," Hank said, giving her an opening if she wanted to take it, to blame him for sending her into a tailspin with the holiday breakup. But June seemed more interested in the drawing in front of her. He pressed on. "What are you working on?"

June put her pencils down, and very slowly, as if she was still undecided, turned the pad of paper around, slowly pushing it across the table in Hank's direction. The image was an overhead view of an automobile fishtailing its way down what looked like a snow-packed country road.

"I don't remember much about what happened after everyone went home," June said. "But I felt like the driver of that car, and it's an icy road and I turn the steering wheel one way, but the car's got a mind of its own and it's heading someplace else and nothing I do seems to straighten it out." She took a deep breath, as if the recollection had required all the energy she could muster. She looked at Hank. "I hope I'll be better soon," she concluded.

Hank slid the pad back across the table. "I think you're going to be fine," he answered, deeply disappointed that was the best he could come up with. June turned her attention back to her drawing. Hank sat for a while and watched her draw, not feeling the need for conversation, content just to keep her company. When, finally, he stood to leave, he promised he'd come back to visit again. He did so each week into the spring when June was discharged into her parents' care. Every visit, he encountered another extravagant personality disorder, from the wannabe Messiah to a self-proclaimed Ethiopian princess who insisted that her grandfather, Haile Selassie, was still alive and on his way to take her home.

Everything about the world in which June suddenly found herself fascinated Hank. He wanted to learn more, and he wanted to write about it, but he didn't know where to begin. Until it occurred to him that the beginning was precisely the place to start, to the moment of crisis that, as it did in June's case, required an emergency intervention. He made an appointment to speak with the facility's medical director, Dr. Lena Stratton, a short, no-nonsense woman with gray hair tied back severely in a bun.

He explained that he wrote for *The Daily Iowan*, and that one of his friends from the paper had suffered a breakdown but was slowly putting her life back together. "Students don't want to think about mental health services, and they sure don't want to think that they might need them someday. With your support, I think I can help remove the stigma and let them know that what they're going through is a lot more common than they might think, that it's okay to seek help."

What he really wanted to do was ride along on an emergency call, but he was pretty sure that if Dr. Stratton got even a hint that he was some sort of crisis voyeur she would toss him out of her office. So he put on his most sincere face and, to his surprise, she liked the idea, promising to take it up with the county's director of emergency services.

Two weeks later, Hank was climbing into the front seat of a bright yellow and white Iowa City Fire Department ambulance, a big boxy van, waiting for the shift commander to get behind the wheel. A second EMT had already jumped into the back.

The emergency call that had come in over the radio moments earlier was impenetrable to Hank: *Engine 202, Medic 205, K Deck, 10-96, 1114 Arthur Street.*

"Okay, Jimmy Olson, you're up," shouted the shift commander as he and the other EMT on duty threw on their jackets.

They headed east across the Iowa River and ten minutes later were driving through neighborhoods south of Highway 6 that bore little resemblance to the leafy streets around the campus, home to UI administrators, faculty members, and medical staff from the university hospital.

"Do you know anything about the woman we're supposed to pick up?" Hank asked.

The chief shook his head. "Nope." Then he pointed ahead to his right. "But it looks like we're here."

On the curb in front of a small dark house was a young woman with a coat thrown over her shoulders flagging down the ambulance. Beside her were two police officers.

"She won't come out of the house, and my little brother Robert won't let anyone in," the young woman said, her hands folded tightly in front of her. "He's with her now. All she talks about is how someone's trying to sneak into the house and kidnap her."

A moment later, she was leading everyone toward a short flight of concrete steps on the side of the house that led to a tiny basement apartment. She extracted a key from the folds of her dress and fumbled with the lock on the door at the bottom of the stairs.

"How old is your brother Robert?" the chief asked.

"He's fourteen. He's a good boy. He's just upset to see his mama this way."

She swung the door open and walked inside, accompanied by the chief, who left Hank and the EMT waiting outside. He returned quickly. "It looks like she's in her bedroom. The son is sitting by himself." The chief motioned to the other EMT to join him and told Hank to follow. To the police officers he said, "I don't think two uniforms are going to help much inside. But I'd appreciate it if you'd stand by." As Hank crossed the threshold, the chief said, "Your job is to stay out of the way."

The apartment was in shambles. A small mountain of dirty dishes was growing out of the sink, and discarded clothing and magazines competed for space on the floor. In the corner, a television was on, and so was every light in the room. The shades were tightly drawn.

The mom was nowhere in sight, but her son was sitting on the arm of a couch, his eyes bouncing off the intruders nervously.

"I know she brought you here, but I'll kill you if you try and touch my mother," he said with as much bravado as he could muster. He seemed uncertain what to do with his hands. He tried folding them across his chest but dropped them quickly and left them in his lap, loosely joined, looking curiously polite. Behind the couch and to the right was a door, closed tightly. On the TV, a game show contestant was jumping up and down. "Philip told me to call him if you tried any more of this hospital bullshit. He said he'd come over with his gun. Then we'll see who goes to the hospital." As if he'd reminded himself that he had forgotten to do something, he jumped to his feet and moved across the room toward the phone.

Just as he lifted the handset, the door behind the couch opened and his mother appeared. She looked rumpled, as though she'd been sleeping and had been awakened by their voices. Her hair was gray and needed a good combing. She looked across the room to where her daughter and the men she didn't recognize were standing but gave no indication that their presence bothered her. She seemed to be looking for something.

Robert spun around when he heard the door open. "Mama, I told you to stay in your room!" he shouted, but his mother silenced him with a wave of her hand. She picked up a single bedroom slipper from the floor in front of the TV and returned to her room, closing the door behind her without so much as a second glance at any of them.

Robert turned back to the phone. "Philip does have a gun," his sister said.

The chief turned in her direction. "Why don't you wait outside for a minute? Tell the police officers about Philip just in case he shows up."

The chief leaned toward the other EMT, who hadn't moved since entering the apartment. "What's the play?"

"Let me talk with the boy," the EMT replied. And he did. While he talked, he moved slowly but deliberately in the direction of the woman's bedroom.

"She's already seen a doctor and he didn't help her at all," the boy said to no one in particular, still clutching the phone—still waiting, it seemed, for Philip to answer, to be there like he promised he would. But after a while, he laid the phone back down in its cradle. "He must be on his way . . ." he said, and nothing more. He had stumbled over a lump in his throat; tears were welling in his eyes.

The EMT walked quietly past him and knocked gently on the bedroom door. "Ma'am, we're ready to go now. I'll open the door and come in and help you get your things together." He turned the knob, swung it open, and disappeared into the room. Hank could hear his voice, calm and reassuring.

A moment later the two of them emerged, the woman in a housecoat and slippers, carrying one of those reusable grocery store bags into which she seemed to have packed her clothes, as if she had been waiting for someone to come for her. She walked by Robert and laid a hand gently on his head as she passed. He didn't move. Everyone else walked outside and escorted her to the van, helping her climb into the back. Hank returned to the front seat, and they drove to the hospital.

CHAPTER SIX

Iowa City, Iowa
2001

The following week, Hank devoted his column to the issue of mental health on campus.

> *A friend of mine suffered a nervous breakdown over the holidays,* he began. *I'm not a doctor, and that's not a medical diagnosis, but somewhere along the way things just slipped out of her control, and she needed help urgently. Fortunately for her, for all of us really, she seems to have received it. I say all of us because there are a lot of people on this campus who are wrestling with anxiety or depression, and any one of us may need urgent intervention someday, just as my friend did.*

Hank went on to describe his ride-along.

> *My friend, when she desperately needed help, benefited from the same sort of professional care that I witnessed in that little house in the east end. I've been to visit her on several occasions since returning from the holidays and am happy to report she's doing much better and looking forward to returning to campus soon.*
>
> *My point in telling you all this, dear reader, is to reassure you that resources are available if you begin to feel sad or lonely or burdened by expectations that seem impossible to meet. Seek out that help. There is no stigma attached to doing so, no more than*

> *if you go to the student health center for help with a migraine. Beyond that, be assured that if you or someone you know seems to be at risk of slipping off this tightrope that is our daily life, there are people standing by with a safety net to catch you and help you get back on our feet.*

The column struck a chord on campus. The student health center's psychiatric staff followed up with a town hall meeting to explain in detail the services available to the campus community. To Hank's surprise, his column even caught the eye of people not immediately connected to the university. A couple of days after the column ran, he received an email from the chief of *The Des Moines Register*'s bureau in Iowa City, who said he had been impressed by Hank's display of public-service journalism.

The email was short. *We'll be in the market for a campus stringer at the end of the year, and I hope I can interest you in the job. You've got the right instincts, and it's a great resume-builder. Think about it and get in touch with me if it sounds like an opportunity you'd like to pursue.*

Hank didn't need much persuasion and, so, as his senior year at UI began, he became the *Register*'s resident campus reporter. He covered the university and events around town that the bureau chief couldn't—or didn't want to—cover himself: a routine meeting of the Iowa City school board, a ribbon-cutting ceremony at the new landfill. Then, after graduation, he got his wish and landed a full-time job, one of two reporters at the bureau in Iowa City.

He was busy, and he was happy. He had a group of friends, most of whom had gone to UI and, like him, decided to stick around, because life was good in the shadow of the university—in a city so progressive by Iowa's standards that it was dubbed "The People's Republic of Johnson County."

And he had a great boss. Curt Avery was a local kid who had become something of a role model for every ambitious Iowa teen who dreamed of their future unfolding someplace other than corn country. He went to Brown on a full scholarship and landed a job right out of school with *The Boston Globe*. From there he'd gone on to *The Washington Post*, covering national politics. He traveled with the Clinton campaign during the '96 election and came back to become a White House reporter. His star was on the ascent. And then, after twenty years away, married with a newborn daughter, he decided he wanted to come back home and get away from the politics of the big-city newsroom. He wanted his daughter to grow up in the Midwest he remembered, with tree-lined streets and neighbors who looked out for each other.

So, he circled back to where he began, and now he was the unlikely bureau chief in a city of fifty-two thousand people, if you didn't count the twenty-five thousand or so who called the university home nine months of the year.

But he was still a top-flight newsman, and he looked the part, inclined to bow ties and tweeds and dishing out juicy little tidbits about politicians whose names everyone recognized.

He was also good at dishing out advice. One afternoon, Hank was on his way to interview the manager of a local paper mill whose employees had just walked out on strike. Hank had done his homework, read about the workers' demands and management's response, but he was still wound up about the interview.

"I just know I'll ask some stupid question and embarrass the shit out of myself."

"Don't worry about your questions," Avery said without looking up from the Metro section of the *Chicago Tribune* that was splayed across his desk. "We only print the answers."

Now, seven years later, sitting on what might well have been the same park bench he had chosen right after his interview at the *Register*, Hank could only shake his head at how things had turned out. He had been doing so well. He was going places, or so he had thought, until he was accosted in the parking lot of the PX at Fort Dodge Air Force Base and everything fell apart. Suddenly, even Hank, so accustomed to walking away unscathed from his transgressions, was forced to conclude there would be no easy fix this time.

He had just lost his job and had no idea which way to turn. He couldn't stay in Iowa City, and he couldn't go home to Cedar Rapids. But there was one place he could go, one person with whom he always felt at ease. First, though, he had to return to Iowa City, clean out his desk, and tell Curt Avery that he was leaving the paper.

CHAPTER SEVEN

Sana'a, Yemen
1928

"Silver has been a part of Yemen's history for almost as long as people have lived on this land." Moishe listened attentively. The man speaking was Ibrahim al-Arifi, the preeminent silversmith in Yemen, an artist so proficient that the unique jewelry he pioneered was said to be made in the Arifi style.

"If we were able to walk back in time, back almost one thousand years to the tenth century," he continued, "we would hear people tell of a large silver mine near here. That was the age of the Silk Road that linked China with Europe, and traders passing through here exchanged their merchandise for silver coins." As he spoke, Arifi's weathered hands were busy weaving fine silver threads into intricate designs. Moishe listened, but most of all, he watched. He had been apprenticed to Arifi, and he was expected to learn each technique the master shared with him.

Moishe had grown up in a family of silversmiths, but his own father never took to the silver trade, choosing instead the life of a merchant and a fabric trader, cottons from Egypt and silks from China. It was not uncommon for Jews in Yemen to make their livelihood as traveling salesmen. Still others became street vendors and shopkeepers. But Jews were most prominent in the trades, working as carpenters, tanners, cobblers, and, especially, silversmiths.

Moishe's skills were such that when he turned eighteen, his grandfather took him to Sana'a to meet Arifi, who was so sufficiently impressed that he invited Moishe to apprentice in his workshop for two years. There, Moishe became fluent in the most intricate techniques. He learned granulation, the process of cutting fine pieces of silver wire and melting them over a steady flame until surface tension rolled them into perfectly round balls. He became skilled in the art of filigree. His whale and flower motif, known in Arabic as *hut wa zahr*, was so delicate people said the eyes of the whale seemed to sparkle.

Arifi spoke reverentially of Sana'a, Yemen's capital. Its location, he said, at the crossroads between the Indian Ocean and the Red Sea, placed it squarely at the center of the commercial and cultural traffic that flowed along the Silk Road. Over generations, the city became a hub, hosting travelers, traders, and scholars, all of whom helped to shape its urban architecture and cultural life. In this milieu, the silver trade flourished.

But nowhere, he insisted, was silver more integral to Yemeni society than when it came time for marriage. "You know, of course, that a Muslim man pays the family of the woman he wishes to marry in silver coins," he said to Moishe one day as they worked together. He went on to explain that this bride price, known in Arabic as the *mahr*, was part of the engagement contract drawn up by the groom and the father of the bride. A percentage of the mahr would be spent on silver jewelry for the bride, which, according to Muslim law, became her own personal wealth.

The jewelry, Arifi continued, declared her status as a married woman of property. The fact that it was sold by weight enabled her to precisely calculate the value of the pieces she owned. When the need arose, she could sell some of her collection. During good times, she might buy additional pieces. Arifi chuckled. "The women of Yemen wear their wealth for all to see, but they reveal only a small portion of what they own."

Now well into the second year of his apprenticeship, Moishe knew that virtually all Yemeni silversmiths used melted-down Maria Theresa thalers as the basic stock for their handmade jewelry. The silver coins were originally minted in Austria in 1741 at the end of Maria Theresa's first year as Empress of the Habsburg Empire. Passed from hand to hand by traders throughout the nineteenth century, Maria Theresa thalers circulated widely in Yemen, based principally on the export of coffee and indigo. Authentic Maria Theresa thalers were prized for their design, and because they were minted with the most stringent control of silver content. Each one comprised 83.3 percent silver and weighed 28.0668 grams.

Wherever it circulated, the Maria Theresa thaler was subject to almost obsessive scrutiny to ensure its authenticity. While engravings on its edge made the coin difficult to counterfeit, merchants would invariably count the number of pearls on the empress's oval brooch, or the feathers on the imperial eagle that appeared on the reverse side. If there was any discrepancy between what they saw and what they knew should be the case, the coin was rejected.

Yemeni silversmiths would often use the coin itself in jewelry they crafted, sometimes heavily embossed with stones or fringed with bells and chains. Moishe had once seen a woman from Beihan wearing a necklace that consisted solely of Maria Theresa thalers suspended from two separate strands draped one above the other, twenty-two coins in all.

Just as often, the silversmiths would melt the coins along with old discarded pendants or bracelets and create new designs, particularly for bridal jewelry. For a family of means, Arifi's shop might create as many as a dozen pieces for a bride: a head ornament with small trinkets, a necklace or two, armlets, bracelets, anklets, bangles, earrings, and finger rings.

When a bride's family wanted a higher percentage of silver than the 83.3 percent found in the Maria Theresa thalers, silversmiths would use the rial of neighboring Saudi Arabia, which was roughly 93 percent pure.

Slowly, under Ibrahim al-Arifi's tutelage, Moishe's silver creations grew finer and more sophisticated. But he wasn't just a creator of fine jewelry, he also was a collector. As he began to earn money from the sale of his own work, he quietly purchased jewelry made and signed by his mentor and others whose craft he admired, worried that those exquisite pieces otherwise would be lost, carried from Yemen to Europe and beyond, sold and sold again. Over the years, as he grew more proficient, he added some of his own creations to the collection. It was a nest egg for his children, something they could use to begin their own lives when the time came.

CHAPTER EIGHT

Sana'a, Yemen
1928

During these early years in Sana'a, Moishe and Abdullah Alloush were inseparable. When they first met, Moishe was working on the stone steps of Arifi's shop in the heart of the Old City to take advantage of the sunlight that poured into the street on cloudless days. Abdullah appeared out of nowhere, approached quietly, and sat without speaking while Moishe worked.

"*Asalaam aleikum*," Moishe eventually said, curious to know if the slender boy with the delicate hands watching him so intently was mute or simply uninterested in conversation.

"*Wa aleikum a salaam*," Abdullah replied, reciprocating the wish for peace. For the first time, he looked up from the intricate patterns Moishe was making with his hands.

"How did you learn to do that?" he asked.

"I have been blessed with wonderful teachers," Moishe replied. "Do you wish to become a silversmith?"

"I do, but my father won't hear of it. He says it is work for Jews, but I know that is not true. I know many Muslim silversmiths here in the suq. But I don't know many who can do what you are doing. And you are young."

"I am nineteen," said Moishe. "How old are you?"

"I am seventeen."

Abdullah returned several times a week, and Moishe was flattered by the attention the younger boy paid to his craft. He was also pleased to have someone close in age to talk with. He assumed the role of teacher, and Abdullah was an eager student, quickly picking up basic techniques, learning to shape beads from discarded silver that was carefully swept into a pile for reuse.

Some days, the two of them would wander through the suq together, and Abdullah would introduce him to places in the Muslim market on the eastern side of the Old City that Moishe had never seen. On these excursions, Moishe would conceal his sidelocks beneath a shemagh, the head wrap favored by Yemeni men. A bakery behind the Grand Mosque became a favorite stop. It produced a delicate, flaky honey cake every morning, the aroma of which drew the boys down the narrow streets until they fell into the knot of people waiting impatiently for the bakery doors to open.

In Arabic, the cake was called *bint al-sahn*, "daughter of the plate," and it was made of delicate layers of dough and generous amounts of butter, then topped with seeds of the nigella plant, which to Moishe's eye looked like black sesame seeds, but left a hint of onion on his tongue. What Moishe loved most, though, was the honey that was poured over the cake as soon as it came out of the oven. Sticky and sweet, the two of them would devour an entire cake in one sitting.

Moishe, in turn, introduced Abdullah to the Jewish Quarter, where he had discovered a bakery that made *kubaneh* just like his grandmother's every day of the week. Traditionally, the sweet, buttery cake was prepared in Jewish homes on Friday afternoon and baked slowly overnight in a lidded tin so that it would be ready for Shabbat breakfast the following morning.

It would emerge golden brown in a soft cloud of steam, the heavily buttered dough rolled into long tubes and then wound into coils before being packed tightly together in the cake pan. He and Abdullah would buy one and tear into it as they walked, the heat of the fresh cake warming their hands through the folds of the paper in which it was wrapped.

As they wandered the streets of the Old City, the two friends would talk, as young men do, about what their lives might be like one day.

"I would like to make such fine silver jewelry that people will come from all over to purchase it," Moishe said. "My village will become famous as the home of Yemen's finest silversmith."

"I will be among those who come to buy your work, Moishe," Abdullah said. "I know I'm not meant to be a silversmith. I'm not gifted as you are. And I must respect my father's wishes. Even now, I keep the simple pieces I have made in a special hideaway on the top floor of my house because my father would be angry if he discovered them. It is a secret space I created myself in the floor of our *mafraj*. My father sits near it often when he is entertaining his friends, but I know he will never find it, or what I have hidden there."

CHAPTER NINE

The British Protectorate of Yemen
1949

Yosef Halevi paced impatiently back and forth across the decrepit wooden floor of the abandoned army barracks, unable to conceal his disgust at its condition. Rodents skittered across the floor and the building looked as if it might collapse in a stiff breeze. The British authorities had promised weeks ago that repairs would begin immediately and still nothing was happening. It was clear to Yosef that they simply didn't grasp the urgency of the moment. There were nearly fifty thousand Jews in Yemen, and already several thousand had made their way to Aden, where they now languished in the desert in makeshift camps, or along the streets of the city itself, because there were no accommodations for them elsewhere. They had left behind their homes and virtually all their possessions, persuaded that the promise of the Old Testament was about to be fulfilled: they would soon be lifted on eagles' wings and carried to safety.

Yosef had been sent from Israel to coordinate their departure. His family emigrated to Palestine years ago when Yemen was still part of the Ottoman Empire. He spoke Hebrew and Arabic and English, although at the moment he was speaking Arabic to the man the British sent, who was to renovate the old Army base and make it livable for families arriving from Yemen.

"This building is a disgrace," Yosef complained to the man. "I wouldn't keep my goats in here. How can we ask families with small children and elderly grandparents to spend even one night in this filth?" He stormed off, leaving the man behind, intent on taking his concerns directly to Ephraim Naadi, the head of the Jewish Agency's office in Aden.

"We must be patient," Ephraim told Yosef after he rushed into his office, fuming about the delays. "Our colleagues in London are working hard to finalize plans, but the British are nervous. They tell us they support what we are doing but do not want it to become an issue for them with Arab countries. They are insisting on maintaining secrecy."

"How will we keep the migration of tens of thousands of Jews from all over Yemen to a single city on the southern tip of Arabia a secret?" Yosef asked.

"With God's help, and careful planning, Yosef. And patience."

But Yosef was not a patient man. And he didn't care in the least that Britain's relationship with Arab states might be jeopardized by facilitating the migration of Yemeni Jews to Israel.

He'd already traveled to Sana'a and met with the leaders of the Jewish community. He'd needed their advice on how to persuade the Imam of Yemen to issue exit permits that would allow the Jews to depart.

The rabbis talked it over among themselves and decided to enlist the help of Yitshak Korah, the son of wine merchants and rose water traders who supplied alcohol to the imam's family. Korah agreed to travel to the southern city of Taiz, where Imam Ahmed had settled after his father, Yayha, was assassinated and the family splintered over control of the imamate.

When Korah arrived, Imam Ahmed greeted him warmly, and the two men withdrew into a small sitting room to meet privately. Korah wasted no time delivering his message: the creation of the state of Israel was focusing the world's attention on the plight of Jews everywhere, including Yemen. "You allow your brother to rule Sana'a and its surrounding towns as he sees fit. He mistreats virtually everyone but seems especially hostile toward the Jews. His actions are going to jeopardize your own standing with countries it is not in your interest to anger. Many Jews are ready to leave Yemen. Let them go,"

Korah counseled. "If they are not here, they can't become a problem."

Ahmed agreed but insisted that the Jews would have to sell all their property before they departed. Korah traveled to Aden to report the outcome of his meeting to Yosef. "He is willing to let our brothers and sisters depart, particularly if he reaps a windfall as they are forced to sell their property and land for a pittance of what it is worth. He'll make sure that his own people are standing by to purchase as much as possible. He'll grow wealthier on the backs of Jews even as they make their way out of Yemen."

Korah continued. "But we must move quickly. Ahmed is mercurial. He can change his mind without warning and if he does, the border to Aden Protectorate will close again, and our brothers and sisters will have no homes to return to. They will be completely destitute."

"I understand," Yosef had said. "I will return to Sana'a tomorrow and convey your message to the rabbis."

Yosef made his way to Sana'a in a truck owned by the Jewish Agency. It was only one hundred eighty miles, but the drive was difficult as the terrain changed from the flat, arid deserts of the south to sharp inclines that led up to the Yemeni highlands, requiring dozens of harrowing switchbacks on narrow, mountainous roads.

Sana'a itself sat at seventy-five hundred feet, and Nuqm Mountain, which rose behind it, was over twelve thousand feet. Yosef could feel the altitude as he walked the next morning to the chief rabbi's home from the small guest house in the Jewish Quarter where he had spent the night, a distance of a few city blocks. The home was modest, and unlike the traditional tower houses in the eastern quadrant of the Old City that rose to six and seven stories, it had but two floors. By law, the homes of Jews had to be lower in height than those of Muslims. Gathered in the main room of the home were community leaders from nearby cities and towns who had come to hear what Yosef had to say.

"I have met with Yitshak Korah. The imam has agreed to issue exit permits, and the British are going to provide lodging in Aden where our brothers and sisters can wait while arrangements are made to fly them to Israel. Go back to your villages and tell everyone to make the necessary preparations. They must first sell their homes, their livestock, and their worldly goods, and then they must carry the records of these sales with them, or they will not be allowed to leave Yemen. Urge them to carry their sacred scriptures, for these are the pillars of our faith."

After Yosef had spoken, there was silence. Then, one of the rabbis, an old man, stood with some difficulty. He spoke slowly and carefully. "I have listened to your words. Until this moment, I have not known how to respond to the pleas from the faithful for a clear direction. But now I understand that the Aliyah is upon us. Now, I can say to our brothers and sisters: 'God is with you and with those who have come to Yemen to support your journey.' I will say this on Shabbat in the synagogue."

CHAPTER TEN

Amran, Yemen
1949

Moishe and Shamaa sat on a worn carpet in the small room of the rabbi's house, surrounded by the eight other Jewish families that remained in their village. The rabbi had just delivered the most stunning news: "The deliverance we have prayed for is here. The Promised Land awaits. You are free to go."

If it hadn't been their own rabbi who uttered these words, they wouldn't have believed them. But he stood right there, in the center of the makeshift synagogue where they gathered each Saturday to keep Shabbat, and offered assurances that the way had been cleared.

"Don't be fearful," the rabbi almost whispered, his voice muted by the weight of the years he carried, his white hair gently framing his narrow face. "I am too old to make this journey. But my peace will come knowing that each of you has been released from the hardships of our lives here and will soon be safe in your new home, free."

At that moment, the room erupted in cries of joy that were quickly silenced by the rabbi. And still Moishe and Shamaa sat, the enormity of what lay before them heavy on their minds. He took his wife's hands, but she looked away. "Come, Shamaa. Let's go home."

As they walked, Moishe acknowledged his wife's fears about the journey, and what their new life would be like in another place, even if it was the Promised Land. They had heard stories of Mizrahi Jews, those who emigrated from Muslim-majority lands, being swindled and mistreated by the Ashkenazi, who had come from Europe to settle in

Israel. The idea that Jews would prey on their own brothers and sisters was heartbreaking, but for now they had more pressing concerns.

"We must sell our home, my shop, the possessions we cannot take with us. And we can take very little. Those who have made the journey to Aden have sent back news of bandits on the roads who will steal anything of value. I'm sure the police in villages we pass through will also be interested in what we carry, not to mention guards at the border crossing."

"What of your jewelry then, Moishe? It is your life's work. How can you leave that all behind?"

"This has been weighing heavily on my mind, Shamaa. I have decided to take it to Sana'a. I have spoken to you of Abdullah Alloush, who became like a younger brother to me when I lived in Sana'a. Years ago, he created a secret space in his home for the silver pieces he made as a teenager. I tried my best to teach him what I was learning myself, but the truth is he was just not meant to be a silversmith. Or perhaps I was never meant to be a teacher. But I will ask him to place my jewelry in that secret space he described to me until I can return to claim it."

"Return to claim it? Do you seriously believe you will ever return to Yemen, Moishe?"

"I want to believe so, Shamaa, but in my heart, I think that when we leave it will be forever. Still, I have it in my mind that I will come across someone with the means of traveling to Sana'a and recovering the jewelry. I'm leaving it behind so that it can be kept safe and, hopefully, one day enjoyed by others."

"Oh, Moishe," Shamaa said, leaning heavily against her husband. "This is all so hard to imagine. I lie down at night and hope that sleep comes quickly, so that I may be freed from the weight of this worry I carry around all day, but it eludes me. I think of what lies ahead and I am already so tired."

They left within the month, nearly forty of them, virtually every Jew in the village. They walked away from their homes before dawn when only a few others were up and about, so as to avoid being harassed, or worse, robbed before they even got on their way. But robbed of what? They had sold almost everything they owned to eager neighbors and others they didn't know at all, who swept into their village as soon as word of their plan to leave Yemen began to circulate. The Jewish families took almost nothing: small bedrolls in which they had wrapped their clothing, some water and food, flatbread, honey and dates, and all the money they had, which the women tucked away in the folds of the heavy robes they wore. And each family carried their sacred scriptures, wrapped carefully and concealed to avoid prying eyes.

Many, like Moishe, had decided to stop first in Sana'a, to bid farewell to family, or to buy provisions for the journey that lay ahead. The capital lay thirty miles to the southeast, and they would cover the distance in two days so as not to exhaust the children and elderly in their group. Everyone was in good spirits, their minds focused only on what lay ahead, not the homes or possessions or livelihoods they were leaving behind.

CHAPTER ELEVEN

Buzzards Bay, Massachusetts
2010

Dewey Poe slowly made his way down the back steps of his small house, tightening his grip on the railing as he descended. It was a cold, damp autumn morning on Cape Cod, the kind of weather that made Dewey's knees complain loudly and set him to wonder how he'd managed to climb in and out of airplanes so easily for so many years. Still, he loved the offseason, when the day-trippers cleared out, the summer rentals shut down, and the Cape returned to its slower rhythms. The roads would soon be almost as deserted as the beaches, which suited Dewey just fine.

He ran his hand along the rear wall of the house as he walked. The cedar shakes seemed to be aging right along with him, slowly turning gray and brittle with each passing year. He looked up at the late September sky, waiting for the sound of the aircraft from Joint Base Cape Cod to signal the official beginning of the day. He'd chosen his house precisely because of its proximity to the air base, because of the opportunity it would provide for regular serenades as the planes next door went to work.

"I've spent my entire life in and around airplanes," he'd told the realtor when she suggested he might like a quieter neighborhood. "Nothing relaxes me more than the sound of a well-tuned pair of engines lifting a big metal bird into the sky."

Cape Cod appealed to him for another reason: he'd developed a fondness for the ocean after spending so many years crisscrossing the earth's broad expanses of water. Here, the Atlantic Ocean was just a half mile to the east, behind a stand of scrub pines that served as a windbreak for his house, down a narrow, winding path and across the beach road.

Dewey lived alone but didn't mind it. He'd been married for forty-six years to the same woman, and their last years together weren't always what he had imagined they might be. Sylvia had contracted fibromyalgia after hip surgery and was in constant pain. It was everywhere, and it was all the time. She was always tired, and when she wasn't sleeping, she was medicating herself to dull the pain. Dewey was ashamed to admit that he felt relieved when she passed away, but it was true. Relief for Sylvia, who was finally free from the misery that was each day's only certainty, and for himself, who couldn't comfort her the way she needed, and had to watch the only woman he had ever loved turn into someone he hardly recognized.

But today was going to be a good day. The air base was stirring, the early morning cloud cover was beginning to burn off, and his grandson was coming to visit. The grandson he nicknamed Scooter when he was just a toddler because he was always busy moving about on his little baby legs. It was no coincidence that Dewey also happened to be a big fan of New York Yankee second baseman Phil Rizzuto, who was dubbed Scooter early in his career because of the short strides he took when running the bases, which he did a lot of during his career, playing on seven championship teams.

Dewey's fondness for nicknames dated back to his time in the Navy. In fact, Dewey was a nickname. His real name was Dwayne, but that hadn't lasted more than a couple of minutes once he enlisted. That was in the spring of 1942, six months after Pearl Harbor and two months after Dewey had turned seventeen. Not that the Navy recruiter ever really inquired. Dewey was a big kid, with deep brown eyes and a quick smile that put people at ease. The Navy recruiter told Dewey he would do his best to get him into flight school, and that's all that Dewey needed to hear. Bullheaded and determined to see the world beyond the coal mines of southern Illinois, he persuaded his parents to sign the enlistment papers attesting to his age and never looked back. He began his career as a flight engineer, eventually qualified to become a Navy pilot, and flew more than one hundred missions in his beloved C-54 Skymaster over the course of the war.

Dewey heard a car arriving, the tires crunching over the crushed seashell driveway that arced in a half-moon in front of the house. It was Dewey's pride and joy, his personal security alarm. No one approached the house, on foot or in a vehicle, without the sound of seashells alerting him.

He walked around the side of the house and watched as his grandson climbed out of the car. Hank looked different since the last time Dewey had seen him. Still lanky and tall, certainly taller than Dewey, but that wasn't hard these days. Dewey was shrinking as he aged, the years shaving inches off his height and dozens of pounds off his weight. He remembered when he stood 5'11" and weighed 185 pounds, but that was a long time ago. His pants hung long over his shoes now, and he had grown accustomed to punching new holes in his belts to ensure they cinched tightly around his waist.

Hank stretched against the car, and Dewey marveled at the handsome young man his grandson had become. He still had the full head of dark wavy hair he had inherited from his father, but his features were his mother's, one hundred percent. When Hank smiled, Dewey saw his daughter all over again.

Hank heard Dewey emerge from the side of the house onto the driveway before he even saw him. "I see your security system is still in place, Gee." Years ago, Hank had created his own nickname for his grandfather, deciding that none of the available options—Grandpa, Gramps, Granddad—was to his liking. He simply called him Gee.

"Works like a charm. Always has. Come here and give your grandfather a hug."

The two embraced and then Hank stepped back. "What's up, Gee, aren't you eating anymore? We're going to have to get you bulked up in time for beach season."

Dewey laughed. "Just what I was thinking. We can start today.

Fish and chips for lunch, with my homemade tartar sauce. Now get your bag and come on in."

They ate, as they always did, at a small round table in Dewey's kitchen. It sat right next to a window looking out onto the carefully tended vegetable garden in his backyard, ringed by a wire fence to keep out the rabbits and deer.

Hank wasted no time getting to what had happened at Fort Dodge. He hadn't shared it with anyone, not even Curt Avery, but he knew that, eventually, he would have to go through the whole episode with someone who could help him understand what had happened and why. He briefly considered telling his parents the real reason he was leaving the *Register*, but that suggested a conversation with them he had successfully avoided all these years, so he decided it was best to stick with Mort's advice and simply said he needed a year to get away, recharge, and think about what he wanted to do next.

He'd always idolized his grandfather, whose visits to Cedar Rapids when Hank was a kid were few and far between, but memorable for the tales he would tell of exotic countries he'd been to and adventures he'd had.

Hank would wait patiently until the dinner table was cleared and the coffee was served, when Dewey would share a story or two from his latest travels. He would always begin by setting the stage. "We had an unexpected layover in Calcutta a few months ago," began one of Hank's favorites. "We discovered an oil leak, and my flight mechanic had to jerry-rig the damaged part to get us back into the air until we could fix it properly when we landed in Tokyo.

"So there I am, sitting in my hotel room after dinner, reading, and I hear this scratching sound. I don't see anything, so I go back to my book, and then I hear it again. I look around, and I'll be damned if there isn't a monkey sitting on the ledge of my hotel window trying to open it from the outside. I walk over to the window and the two of us stare at each other through the glass. I rap on the window, and that little monkey did the same thing."

Hank was eight when he first heard that story, and he blurted out "Monkey see, monkey do," which Dewey said was exactly what he had learned that night. That, and the importance of making sure your windows were locked up tight before going to sleep, especially if you were staying in Calcutta.

Hank knew there wouldn't be any drama with his grandfather. Dewey was a practical man who fixed things when they were broken and moved on, which is just what Hank needed to do. Getting through the story was easy. It was much harder to acknowledge that, even now, as an educated and—until recently, anyway—gainfully employed adult, he still found it hard to resist the temptation to take something that he knew wasn't his.

"That's what worries me most, Gee. I didn't go into the base PX thinking it would be a great chance to take home a new set of steak knives. It's more like I walk into a store and it's game on, and I can't resist seeing if I can outsmart them." Hank shook his head. "Where did this come from? I think of myself as pretty normal, but a part of me just wants to prove how clever I am. And look where it's gotten me now." Hank looked away from his grandfather, embarrassed by his own admissions.

"Well, son, you put your hand over that flame once too often, and this time you got burned but good." He looked at his grandson over the last bit of fried haddock he had speared onto his fork. "Guess the question now is: have you learned anything?"

"Yeah, I get it, Gee. This can't happen again. I'm not twelve years old anymore and no one's going to give me a pass when I do dumb shit. I grew up thinking I could keep walking off with stuff and never face any consequences. That didn't work out as planned. And as my reward for being so stupid, now I have to figure out all over again what I'm going to do with my life."

"And how do you plan to do that?"

"Not sure just yet. Maybe taking a year off isn't the worst idea in the world. Maybe I can use the time to work on a few things, clear my head. Truth is, I don't know what I'm going to do, Gee."

Dewey thought for a moment, and then said, "Seeing as how you've got a bit of free time on your hands, I've got something I've been wanting to show you. Let me get it."

He got to his feet slowly and disappeared for several minutes, returning to the kitchen as Hank was clearing the lunch plates from the table. In his hand was a sealed manila envelope. He took a paring knife and sliced it open along one edge. Inside were two pieces of paper that Dewey carefully unfolded. He handed them over to Hank, who looked at the script. It was indecipherable.

"What is this, Gee?"

"Remember I told you how I flew in and out of Aden in 1949 to airlift Yemeni Jews to Israel? One of them handed me this note when we landed in Tel Aviv after my very first flight. It's written in Arabic, at least that's what I was told by one of my crew back then. To this day, I've never had it translated. Why don't you look into it, Hank? Who knows, maybe there's a story worth telling in there, something you can work on while you're figuring out what to do with yourself."

CHAPTER TWELVE

British Protectorate of Aden
1949

Moishe sat on the desert floor surrounded by his family and the dozens of others who, like him, had decided to leave their homes and make their way to Aden the only way they could: on foot. He couldn't stop rubbing his eyes, which had been burning ever since a sandstorm erupted right after they crossed the border from Yemen into the British Protectorate. The afternoon light was fading quickly, and children scampered here and there looking for wood their parents could use to build a fire for warmth and comfort until sleep overtook them.

He, Shamaa, and their two children, eleven-year-old Miriam and eight-year-old Benyamin, had been walking for more days now than he was able to recall. The first leg of their journey, to Sana'a, had gone easily and without incident. He located Abdullah Alloush, who owned a successful jewelry shop in the Old City, where he happily displayed and sold the work of Yemeni silversmiths, Jews and Muslims alike. He agreed to hold Moishe's precious collection for safekeeping in the hideaway he had described those many years ago, under the floor of the mafraj, the sitting room on the top level of the home in which he was raised, and which he had inherited when his father passed away. He laughed when he told Moishe that he still kept his early attempts at silver jewelry in the secret space and would quietly look in on them from time to time.

"It reminds me that I made a very good decision when I chose to become a jewelry merchant rather than a jewelry maker," he said. "You should ask for my brother Hazem if I am traveling when you come for your jewelry. I'll tell him you are to be trusted. He'll take you to the mafraj." He told Moishe where to find the secret hiding space and how to look for the floorboard that concealed it, should it ever be necessary. "But why don't you just sell me the pieces, Moishe? I'll pay you generously, you know that."

"I know that, my friend, but I can't bring myself to sell them yet," Moishe replied. "Perhaps someday."

Once Moishe was assured his jewelry was in safe hands, he grew impatient to resume the trip. After a couple of days, the small group of travelers departed, making their way down the steep, winding trails from the highlands in the direction of the city of Taiz, one hundred twenty miles to the south.

Progress was often slow, heavily dependent on the stamina of both the very young and the very old members of their party. On good days they managed to cover as many as fifteen miles, but those days were outnumbered by others that were punctuated by endless stops and starts to accommodate someone who was ill or injured, or to wait out a storm under whatever shelter they could find.

It took them just over two weeks to reach Taiz. They rested there briefly, sleeping in a small wooded area some distance from the city, uncertain of the reception they would receive if they wandered into Taiz as a group. Over the next two days each family walked into town on their own and bought what they needed. They resumed their journey under a hot sun that followed them all the way to the border that separated Yemen from the British Protectorate.

By then Moishe was beginning to lose track of how many days it had been since he left his home. Eighteen, maybe twenty, they all blurred in his memory. Days of nothing but walking, carrying Miriam or Benyamin in his arms while they slept. The hardest part, though, was telling the children, who were always hungry and thirsty, that there would be no food or water until the next day because they had to ration what little they had until they made it to the next town and could find more.

The money they carried with them was rapidly dwindling, some spent on food when they were able to buy it, some handed over for payment of "taxes" along the way, either to bands of criminals who hounded those making the trek to Aden, or to local authorities. As far as Moishe was concerned, there was no difference between the two. Every day they walked with a group of other families who, like them, had given up virtually everything they owned except for what they wore on their backs and carried in their arms, intent on making their way to a new home.

The day they walked out of Yemen and crossed into the British Protectorate should have been a happy one. They had reached the final stretch; Aden was now within reach. The protectorate was the territory the British were satisfied to leave in the hands of sultans and tribal sheikhs in exchange for a promise of loyalty to the Crown. Moishe's ragged band of travelers arrived at the border late in the afternoon. A small hut hugged the road, and two men sat in front on their haunches, their rifles leaning against the building.

"*A salaam alaikum*," Moishe said, greeting them in Arabic.

"*Wa alaikum a salaam, yahud*," the younger of the two replied, addressing them as Jews, twirling the index finger of his right hand next to his temple and giggling with his companion over Moishe's *peyot*, the traditional sidelocks.

"We are on our way to Aden. We have our exit permits and all our papers in order." Moishe approached the two men and offered them the documents. Neither seemed interested.

"Tax," the one said.

Moishe sighed. "How much?"

"How many are you?"

"Perhaps thirty."

"Then the tax is thirty rials."

"We have been walking steadily for many days, my brother. We have little money and need to buy food and water for the children."

"Keep talking and it will be two rials each." He looked at his companion and the pair laughed again.

Moishe saw no benefit in further conversation. He returned to the group and delivered the news. Everyone looked alarmed.

Shamaa spoke aloud what the others were thinking. "Moishe, that is virtually all we have left. What are we to do without any money?"

"The Lord has brought us this far and he will not abandon us now," Moishe said. "And the longer we linger here, the more likely these two will decide to cause us trouble."

Shamaa reached under layers of clothing and extracted a small cloth purse. She unwrapped it and handed a handful of currency to Moishe.

"I pray the Lord is not too busy these days, Moishe. It would be easy to lose track of a handful of Yemenis wandering through the desert."

"Shamaa, have faith."

"I have faith, Moishe. It is our lack of everything else that troubles me."

He finished collecting the money and returned to pay the guards, who sent them on their way.

The sandstorm struck that evening, as they gathered around a small fire. It had been hot all day, and the children were thirsty and their water was nearly gone, and some of their companions were sick and barely able to get up from the ground, much less contemplate another day of walking.

It was not the first sandstorm they had endured as they crossed the deserts of Yemen, but it was the fiercest. The wind howled and the earth seemed to heave beneath them. Shamaa stretched up to Moishe's ear and said, "It is as if Yemen itself is punishing us for leaving it behind."

The wind paused at some point, and they thought the storm might have passed. Then it resumed, and one of the men began to laugh wildly. "Look at us," he said. "We have left the green mountains and the rich soil of Yemen so that we can spend our days and nights in these pitiless deserts."

No one replied. They simply huddled together and tried to protect their children from the sand that stung their exposed skin and crept into their eyes and mouths and noses no matter how tightly they covered them.

They walked into Aden the next day, exhausted, hungry and sick, the remnants of the sandstorm still clinging to their hair and their clothes. A jeep carrying a handful of British soldiers approached.

"What in bloody hell happened to you?" asked the one in charge.

"Sandstorm," was all Moishe could muster in the way of response. The soldiers went around to the rear of the jeep where a large jerrican of water was strapped to the chassis. They moistened rags so the travelers could wipe their faces and passed water around in small aluminum cups until it was gone.

"Are many others like you out there?" one of the soldiers inquired.

"Many," said Moishe. "Some left after we did. Others said they were going to take the eastern route because they heard it was safer."

The jeep continued on its way, leaving Moishe and his family and those traveling with them sitting in what little shade a handful of date palm trees provided. After some time they got back onto their feet and resumed walking. The city seemed to wrap itself around them as they went, buildings, sidewalks, and shops hemming them into narrow streets through which they moved quietly, too weary to speak.

Still, they pressed on. The city was crowded and dirty, and it didn't feel safe. People seemed to be living on virtually every street corner, out in the open, cooking food over small fires. Moishe thought most looked as forlorn as his own family, their children listless, their clothing disheveled. He asked a small knot of men standing on the street for directions to the camp he had been told awaited them, and his question elicited scornful laughter and an unwelcome truth: there was no camp. Work on the site hadn't even begun.

There was nothing else to do but keep moving until they could find an unoccupied patch of ground to spend the night. The location they finally stumbled upon was in the shadow of a large mosque's dome.

They quickly claimed the space, too exhausted to worry about how the Muslim congregation might feel about a couple dozen Jews deciding to become their neighbors. All they knew for certain was that they were too tired to walk any farther.

Moishe and his family ate quietly: bread and oranges they had bought at the first market in Aden they'd come upon. As the sun set, and the time for evening prayer approached, activity around the mosque quickened. The *adhan* rang out, summoning the faithful to leave behind worldly matters and raise their voices in prayer. As the congregation departed, the imam approached. Moishe rose and walked over to greet him.

"*A salaam aleikum.*"

"*Wa aleikum a salaam.* We have been expecting you. So many of your brothers and sisters have come before you but none to this spot. We believe it was because they feared us as Muslims. You have no need to, although it saddens me that even our community is torn over Islam's approach to strangers who do not share our beliefs. Some of us hold the view that, because we are all children of the Book, we should treat you as we would our own brethren. Others fear you, and argue that we should close our doors, and our hearts, to you and your families. We have struggled with this question, and after much discussion have reached a compromise, which I hope you will understand and accept."

He reached into a pocket under his robe and extracted a small pouch. "In this pouch are Indian rupees, our currency here in Aden." His eyes swept over the thirty or so Jews who sat watching from a distance. "We cannot offer you much because we are working people, but we hope that what we are able to offer will help sustain you." The imam paused. "But our generosity seems to have its limits. And so, while you are welcome to spend the night here where you are, I must ask that you depart tomorrow. This is the compromise we have reached among ourselves."

Moishe felt what little energy he had left drain from his body as the reality of moving once again the next day sunk in. Nevertheless, he thanked the imam and his congregation for their generosity and agreed that they would depart in the morning. To where, he had no idea.

"There is a man here in Aden," the imam said as he turned to go. "He is a Yemeni Jew who has come to help pilgrims such as yourselves. He has come by to reassure us that the influx of Jews will be short-lived and you all will be on your way to your Promised Land very soon. I will send word to him so he knows you are here. He seems to be very resourceful."

Moishe returned to where his family and the others were waiting. "We will be safe here tonight," he said, "and the imam has given us money that I will distribute to each family equally. But we cannot stay here. So sleep well and gather your strength, because tomorrow we must move to another place."

Moishe walked over to Shamaa and the children and sat heavily on the ground. He felt utterly spent but unable to sleep. After a long time, as sleep finally came to him, his last thought was this: If the Lord wants me to go any further, he will wake me. Otherwise, I will die here where I lie.

The following morning, as they gathered up their belongings and prepared to move on, a truck pulled up and three people, a man and two women, got out. The man said his name was Yosef, and that he had received a message from the imam regarding a group of Jews spending the night next to the mosque who were in need of his assistance.

As he spoke, the women began to weave their way among the small clusters of families, searching out the ones who needed care immediately, offering water and dates and assurances that there soon would be shelter for everyone, it would just take a bit of time.

"We will take you to another location in our truck," Yosef said. "There are other families there and you won't have to move again."

That had been how many days ago? Moishe wasn't sure. Almost as long as they had walked, it seemed. Long enough for him to forage enough scrap lumber and fabric to build a makeshift shelter that provided a bit of relief from the heat of the Arabian sun. At least food and water were less scarce now. People came every week with some provisions. And each time they departed they made the same promise, in Hebrew: you will be on your way very soon.

That morning, Moishe woke to their familiar voices, only this time Yosef's tone was more urgent. "Come," he said, urging people to climb into the back of his small truck and another that followed. "There is an airplane on its way, and it will carry you to the Promised Land," he continued, encouraging those stirring slowly from another night of sleep on the hard-packed earth. "This is the day you have dreamed of."

Shamaa looked at Moishe, as if to ask, "Do we dare believe this crazy man?" It was a question Moishe was asking himself at that moment. And yet, these were the words they had come so far to hear, so they collected everything one more time, got into the bed of the truck, and, along with as many others as could fit, were driven to the British military base, out onto a hot, exposed expanse of concrete where they were told to sit and wait.

Before that moment, Moishe had never seen an airplane, and suddenly he was surrounded by them. Small, steely gray-winged machines parked everywhere. To Moishe they resembled overgrown insects that might lurch forward and sting you fatally without warning. Some had teeth painted across the tip of the airplane's nose, making them look even more menacing. But not one of them was large enough to carry more than a couple of the people slowly filling the space around him.

Then someone was pointing to the sky, and someone else said they could hear an airplane, and another said *yes, there it is*, and the people around Moishe stood up excitedly, their eyes sweeping the heavens, fingers pointing here, no there. Moishe didn't stand. Nor could he see or hear anything that might have been an airplane, but the prospect of one coming down from the sky seemed to agitate the British soldiers, who approached in small vehicles, jumping out quickly and telling everyone to get up and move. "Clear the runway!" they were shouting, which didn't mean much to Moishe, although he had the distinct feeling he was very close to it, given the way the soldiers were insisting that he and everyone else vacate the area where they were sitting.

"Here it comes," someone behind Moishe said, and this time he could see the airplane swooping down from the sky and slowly approaching earth. When its wheels touched the ground, it bounced from side to side and then settled into a steady roll, which eventually brought it to a stop just a short distance from where he stood.

The airplane was larger than most of the others on the ground, with a long silver body and wings on which were mounted four propellers that Moishe couldn't believe were sufficient to lift something so large into the sky. A row of small windows ran along the side of the airplane. Moishe wondered if it was full of people. He couldn't imagine who would come to Aden other than Jews from Yemen seeking to leave.

Minutes later, a man in a brown leather jacket appeared, slipped on a pair of dark glasses, and climbed down a small ladder at the rear of the plane, followed by two women. The man seemed to be in charge, because Yosef wasted no time rushing over to him, followed closely by a British military officer who spoke to Yosef sternly before gently steering the man away from the plane to a place where they spoke quietly.

The British military officer handed the man, whom Moishe heard referred to as the pilot, a message, which he read and then tucked into his shirt pocket. He didn't seem at all perturbed by the people milling around him or his airplane. He didn't raise his voice or berate anyone. Four other men, dressed much as he was, climbed down the same small ladder onto the tarmac. Two of them walked around the airplane together, examining this part and that, while the others waited.

At that moment Moishe decided that he would entrust his jewelry to the pilot. Surely, if he could make something so large defy gravity in order to deliver them to the Promised Land, he would understand how important it was that Moishe's life's work didn't languish in the darkness beneath the floorboards of a childhood friend's home.

The momentary sense of relief his decision had brought was quickly dampened by Yosef, who announced that their departure had been delayed until tomorrow. They would have to get back into the trucks and return to their desert encampment.

Still one more night sleeping on the ground as the desert temperatures plummeted. At least it would give him a chance to write the pilot a note. He didn't know how or when he would give it to him, but he was confident the Lord would present him with the opportunity.

CHAPTER THIRTEEN

British Protectorate of Aden
1949

Darkness was closing in and once again Moishe was having a hard time seeing, but he was nearly finished. He had written the note in Arabic. This surprised him at first, but he decided that this message should be in Arabic, the language of Yemen, which was, after all, his homeland. He'd lived there for his entire life and had never imagined leaving—until now. He read the note a final time:

> *I am Moishe Azani, a Jew, a silversmith, a Yemeni. But I can no longer live in my own country and, with God's blessing, will soon begin a new life with my family in the Promised Land of Israel. To make this journey, I have left behind everything, including treasured pieces of handmade jewelry I could not bring myself to sell. I wanted to believe I would return to claim them one day, but now I know that my wife, Shamaa, is right. I will never come back to Yemen.*
>
> *I have given this note to you because I believe you will be able to go to Sana'a where I have hidden the jewelry and retrieve it. Each piece is special in its own way, a contribution made to Yemen's culture by Jews like me. My fear is that as we leave, these traditions will be lost, and the world will slowly forget that the generations of Yemeni Jews created beautiful art with our hands. I make no claim that my work is of extraordinary value, although it has allowed me to earn a living and provide for my family. I*

hope to continue my craft when I am settled in Israel, but I am prepared to do whatever the Lord asks of me. I have watched you and believe you are a trustworthy man, so I am placing my life's work in your care and ask only that you find a way to share it with the world.

There are twenty-two pieces wrapped in a thick, woven cloth bag. It is hidden in a house at 13 Hamdan Street in Sana'a that belongs to the Alloush family. My friend, Abdullah Alloush, has agreed to conceal the package in a space only he and I know about.

In the event Abdullah is not present when you go to his home, you should ask for his brother, Hazem. He will take you to the top floor of the house, to a room known as the mafraj. In the northwest corner, beneath the cushions and the carpets, a small piece of the floor can be removed intact. In this space you will find the cloth sack with the jewelry that Abdullah has hidden for me. Do what you will with it, although I hope you will see in each piece a bit of Yemen's history that deserves to be celebrated and shared. May God bless you.

Moishe signed it. He unfolded another piece of paper, a list of everything he had left behind. He ran his hand over it, smoothing out the wrinkles, wishing he could hold in his hands the objects described on the page.

Before leaving his home he had carefully inventoried each item. First was the distinctive jewelry of his mentor, Ibrahim al-Arifi:

>*gilded filigree box*
>*amulet box*
>*amulet with beads and dangles*
>*hinged bracelets (2)*
>*upper-arm bracelets (2)*
>*necklace with Russian coral and pendants*
>*woven belt with agate stones and whale and flower motif*

Much of what Moishe had acquired was modest, and he wished he'd been able to purchase more, but he could scarcely afford those pieces at the time. There was another piece, unsigned, which Moishe was certain was an Arifi because of its unique design. It was, he thought, one of his mentor's finest pieces. In his inventory he had written:

> *necklace with three hollow triangles suspended from gilded collar studded with coral. Fine filigree and granulation with arabesque designs. Believe it to be an unsigned Arifi.*
> Most of the rest was Moishe's own work:
> *bracelets (2), filigree studded with small, beaded clusters*
> *bracelets (2), hinged, with braided wire and double rosette*
> *coral necklace with silver amulet. Made as a gift for Samaa on the occasion of Miriam's birth.*
> *necklace with six silver strands and pendants encrusted with semiprecious stones*
> *amulet with filigree and granulation*

Finally, there were a few pieces made by others that Moishe had admired and purchased or, in some cases, bartered for:

> *rings (2) with coral insets, one large, one small*
> *headpiece with coral beads and fringed with silver*
> *earrings (2) with filigree*

He folded both pieces of paper together and tucked them carefully inside his shirt. He felt as though a great weight had been lifted from his shoulders.

CHAPTER FOURTEEN

Buzzards Bay, Massachusetts
2010

Hank looked intently at the piece of paper in his hand, as if staring long enough would suddenly render the impenetrable script legible.

"Arabic?" he asked. "Yes, it does look familiar. I learned a few words when I was researching my story on Guantanamo, but I don't claim to know much about the Middle East, Gee. And I'm a little embarrassed to say this, but I guess I never paid sufficient attention to your experience airlifting the Jews from Yemen, so refresh my memory if you don't mind."

Dewey gently took the note from Hank's hands, as if to suggest such a lack of attention disqualified him from holding it. He gently folded the two pages and returned them to their envelope.

"Next to my service in the war, it was the single most important thing I ever did in my life. I got to help people leave a country where they could no longer live with dignity and get to a place most had only dreamed of ever seeing. By the end of the airlift, Flagstaff flights had moved over forty-eight thousand souls to Israel, virtually the entire Jewish population of Yemen. My crew and I alone carried over a thousand. Most had to walk for weeks from their homes all over Yemen to board one of our planes."

Hank looked puzzled. "But how did a small US airline get roped into flying Jews out of Yemen?"

"It's what we did, son. After the war we were flying air charters just about everywhere you could imagine. We had the planes, the crews, and the experience with long-haul flights. Management was approached by an organization in the US called the Jewish Agency, whose mission was to populate the new state of Israel." Dewey paused while a plane from the air base passed overhead. "We started out flying Jews from Shanghai and then the focus shifted to Yemen. In all, there were more than five hundred flights over two years. We never had an accident, and never lost a single life."

"So tell me about the flight that day, Gee. This time, I promise to listen."

Dewey pushed his chair back from the table a bit and thought for a minute. "What I remember most about that first flight was the hundreds of people crowding onto the runway in Aden the day we arrived, and the urgency we all felt to get them on their way." Dewey smiled as he recalled the events of that day. "I can remember a group of us standing around on the tarmac trying to figure out how we were going to do it. There was the RAF commander who was in charge of the base, an Israeli originally from Yemen who had come back to provide housing for the arrivals, and me and my crew. The Israeli kept asking how many people we could squeeze onto the plane."

CHAPTER FIFTEEN

British Protectorate of Aden
1949

It was hot and Yosef's patience, always in short supply, was just about exhausted. He had asked several times about the capacity of the aircraft that sat on the runway behind him but had not received an answer, so he asked again.

"This is a Douglas DC-4," the pilot replied. "It's designed to carry up to sixty passengers." Dewey looked at his crew, who gathered around him in a small knot, trying to take advantage of what little shade the plane's fuselage provided. "If anybody has any bright idea how we can do better than that, speak up."

Joe Worsley, the flight mechanic, said, "It's a little risky, I suppose, but if we rip the seats out and let everyone sit on the floor, we can double our seating capacity."

Dewey asked, "Anybody see a problem with that?"

Ed Burdette, his copilot, spoke up. "We'll have to do something to keep people from getting up and moving about the aircraft."

Dewey thought about that prospect for a minute and replied, "I have a feeling we're about to pack this plane so tight that there won't be any room for folks to get up and move much, even if they wanted to. What's our maximum payload?"

"DC-4 maxes out at twelve thousand pounds, Cap," Worsley said.

Dewey looked over the crowd again. "Almost everyone I see out here is pretty slender, and a lot of them are children. If we figure an average of eighty pounds per person, we should be able to accommodate almost one hundred fifty at a time."

"We're talking about flying without seatbelts. That's an FAA violation." It was Steve Reeder, his navigator.

"Force majeure, Steve. Besides, I don't expect we'll be entering US airspace. Let's get it done." Dewey turned to Walcott. "We'll need fuel, Commander."

CHAPTER SIXTEEN

British Protectorate of Aden
1949

As they had the day before, Moishe and Shamaa awoke to the sound of small trucks entering their desert encampment just as the sun was rising. It was already warm, and the sky promised little relief from the heat that seemed to adhere to their skin like a robe they couldn't shed.

They carried their children onto one of the trucks and were taken to the same tarmac where they had spent most of the previous day. They watched as the men who had exited the plane the day before walked together out of the terminal building. They walked around the plane, carefully examining it from front to back.

They climbed the ladder and disappeared inside for several minutes, then returned. The pilot looked at some papers that were given to him before climbing back inside. The others followed: four men and two women. Moishe knew the women spoke Hebrew—they had offered greetings as they passed the spot where he, Shamaa, and the children sat.

Some time passed. The man in charge appeared at the top of the ladder, turned around, and descended effortlessly. He said something to the British military officer standing next to the plane, who gave a signal to Yosef, and suddenly everyone seemed to be in motion.

Moishe had imagined delivering his note before everyone got into the airplane, but he didn't dare try to cross the line of soldiers, who were trying without much success to maintain order, and seemed to be growing increasingly impatient as a result.

Off to his left, Moishe heard shouting. An agitated group of people clustered around one of the rabbis, who was trying to make himself heard over the protestations of those afraid to board the airplane. "Brothers and sisters," the rabbi pleaded, "you needn't fear. Remember what the scripture has promised: when the time for Aliyah comes, the Lord will give you strength and bear you up on eagles' wings. These are your wings. Go now."

His words seemed to reassure most of the group, although some continued to pray loudly as they rejoined those waiting to board the plane.

Eventually, something resembling a line formed and people began to board. Moishe and Shamaa carried their children to the rear of the plane, which was quickly getting very crowded. People were squeezing themselves into what space remained on the floor, now stripped of all its seats, and Moishe and his family joined them.

It seemed to take forever to get everyone on board and settled, and then one of the women who spoke Hebrew announced they would need eight or nine hours to fly to Israel, so they would have to sit quietly and not move about, which seemed a foregone conclusion to Moishe, given the number of people occupying every inch of floor space on the airplane.

The sound of people's voices—praying, weeping, offering assurances to one another—filled the plane until the moment the small rear door through which they had boarded was closed and, suddenly, all the noise seemed to stop. It was, Moishe thought, as if everyone was holding their breath, afraid that something would go wrong, that they would have come this close to their deliverance only to have it snatched away.

He looked around, a growing discomfort creeping over him that the large circular drum of the airplane in which they sat was little more than a coffin on wheels.

He pushed the idea from his mind as the engines of the plane rumbled to life, throaty and powerful. In a matter of minutes, they were moving. The sound of the engines grew louder and, as it did, so too did the prayers of those on board. For a long time the airplane rolled along the ground, turning left and then left again. It paused very briefly, as if to catch its breath before attempting the impossible task of lifting itself from the earth. Just as quickly, it began to move. The sound of the engines on either side grew louder as it picked up speed, and seconds later the nose of the plane tipped upward, and it was in the air. It was truly a miracle, Moishe thought. He said a quiet prayer of thanks and pulled Shamaa and his children close to him. They lay down as best they could, and they slept.

CHAPTER SEVENTEEN

Buzzard Bay, Massachusetts
2010

Hank brought his grandfather another cup of coffee while Dewey reflected on how long it had been since he'd given much thought to that first flight from Aden. Recounting the story now, the details seemed as clear in his mind as the sky had been that August day sixty-one years earlier. He could clearly remember the temperature on the runway starting to climb as the morning dragged on and they struggled to get everyone on board.

Dewey had been sitting in the cockpit going through his preflight checklist when Ed Burdette ducked his head in. "We're going to need another couple of minutes before we can start the engines, Cap. There's a lot of people trying to settle down back there."

Glancing out the window onto the tarmac, Dewey saw a couple dozen people milling about near the plane's stairs. Most had obviously never been near an airplane before and were clearly uneasy about climbing inside. Their voices filled the airplane as they boarded. Some seemed to be praying, and plenty were crying, adults and babies alike. Then the passenger door at the rear of the plane was closed and, as if it were a signal, the noise stopped.

Dewey rolled the plane to the runway and waited for the go-ahead from the control tower. As he began to accelerate into his takeoff, the sound of voices rose again.

Dewey climbed to his cruising altitude of nine thousand feet and leveled off. Just ahead was the Red Sea. Dewey banked into his turn and headed north. The flight to Lod Airport in Tel Aviv would take the better part of nine hours. Joe Worsley, the flight mechanic, reported that most of the 152 passengers seemed to be trying to find enough space on the floor of the plane to lie down and go to sleep. "They're packed tighter than sardines back there," he said.

They followed their usual route straight up the Red Sea, using a radio beacon at Jeddah in Saudi Arabia to maintain course. They made their way past the northern tip of the Sinai Peninsula, making sure to stay clear of Egyptian airspace. Before long they were passing through the Straits of Tiran, entering the Gulf of Aqaba, so narrow they could see shoreline on both sides.

Dewey looked to his right, to where Ed Burdette seemed to be fidgeting with the fuel gauge. He tapped it with his knuckle, as if trying to wake it up. "Cap, we're burning way too much fuel," he said.

"How much is way too much?"

Burdette was slow to respond. "Hard to say, Cap . . ."

His voice trailed off, as if the answer to Dewey's question was better left unspoken for the moment. Instead, he asked Steve Reeder, the navigator, for a clear fix on their position and how much fuel they would need to reach Lod Airport.

Reeder's calculations were grim. "Given our current burn rate, we're going to run out in a hundred eighty miles, and we've still got three hundred thirty miles to Tel Aviv."

Dewey knew what had gone wrong: completely unaccustomed to carrying the maximum weight limit, they had miscalculated how quickly the DC-4 would consume its fuel supply. "Run those numbers again, Ed," he said. "If I'm going to press the panic button, I want to make sure there's good reason."

The numbers came back the same. Dewey asked Jimmy Vargas, the radio operator, to check for a secondary airport somewhere else in Israel. Vargas radioed Lod Airport and was told that Tel Aviv was the closest, unless, of course, they wanted to divert to Egypt or Jordan.

"How about that," Burdette said. "The simplest solution is right here on either side of us, but we can't touch down in either country because they're both at war with Israel and we're carrying a planeload of Yemeni Jews."

"What if I throttle back to fifty percent airspeed?" Dewey asked.

The answer came back quickly. "At fifty percent, we'll burn sixteen hundred pounds of fuel per hour," Reeder said. "That will get us as far as Beersheba, but that's still fifty-seven miles south of Tel Aviv."

"Oh, for Christ's sake," Dewey said. "Am I going to have to put this down on a fucking highway?"

"We can kill one of the engines," Ed Burdette said. "That will conserve fuel. Joe, we can do that, right, and still keep this bird in the air?"

"In theory, yeah," replied Joe Worsley, the flight mechanic. "I've never heard of a real-life case when that was done while flying with a full payload, but the DC-4 is designed to fly with just two engines, although I strongly discourage cutting more than one."

"All right, let's give it a try," Dewey said. "Prepare to cut starboard engine number four."

The plane slowed noticeably with just three engines, and Dewey lowered his cruising altitude to seven thousand feet, which he was assured would be well clear of anything on their flight path into Lod Airport.

Once they settled into the new airspeed and altitude, Steve Reeder ran the numbers on the fuel consumption again. "I think we got it, Cap," he said. "We should touch down at Lod Airport with enough fuel to fill a five-gallon gas can."

"That'll work just fine," Dewey replied, and the crew seemed to exhale all at the same time.

When Lod Airport finally came into view, Dewey deployed the landing gear and came around so the nose of the plane lined up with the assigned runway. He touched down smoothly with plenty of runway ahead of him and came to a stop about a hundred yards from the terminal.

They sat on the tarmac for a couple of minutes, waiting for instructions from the control tower. Steve Reeder pointed to a set of headlights coming toward the plane in the waning daylight. It was an Israeli military jeep. It turned around in front of the plane, and the driver signaled for Dewey to follow him. The jeep led them to the terminal building, where Dewey taxied to a stop and shut everything down. Suddenly, the sound of a hundred fifty voices rose from the rear of the plane, reminding Dewey of just how many others were on board.

An Israeli military officer approached the plane. Dewey opened the cockpit window. "You have Yemeni Jews on board, is that correct?" Dewey confirmed it was, and the Israeli relayed the information via radio to the terminal. "Ground crews are coming immediately to off-load the passengers."

Dewey and Joe Worsley made their way to the rear of the plane, where one of the flight attendants had opened the hatch and was deploying the stairs. As Worsley made sure the locking pins were inserted into the landing gear and the wheel chocks were in place, the process of unloading the aircraft had begun.

"To this day I remember the joy on their faces as they stepped onto the tarmac," Dewey said as he sipped the last of his coffee. "So many lifted their eyes to the sky and gave thanks, others knelt and kissed the ground. That's when this man approached me. He was carrying a young child. He looked to be around forty years old. I thought he was just coming over to say thank you, but he brought one of the Israeli flight attendants with him. He was speaking very rapidly, and he seemed to be asking her to translate.

"'Because of you,' he said, 'we have made a journey I never thought possible. I wish to give you this.' He handed me these two pieces of paper, all folded up, grasped my hand, and said, 'Thank you. May God bless you.' And just like that he was off, melting into the crowd of arrivals along with everyone else. I looked at the stewardess, and she just shrugged.

"'I have a feeling you will receive many such notes, Captain,' she said. 'People will want to thank you for bringing them home. I do, too.' And then she walked to the rear of the plane to help with the offloading. I stuck the note in the pocket of my jacket and didn't think about it until I came across it as I was packing my bag to head home some months later. I looked at it carefully for the first time and had pretty much the same reaction you did. I figured that someday I would have time to get it translated and see what exactly it said, but I never got around to it. Seems a shame to never find out, don't you think? And you being a newsman and all, I figured you'd know how to get it done."

"Unemployed newsman, Gee," Hank reminded him. "But yeah, I'm kind of intrigued myself. And I might know someone who can help us find out."

CHAPTER SIXTEEN

Sana'a, Yemen
2010

Haitham Batarfi positioned himself well clear of the crowd that was forming near the doors. Soon, the passengers arriving in Sana'a on the Lufthansa flight from Frankfurt would be passing through them. It seemed to him that only about half of them were family members waiting to greet loved ones on their return to Yemen. The rest were hustlers of one sort or another: petty grifters, cab drivers looking for fares, tourist "guides" looking to usher newcomers around the capital and, of course, sprinkled in among the crowd, a handful of *mukhabarat*, the Yemeni secret police, always looking for someone arriving who might warrant a little extra scrutiny.

Haitham was none of the above—he knew exactly who he was looking for, and she knew him. So, he waited at a distance and watched the ebb and flow of the crowd. Then the glass doors slid open, the first of the arrivals made their way into the terminal, and the doors closed behind them. The crowd seemed to swallow them up and then, just as quickly, released those who weren't absorbed into small family clusters, or hadn't stopped to negotiate the fare into the city with one of the cab drivers.

The arrivals continued to trickle out for the next ten minutes until Haitham saw Kit Salem make her way through the door, wheeling a small blue suitcase behind her. She was wearing a lightweight down jacket, jeans, and running shoes. She had a knit cap pulled over her head, but it failed to tame the raucous mane of red hair that fell to her shoulders. She made her way through the crowd, ignoring all the voices directing queries and invitations in her direction, then looked directly toward the spot where Haitham always stood while waiting for her. He waved, and she smiled broadly when she saw him.

"*Al-humdulelah salaame*," he said, offering the traditional Arabic greeting to a traveler.

"*Allahusalaamak*," Kit replied in return. "How are you, Haitham?" They hugged quickly.

"I'm fine, Kit. Glad to welcome you back. Come on, my car is just outside in a completely illegal space, but there wasn't a policeman in sight when I pulled up. Besides, a distinguished representative of the world-famous *Financial Times* shouldn't be expected to trudge through airport parking lots after a long flight from London."

"I wish everyone had such an elevated opinion of *FT* journalists."

"What can I say, Kit? You pay me. Making you feel important is part of my job description."

They continued chatting until they reached Haitham's car, an aging Peugeot sedan that he'd bought three years earlier in 2007, shortly after he returned to Yemen from London. Kit tossed her bag into the back seat and climbed into the front. "Any news on the appointment with the interior minister? I really need to see him this time."

"Still waiting for confirmation, Kit, although his office manager promised he would make it happen."

Kit had tried and failed to see the minister in charge of Yemen's internal security the last time she was in Sana'a. She was tracking the movement of a top Al Qaeda operative, and a lot of signs pointed to him being in Yemen, although the trail had gone cold. Still, she wanted to speak with someone who might know whether there was any indication of him having entered the country.

"Well, I've got five days, so I hope something will open on his busy schedule. Not today, though. I want to get to the hotel, take a shower, unpack, and head over to Shaibani's for dinner. In that order."

"*Ala keifik*," said Haitham, "as you wish," and they drove off in the direction of the city.

In the world of international journalists, Haitham Batarfi was a fixer, the local contact who greased the skids for those, like Kit, who flew into another country for a quick visit and didn't have the time, the relationships, or the language skills to schedule appointments with hard-to-see people, find their way around the city, know which restaurants to avoid, or how best to approach locals.

Kit was easier to care for than others in almost every respect. She spoke the beautiful Arabic she had learned from her father, a well-known Beirut lawyer and politician who had relocated his family to America shortly after the outbreak of Lebanon's civil war. With no diplomatic experience but a wealth of family connections, he managed to land an assignment with the Lebanese delegation to the United Nations. Kit's mother was two months pregnant when they arrived in New York City in September 1978, and Kit was born in Lenox Hill Hospital the following March. Two years later, as her father's tour of duty at the UN was drawing to a close, and with the civil war still raging back home, he sought and received political asylum in the US.

Kit's parents had met in Beirut while both were students at American University. Her mother was Irish, the daughter of Gerald Meloy, a historian and archaeologist who introduced her to the ancient cultures of the Abbasids and Umayyads when she was just a child. Every summer she would travel with her father to digs in Syria and Lebanon, and she was conversational in Arabic by the time she turned ten. For her, the Levant was home, and AUB was the only place she ever considered going to university.

Kit inherited her mother's fascination with the Near East, as well as her coloring and her hair. It was red from the day she was born, so distinctive that her father almost immediately stopped calling her by her given name, Katherine, and started calling her Kit, "my very clever little red fox."

Thirty-one years later, Kit Salem was a respected journalist and a frequent visitor to the Arab world, and Yemen was one of the countries she most enjoyed visiting. Haitham himself had gone abroad to study in the UK and had worked for a couple of years for the BBC, but like a lot of Arabs, he missed the familiarity of home and returned to Yemen. He told himself it was because his parents were getting older and could use his help, although his two sisters lived close and were able to pitch in as needed. Mostly, he just felt comfortable in Sana'a. It was where he had grown up. He knew a lot of people, whom to call on when official papers needed to be signed in a hurry, what restaurants didn't care if you brought a bottle of wine to dinner with you. In other words, the perfect fixer. And it kept him busy. Al Qaeda in the Arabian Peninsula had emerged in Yemen, and Sana'a had quickly become a required stop for almost any journalist covering regional security and counterterrorism.

Kit was one of the better ones. It wasn't just that she was fluent in Arabic, it was also that she was smart and tough. She couldn't be bullied, and he had seen a lot of officials in Sana'a try and fail. She pushed right back, and the good ones seemed to respect her for it. It was one of the reasons most of them made time for her whenever Haitham reached out to ask for an appointment.

Which is what happened late that evening, when Haitham got a call informing him that the interior minister would see Kit in his office at 1 p.m. the next day.

CHAPTER SEVENTEEN

Sana'a, Yemen

2010

Abdulaziz al-Kebsi was the scion of a well-established Yemeni family with the easy manner of a seasoned politician and a well-honed flair for the theatrical. He was fond of demonstrating to visitors his familiarity with matters unrelated to internal security, such as Renaissance art and the Bundesliga. He also enjoyed serving freshly brewed cappuccino to his guests in delicate, bone china cups, never failing to remark that Yemen was the birthplace of the coffee bean, a point of friendly contention between him and the Ethiopian ambassador.

He greeted Kit effusively as she was escorted into his office. "Miss Kit Salem, *ahlan wa sahlan*, welcome, welcome. I hope you have been well."

"Thank you, Mr. Minister. Well indeed. Even better now that I can smell the rich aroma of Yemeni coffee." Kit figured it never hurt to spread a little bullshit around at the beginning of a conversation. She found it particularly helpful in the Arab world, where every conversation followed a certain pattern: repeated expressions of welcome by the host and gratitude for the host's hospitality by the guest, most often followed by fervent wishes for the continued good health of the host and his family, which were then reciprocated by the host.

Westerners sometimes had a hard time with this careful orchestration, preferring to get right to business, but Kit had learned early on that the time invested in demonstrating respect for these conventions was time well spent.

Of course, it didn't hurt that she had grown up watching her father engage in precisely this sort of give-and-take when he would receive guests at their apartment in New York and, later, their home in Connecticut. A precocious child, she loved being invited, even briefly, to those occasions, where she would show off her Arabic and her familiarity with Middle Eastern politics to smartly dressed men and women before her father would gently usher her out of his study and close the door.

"Your father is well, I trust?" the minister asked.

"Yes, he's fine, sir. Thank you for inquiring. He's recovered from a bit of a spill he suffered earlier in the year while coming up the front steps of our house, which is a great relief to us all."

"I'm sure it is. Please give him my regards next time you see him, will you?"

"Of course, sir. I hope you and your family are all well. Your boys must be nearly grown by now."

"Yes, one is at university and the other is not far behind. I don't quite know where the years went." He sighed almost imperceptibly and invited Kit to try her coffee. As she did, he shifted in his chair, and Kit sensed that both were signals that the conversational preliminaries had ended. So, she turned to business.

"Mr. Minister, thank you for seeing me today. I know you're busy, but I greatly value the opportunity to hear from you directly. I have been tracking the whereabouts of Ibrahim al-Jubaili for nearly a year now. As you know better than I, French authorities believe Jubaili is responsible for making the explosives used in the attack on the exhibit of ancient artifacts from the Holy Land at the Musée de Montmartre in May of last year. And while they haven't any proof, they worry that he managed to get them through the metal detectors at the museum in the lining of a backpack he carried, because the materials were nonferrous.

"While that explosive charge was small, and the damage was not extensive, counterterrorism officials in Paris and London have told me that they are deeply concerned that Jubaili's quest to build a large nonferrous explosive continues unabated. You can imagine, if he were to succeed, the damage such a bomb could cause if it were able to evade metal detectors at, say, a major airport. They are desperate to find him, and have turned their attention to Yemen, where they believe he is hiding. I was hoping you might be able to share with me your own thoughts on his whereabouts."

She paused and took another sip of her cappuccino.

The minister watched her and smiled ever so slightly. "We are speaking off the record, yes?" He waited for confirmation from Kit that whatever he was about to say would not make its way back to him.

"As you wish, sir," she said. "Although I would like to get a quote from you that I can use in my story, even if it's noncommittal."

"Of course, I understand. Off the record, I can tell you that I have spoken with my British and French counterparts and even an American or two in the past month or so, and all are keen to know if Jubaili has returned to Yemen. My honest answer to them, and to you, is that I just don't know. There are rumors, of course, alleged sightings here and there, but nothing I have been able to confirm. But I have my best officers working the case, and if Jubaili is in Yemen, we will find him."

"And if you find him, sir, will you be able to arrest him? Given his family ties, he might be holed up in one of the more remote tribal areas and protected by well-armed fighters. Are you prepared to go to war with your own people to detain him?"

"Oh, I hardly think we'll have to start a war over Ibrahim al-Jubaili. As you know, he is a Kuwaiti, not a Yemeni, which means that many of those protecting him are doing so for reasons other than personal loyalty. And as you may have heard during your travels here, Kit, you can't buy a Yemeni tribe's loyalty, you can only rent it. In that case, it goes to the highest bidder. And should it be the government of Yemen, then Mr. Jubaili's safe haven begins to look much less secure, wouldn't you agree?"

Kit knew he was sparring with her. She jabbed back. "Although the fact that Jubaili is married to a Yemeni woman whose father is a senior sheikh of the Khalifa tribe suggests to me that there may in fact be some loyalties at play here."

"You've done your homework, as usual."

A staffer entered the office, walked quickly to where the minister sat, and handed him a piece of paper folded in half. The minister opened it and read the message.

"Ah, yes, I'm being reminded that I have a luncheon scheduled with several local dignitaries and am now officially late for my own event." He returned the note to his aide and for a moment, appeared to be getting up from his chair. Then he stopped and looked at Kit. His face brightened and he said, "I have an idea. Why don't you stay and have lunch with us? I think you'll find my guests to be quite interesting. Our friend Haitham can join us, as well. What do you say?"

Kit was intrigued. "You're very kind, Mr. Minister, but I wouldn't want to intrude on your day any more than I already have."

"Nonsense." He dismissed her concern with a patrician wave of his hand. "This will be a treat. We'll just need a moment to rearrange the seating. Make yourself comfortable. I'll see to that and be back directly."

Ten minutes later, he was escorting them to his private dining room, which was just down the hall, behind ornate wooden doors that were flanked by two guards wearing dark suits and blank expressions. One reached across and opened the door as the minister approached. Kit and Haitham followed him into the room.

A dozen tribal sheikhs were sprinkled around a large rectangular table. They each wore the traditional *thobe*, an ankle-length white robe favored by Yemeni men. Most wore a suit coat over the thobe and *keffiyehs* wrapped turban-style around their heads. All had a *jambiya* tucked into a broad piece of ceremonial cloth tied around their midsection. Kit knew the large curved knife was carried by virtually every Yemeni male from the time they were boys. According to tradition, you never drew the jambiya from its scabbard unless you were going to use it. The quality of the jambiya, its handle and its scabbard, said much about the social status of its owner.

The minister quickly circled the table, embracing his guests and kissing each on one cheek and then the other.

He returned to where Kit was standing and introduced her in some detail, making a point of mentioning her Lebanese origins and her fluent Arabic. He introduced Haitham and invited him to sit at the far end of the table between two men younger than all the others present. Glancing at them, Kit thought they must have accompanied their fathers to the luncheon, a training exercise for the life that awaited them. Haitham sent her a look across the table that suggested he had drawn the same conclusion.

The minister ushered Kit to a place of honor, near the top of the long side of the rectangular table. To her left sat a heavyset man with a modest, neatly trimmed beard who seemed vaguely uncomfortable having a woman to whom he was unrelated sit so close. To her right, between her and the minister, sat an older man with an almost military bearing. The minister wasted no time making introductions.

"Miss Kit, to your left is Sheikh Abdulrahman al-Ahmar, a dear friend who joins us today representing the Hashid tribal confederation. To your right is Abdulwahab bin Hamad al-Akli, the paramount sheikh of the Khalifa tribe." He leaned forward just a bit, as if to signal he was about to share something confidential. "I've informed Sheikh Abdulwahab of the issue we were just discussing in my office." And then he broke into the most devilish smile.

So, Kit thought to herself, that's what this is about. A little test for the inquisitive journalist. But as the minister had acknowledged earlier, Kit had done her homework. She recognized the name of Ibrahim al-Jubaili's father-in-law. And now she was sitting right next to him, the man most likely to know the whereabouts of AQAP's principal bombmaker. She smiled at the minister, nodded politely to the man on her left, and turned her attention to the man on her right, who occupied a seat of honor closest to the host.

"I hope that unexpectedly finding yourself seated next to an American journalist won't rob you of your appetite," she said brightly.

He may have heard what Kit said, or he may not have; it was impossible to know from his reaction. Slowly, he reached into the center of the table for a basket laden with warm pita bread and offered it to Kit.

"I've learned in the course of my life to eat when there is food, even if conditions are not ideal," he said dryly, still holding the basket of bread. Kit took one and returned the favor with the bowl of hummus that was in front of her. For a moment, they didn't speak. Then, without turning to her, he said, "I understand you are interested in the whereabouts of my son-in-law."

His directness surprised her. She took her time finishing what she was eating and drank a sip of juice. She didn't want to appear too eager. "Yes, sir, that is correct. I would like to speak with him. I would not divulge his location, of course. I am a journalist, not a police officer."

"And why is it you have come to Yemen in search of Ibrahim?"

"As you may know, sir, Interpol has issued a warrant for his arrest in connection with the bombing last year at the Montmartre museum in Paris. The authorities I have spoken with think that he has taken refuge here, possibly with his wife's family."

"You are American, no?" he asked, a question Kit took as rhetorical since their host already had made that clear in his introduction. "I don't know how familiar you are with Yemen, although it seems you have visited before. But I assure you that the French authorities need not be concerned about anyone living under my protection or within the confines of our tribal land. I take full responsibility for the actions of each member of my family, and the Khalifa tribe, and no one will do anything to dishonor our name."

Kit knew enough about Yemen's tribes to know of this principle, but thought an expression of gratitude for the sheikh's explanation would be the most productive response.

"Of course, sir. I've read a bit about Yemen's tribal culture, but having it explained in those terms is very helpful indeed. Thank you." She paused while a waiter reached around to ladle soup into the bowl in front of her. Aromas of garlic and coriander lingered in the air as she gently stirred the broth.

"Would I be correct to conclude from your comment that Ibrahim is in fact staying with you?"

The sheikh stirred his own soup for a moment, as if he was mulling something over.

"I'm not in a position to say where Ibrahim is staying," he said. "But I will agree to look into your request if you will agree to do something for me."

CHAPTER EIGHTEEN

Sana'a, Yemen
2010

Driving away after lunch, Haitham shook his head in disbelief. "Incredible. Sitting you next to Jubaili's father-in-law."

"Yes, our friend the minister got quite a charge out of that."

"I'll bet he did. Jubaili is almost certainly living with his family in Shabwa province where he's out of reach. And I'll bet the minister has come to an understanding with the old man that as long as his son-in-law doesn't make a mess in Yemen, or do anything else that might draw unwelcome attention to Yemen, he won't be disturbed."

"I didn't know you were so cynical, Haitham."

"The minister's playing a weak hand. I'm sure from where he sits, keeping Yemen out of whatever unpleasant schemes AQAP may hatch is the best outcome he can hope for. If the UK or France or the US, with all their resources, can't stop Jubaili, why should Yemen be expected to do so?"

They rode in silence while Kit scribbled notes in the small journalist's notebook she carried everywhere. She spoke up. "I didn't tell you the best part yet. Do you want to guess?"

"The father-in-law agreed to set up a meeting for you with Jubaili?"

"Not quite. He never even admitted he knew Jubaili's whereabouts. He just said he would look into it. But he wants me to do something for him in return."

"Such as?"

"His oldest son, Ashraf, has been held at Guantanamo for eight years, apparently without ever being charged with anything. He wants me to visit and write a story about him. He seems to think it would help his case."

Haitham looked puzzled. "Do they even let journalists into Guantanamo?"

"I think so, but it takes forever to arrange a visit, and even then you go only as part of a carefully choreographed group tour. One of my colleagues went last year and said it was a complete waste of time. But think of it this way, Haitham. My story just got a whole lot more interesting. Instead of an Interpol-seeks-terrorist story, which, sadly, is all too common these days, now there's an opportunity to develop a portrait of a family in Yemen that has been thrust right into the middle of the so-called war on terror. The youngest son is in Guantanamo, the son-in-law is a notorious bombmaker and international fugitive, and, in the middle, we have this very traditional tribal leader clinging to a code of honor that seems positively quaint in this age of ours.

"First thing I need to do is call my editor in London to explain what I have in mind, and why it will require me to return to the US so I can look into his son's case. I'll need to go to Washington and speak with someone at the Pentagon and the State Department, and I'll need to speak with the attorney who is representing him. The father gave me her name. I wrote it down." She flipped through the pages of the notebook on her lap. "It's McAfee. Carole Ann McAfee. He said they spoke a couple of times right after she agreed to take his son's case. She's a partner at a law firm in DC, so I'll try to see her at the same time."

CHAPTER NINETEEN

Princeton, New Jersey
2010

Hank walked quickly across the quad, weaving his way around students moving casually, or seemingly not at all, along the brick pathway that bisected a carefully manicured expanse of lawn. The train had been late departing DC, and what was supposed to be a three-hour trip to Princeton had taken over four. He called ahead to alert Marwan Darwish he would be late for their appointment, and the grad student who answered the phone said Darwish was expecting him, although he had a class at five o'clock.

Still, Hank hated to be late. It was a small obsession with him, one he often used to his advantage as a reporter. He would always be on time for an interview. If the other person was late, so be it. Many people, he discovered, were genuinely apologetic for keeping him waiting, and it sometimes led them to be a bit more helpful than they might have been otherwise.

Hank wheeled around a staircase heading up to the third floor of Lancaster Hall and nearly knocked over a young woman who had stopped to check something on her cell phone. He muttered under his breath about keeping the traffic lanes free, swung past her, and kept climbing. The third floor was quiet, and Hank walked quickly to Darwish's office. He knew it well, having visited multiple times when he was conducting his research into Guantanamo.

Darwish had established himself as a vocal critic of US counterterrorism policy following the attacks of 9/11. A Syrian

American, he immigrated to the United States as a child with his family. His parents were both physicians, but he had no interest in medicine. He loved history. Especially the history of the Middle East, the extraordinary civilizations it had produced, its scientific achievements, its tales of conquest, and, sadly, its now-familiar reputation for corrupt, dysfunctional governments.

Darwish was an accomplished historian, a popular professor, and, for the past two years, chair of the Middle Eastern Studies Department. The position provided him a high-profile platform from which to condemn the suspension of habeas corpus that became common practice as the US rounded up hundreds of individuals around the world, declared them enemy combatants, and locked them up. The lack of due process, he argued, squandered America's reputation as a nation committed to the rule of law and undermined its ability to criticize other nations for failing to respect human rights.

Hank stepped through a door into a small waiting area. A young man sat at a desk, typing furiously on a laptop. Hank introduced himself and took a seat. The young man got up and tapped lightly on the door to his left. A moment later it swung open and a man of medium build with tightly cropped gray hair and a large smile emerged.

"*Ahlan wa sahlan, ya*, Hank," he said loudly. "Do you remember any of the Arabic I taught you?"

"*Ahlanbik*, Professor," Hank said, returning the greeting, "and I'm afraid that's about as much as I can muster right now."

Darwish took Hank by the arm and ushered him into his office, which, as Hank recalled, was perhaps the most orderly space he had ever seen. Every book, every paper, every picture on the wall seemed to be in precisely the right place. And what Hank found most fascinating: the office didn't have a desk. There was a large rectangular table surrounded by eight chairs where Darwish often worked or held small-group seminars, making the space feel much more like a sitting room than an office.

"Marwan, I would love to come here just once and see a stray pencil on the floor."

"I know it's not healthy, Hank. Basma tells me so each time she comes by. But what can I do? I'm immersed constantly in the chaos that is the Middle East, so I try to create a bit of order where I can. Please, have a seat." Hank did, and Darwish sat across from him in a worn easy chair. "I'm delighted to see you, Hank. It's been much too long. And so it pains me to begin our conversation by pointing out that I have one more class to teach this afternoon. I'll have to run out of here in exactly twenty-five minutes so as not to offend our next generation of leaders by keeping them waiting."

"Understood, Marwan. I apologize for showing up so late. Amtrak couldn't commit to a schedule today." He reached into the pocket of his jacket and pulled out the envelope his grandfather had given him. "I'm hoping you might be able to help with a translation of this, well . . . I'm not sure what it is. In 1949, my grandfather was a pilot for Flagstaff Airlines, which carried thousands of Yemeni Jews to Israel as part of what was called at the time Operation Magic Carpet."

Darwish nodded vigorously, indicating his familiarity with the events.

Hank continued. "One of them handed my grandfather this note when they landed in Tel Aviv, and he never bothered to have it translated. He's curious about what it says, and I said I would try to find out."

Darwish extracted the two pieces of yellowed paper from the envelope and unfolded them carefully. He pulled a pair of eyeglasses from his shirt pocket, put them on, and leaned back in his chair.

"The man who wrote this has beautiful handwriting," he said, not lifting his eyes from the paper. "Like an artist." He began reading aloud. "*I am Moishe Azani, a silversmith, a Jew, a Yemeni.*" He read the rest of the note in silence.

When he was finished, he lowered the paper to his lap and removed his glasses. "*Mash'allah,*" he exclaimed quietly, invoking

God's blessing. "What a moment that must have been in this man's life. Hank, look. I've got a class waiting for me. Why don't you have dinner with us, stay the night, and go back to DC tomorrow? With a bit more time I can write a good English translation you can take with you, and we can catch up. I know that Basma would be delighted to see you. I'll call her now and ask her to add a plate for dinner and clean the cobwebs from the guest room. What do you say?"

"Marwan," Hank said without hesitation, "I would be honored."

CHAPTER TWENTY

Washington, DC
2010

Carole Ann McAfee's cell phone, silenced on her desk, began vibrating. She picked it up and saw a number she didn't recognize. "Hello?"

"Carole Ann McAfee?"

"Yes, it is. Who's this?"

"My name is Kit Salem. I'm a reporter with the *Financial Times*. I'm hoping you've received an email from one of my colleagues, Brett Sorensen, alerting you that I would call on this number, which he was kind enough to share with me."

"I quite likely did, but my email management is dreadful, so I suspect it is buried under a hundred other messages also deserving of my attention. But no matter. Brett's been a good friend for years. What can I do for you?"

Kit explained her conversation with Ashraf al-Akli's father and her wish to develop a portrait of a family emblematic of how violent extremism crept into the lives of people in the most remote corners of the globe.

"I told Ashraf's father that I would try to visit his son at Guantanamo, although I must admit I haven't even started to investigate that piece of the story yet."

"Save yourself the time, Ms. Salem," McAfee replied curtly. "You can ask to be included in a journalists' tour of the prison, but no contact with the detainees is allowed. The United States government would prefer that we all forget about the one hundred seventy or so men being held there, none of whom have ever been given the opportunity to understand the charges they face or the evidence on which those charges are based, including my client. But you didn't call to hear me rant, did you?"

Kit left the question unanswered. "If I can't speak with your client, would you be willing to describe for me how he ended up in Guantanamo? I don't want to put him in any jeopardy, but ever since I spoke with his father, I can't get this story out of my head."

"Let me think about it. This would have to be a net positive for Ashraf. Anything else is off the table." She asked Kit for her email and said she would be in touch in a day or two. "In the meantime," she said, "let me give you the contact info for a journalist named Hank Amato. He wrote a series in 2008 on my work with Ashraf. At the very least, it will provide some useful background on his case."

"His cell number would be most helpful, thank you. I tried reaching him at *The Des Moines Register* but he doesn't work there anymore. I do have his articles with me, though. His profile of your work with Ashraf is pretty much the first thing that pops up when you search your client's name. Anyway, you have my number now, as well, and you can call me at your convenience," said Kit as she ended the conversation. "I'll wait to hear from you, and thanks for considering my request."

Kit turned from the small desk where she sat and tossed her cell phone onto the bed of the hotel room she had checked into the night before. Picking through a stack of papers she had carried with her, she extracted a thick sheaf held together with a large paper clip. She walked to the bed, piled the pillows against the headboard, sat down, and placed the papers on her lap.

The headline on the first of three articles clipped together read: *A Hawkeye's Search for Justice*, and beneath it: *UI Law Grad Battles for Client in Guantanamo*. Just below that, in smaller print, was Hank's byline.

Carole Ann McAfee was hopping mad, it began. *So angry that her hands were trembling and she was having difficulty maintaining eye contact with the young man she had just traveled 1200 miles to meet. It was not her normal response.*

"I've never seen her flinch," said a former colleague. "I've seen her stare down street thugs, gangsters, and career criminals. Look them directly in the eye until they look away, like they knew she could see into their soul, see their guilt. And I've seen her sit and listen patiently to their victims while they described horrific acts of violence," said Philip Chabonne, a law professor at Emory University. The two worked together in the mid-'90s, when both were assistant district attorneys in Chicago. Chabonne, now on the board of the Center for Constitutional Rights, was responsible for putting McAfee in the room where her anger was making her physically ill that day.

The room in question was in a prefabricated building located on Naval Station Guantanamo Bay on the southeast corner of Cuba, 90 miles from Miami. The base, a relic of the Spanish-American War, has been leased by the United States since 1903, much to the consternation of the Cuban government, which has characterized the continued American presence on its territory as an illegal occupation.

Largely ignored throughout the 20th century, Guantanamo suddenly found itself thrust into prominence in the wake of the 2001 terrorist attacks on New York and Washington, DC. The US government saw the base as the perfect location to house the hundreds of individuals it had vacuumed up around the world as part of the so-called Global War on Terror. "It was close to the US mainland, easily accessible, and on territory we controlled, but in their view, outside the jurisdiction of American courts," said Chabonne. "An ideal spot if you wanted to conveniently ignore due process and engage in systematic abuse of prisoners, which seems to be precisely what the US government had in mind."

This was McAfee's first visit to the facility and her first meeting with her client, a slender 21-year-old Yemeni with dark hair and a wispy beard that looked like an adolescent's failed declaration of manhood.

His name was Ashraf al-Akli, and he was escorted into the room by two large guards, despite his diminutive size and the fact that he was wearing ankle and wrist shackles. None of that would have made McAfee flinch, however. What got to her was his face. It looked like he had been run over by a truck.

She recalled the moment: "His left eye was swollen shut and all around it the skin was a deep purple. His right eye was bloodshot. His face had contusions and bruises and when the guards sat him down in the chair across from me his face contorted in pain from the effort. I thought he was about to scream. But he didn't. He looked right at me. We looked at each other. Neither one of us spoke for the longest time. Honestly, I couldn't think of anything to say that might offer him comfort. It just made me so angry. That's when my hands started trembling. And that's when I looked away."

McAfee's client had been IRF'd, beaten by the prison's Initial Reaction Force, for a rules infraction: he had stepped across a no-go line at chow time. Later that night, she said, 'the IRF swept into his cell, five guards in full tactical gear. The prisoners call them Darth Vaders. They beat Ashraf until he lay on the concrete floor of his cell like a dishrag.'

Kit stopped reading, leaned back, and tried to shake the image from her mind. Then she reached for her cell phone and dialed the number she had gotten from Carole Ann McAfee.

Hank answered as he always did. "This is Hank."

"Hank Amato, Kit Salem here. I'm a reporter for the *Financial Times*. Do you have a minute to speak?"

Hank was momentarily disoriented, unaccustomed to being cold-called by a reporter he didn't know.

Kit jumped into the pause that ensued. "I got your number from Carole Ann McAfee. I'm interested in the case of one of her clients, a prisoner at Guantanamo, Ashraf al-Akli. I know you looked into his detention when you profiled Carole Ann for the *Register*. Great work, by the way. I understand you're no longer with the paper. Are you working elsewhere?"

"Is this an interview?" Hank asked.

"Oh my word, no," Kit said. "I'm sorry. I'm just making conversation. But I would like to speak with you about al-Akli. Carole Ann told me there's no way I will get to see him myself, so I'm going to have to rely on what others have learned about him in order to piece together some sort of composite picture."

Hank hesitated. "You know that everything I wrote was either from open sources or from Carole Ann herself, right? I can tell you where to look and save you some time."

"I just flew into New York and I expect to be here for a couple of days, but I don't mind coming to you," Kit persisted. "Where are you located? I see your phone has a 319 area code. Are you still in Iowa?"

Hank's first thought was that his whereabouts were none of her business. Then he quickly remembered how many times his own research had benefited from a total stranger offering to share what they knew. "I'm in Washington, DC. Unless I miss my guess, you're going to have to make your way down here at some point doing a Guantanamo story."

"It's my next stop," Kit said. "My plan is to sneak off for a quick visit with my folks in Connecticut and then get to work on the story."

"Well, give me a call when you get here, and I suppose we can arrange to meet." Hank was surprised that he was still being so prickly, and he realized it was because he was unfamiliar with the feeling of being pushed into a conversation he wasn't sure he wanted to have. He wondered how many of the people he'd called out of the blue during his own career felt the same way when he'd pressed them for information.

Kit said something, and Hank realized that she was trying to set up a time to meet. "Can we plan on getting together next week when I'm in DC? You've got my cell number now. Check your schedule and send me a text. Let me know what day works best for you, and I'll take you to lunch. You pick the spot."

CHAPTER TWENTY-ONE

Washington, DC
2010

Hank had gotten to know his way around DC while he was writing his profile of the Guantanamo lawyer. Carole's office was in a large steel and glass building on the corner of 19th and L streets, not far from Georgetown, where he had found a short-term sublet at a price The *Register* was willing to pay. He liked the city and its neighborhoods. It was one of the reasons he decided to move back when he suddenly found himself untethered. DC was full of young professionals, and much to Hank's liking, it was a low-rise city.

As it turned out, DC also offered Hank a good lodging option while he figured out what to do next. An acquaintance from *The Daily Iowan* worked as a congressional staffer and had a spare bedroom he was more than willing to rent.

Hank recalled meeting McAfee for lunch one day at a restaurant called The Solarium, located a few blocks away from her office. It was just off the lobby of an upscale hotel—bright, unpretentious, and normally not too loud—which is why he had proposed it for lunch with the *FT* reporter.

Sitting at the table waiting for her to arrive, he fidgeted with the collar of the blue and white checked shirt fresh from the dry cleaners that he wore under a charcoal gray V-neck sweater. It was another outfit he saved for special occasions, although he couldn't quite put his finger on why this occasion qualified as special. Nor was he sure why he was feeling a little nervous. He didn't even know this woman, although he had done the requisite internet search to confirm her bona fides—and to make sure he would recognize her when they met for the first time. Her work was impressive, and he knew and respected the *FT*, but he wasn't interviewing for a job, was he? The short answer was no, although he figured lending a hand to a well-known journalist might pay off someday in case he needed a reference.

Hank also had a bit of an agenda of his own. His research revealed that Kit Salem's work often took her to Yemen, a country about which he had suddenly become quite interested. He even brought the translation Marwan Darwish provided of the note his grandfather had given him, although he wasn't at all certain he was ready to share it with anyone. He'd have to see what she was like. And, if he was being honest, Hank also was curious to see if Kit Salem was nearly as good-looking in person as she was in the internet photos he had come across.

And then suddenly there she was, sweeping into the sun-filled dining room in a swirl of navy blue and lemon yellow, the former being what appeared to be a very well-tailored peacoat, and the latter the scarf she told the waiter she'd keep around her neck. "Chilly for October in DC," she said by way of explanation. Hank watched as she got settled. Cell phone on the table, large shoulder bag on a small stool the waiter positioned next to her chair. She wrapped both hands around the thick red hair that was falling over her shoulders and swept it back, securing it deftly into a ponytail with an elastic that materialized from under her sleeve. Then she paused and smiled. Hank was mesmerized.

"Thanks for seeing me, Hank."

"You caught me at a good time," he said, but Kit seemed uninterested in a discussion of his employment status.

Instead, she took a moment to look around. "What a lovely room," she said. "So bright. Do you come here often?"

"When I want to hear what my lunch partner is saying," Hank said honestly. "That's more difficult than you might think in a lot of restaurants downtown."

"Well, thank you for choosing so thoughtfully," Kit said. And just like that, she got down to business.

"Your series on Carole Ann McAfee was first-rate, Hank. It deserved all the accolades it received."

Uncomfortable with praise, Hank turned his attention to the position of his knife and fork on the table. "Thanks," he finally said. "Carole Ann is such a compelling character. It would have been malpractice to blow the chance she gave me to see the world from her perspective."

Kit smiled again, and Hank noticed the tiniest wrinkles at the edges of her stunning green eyes.

"She's agreed to see me this afternoon," Kit said. "I'm going to her office directly from here."

"Good for you," Hank replied. "If your interest is Ashraf al-Akli, she can tell you about him in exquisite detail."

"You never got to speak with him, then."

"Not even close. Only the attorneys of detainees are allowed that kind of contact. I got to the prison on one of the Pentagon's carefully staged tours for journalists, and I may even have seen him, but I'll never know."

The waiter came by to see if they were ready to order. Kit ran her eyes over the menu and quickly decided on a Cobb salad and a lemon San Pellegrino.

Hank opted for the pan-fried trout and an iced tea. The waiter retreated and the two looked across the table at each other.

"Do you mind if I ask you what you remember about your visit? I contacted the Pentagon press office and was told it could be months before they might be able to get me onto the base. Frankly, I don't think it helped that I work for a British newspaper that has been very critical of America's little penal colony on the island of Cuba."

"Sadly, I returned with very little to tell," he said. "There were about twenty-five journalists in my group. We had to go through the usual preliminaries, including initialing all thirteen pages of the ground rules for media—what you can bring, what you can photograph, who you can speak to, and who you can identify. The tour itself was a typical US government dog and pony show. They took us to Camp 6. That's where prisoners deemed compliant are housed. We were told no fewer than four times that it has air-conditioning."

Hank rolled his eyes and went on. "Our tour guide was quite proud of the fact that forty percent of the prisoners attend classes, including life skills training. They actually offer a course called Building a Résumé." Hank smiled at the recollection, and Kit did as well. He thought her smile was just about perfect.

He described the visit to the medical unit, the library, and the kitchen, the glimpse of a cell where a Muslim prayer rug and prayer beads and a copy of the Quran were laid out carefully on a bunk.

"It was all very Orwellian," he said. "Here's a place where fundamental legal rights are suspended, where human rights are regularly violated, and our hosts are all, 'Look at this, we have Harry Potter in Arabic!' I barely used anything I saw or was told during the visit in my article." Just then lunch arrived, giving Hank a chance to jump in with a question of his own. "So what prompted your interest in Ashraf al-Akli?"

Kit looked up from her salad, which had just been placed in front of her. "I met his father during my last visit to Yemen," she said. "He's a very traditional tribal leader who is wrestling with some very twenty-first century problems. His youngest son has been thrown down a black hole by the United States on unspecified charges related to terrorism, and his son-in-law is suspected of being one of the most dangerous bombmakers in the world, the man behind the attack on the Musée de Montmartre in Paris last year."

"I remember that," Hank said. "Some priceless artifacts were damaged, right? I guess everyone was relieved it wasn't any worse."

"Which is why finding Ibrahim al-Jubaili is so urgent. His one goal in life seems to be fabricating a powerful, nonferrous explosive device. If something like that ended up on an airplane, there could be tragic consequences."

"And the man you met, the father-in-law, is he being helpful?"

"He's being a bit cagey, to be honest. He asked me to look into his son's detention, suggesting that might help him decide." While Kit recounted their conversation in Sana'a, Hank went to work on his lunch. Kit watched him as he ate, approving of his dark hair, deep brown eyes, and light olive complexion that seemed to be the exact opposite of the slightly freckled, too easily sunburned skin she had inherited from her mother. He could use a haircut, she thought, but she was a bug about neatness. In that respect, Hank passed muster just fine. His checked shirt under the V-neck sweater looked freshly pressed. She gave him extra style points for his wristwatch, a simple analog with a brown leather band.

They chatted their way through lunch, and walked out of the hotel onto 16th Street, a half dozen blocks north of the White House. McAfee's office was about the same distance to the east, so Hank offered to walk with Kit. On the way, he mentioned his own developing interest in Yemen, based largely on his grandfather's role in the emigration of Yemeni Jews in the years following Israel's creation.

"I'd love to hear more about that, Hank," Kit said, and it was surprisingly easy for him to believe her interest was genuine. "Look, my train back to New York doesn't leave until eleven tomorrow morning. Why don't we have breakfast at my hotel? I'm staying in Dupont Circle. I can tell you about my visit with Carole Ann and you can tell me more about your grandfather's experience in Yemen."

They agreed to meet at eight the next morning, and she was off, through the revolving door and into the lobby of the building that housed McAfee's law firm. Hank watched her through the glass facade. She walked purposefully up to the reception desk and produced an ID for the security guard, who handed her a sign-in sheet. Then, as she walked toward the elevators, she glanced back to where Hank stood and gave a tiny finger wave. At that moment, hopelessly infatuated, Hank decided that maybe his crazy, recurring idea of traveling to Yemen in search of the silversmith's jewelry wasn't so crazy after all.

CHAPTER TWENTY-TWO

Shabwa, Yemen
2010

Abdulwahab rolled over, away from the first light of day that was just now angling into his bedroom through the *qamariya*, the stained-glass, half-moon window that threw patterns of colored light into the room as the sun arced across the sky. He stretched his hand to touch the colors that had made their way onto the wall next to his bed. The day was beginning, and he had yet to sleep.

This was not unusual after a *qat* chew, when his body was still abuzz from the overdose of cathine and cathinone, the latter a close cousin of amphetamines, which he consumed over the course of four or five hours, chewing the leaf of the qat plant and talking a blue streak to anyone within earshot. He could have been talking to himself for all the difference it would have made. Qat just wound a person up and then slowly spooled him out for as long as he kept chewing.

Abdulwahab's cousin, a doctor at the small hospital run by a French aid organization in the nearby city of Ataq, had stopped chewing because he said it was ruining his health and his ability to practice medicine. He also claimed it was slowly eroding the foundations of Yemeni society. He said that when the qat market opened each afternoon, half the hospital staff would simply leave to buy what they needed for the day, and woe to anyone who showed up in need of emergency medical care.

Abdulwahab thought his cousin was becoming a bit of a zealot, although he didn't entirely disagree with the view that chewing had become the center of life for a lot of Yemenis, with few discernible benefits. In the first place, because it was such a cash crop, farmers stopped growing coffee, fruits, and vegetables, which were much slower to mature and bring to market, and started cultivating qat. Now Yemen had to import foodstuffs it traditionally grew in abundance. Qat also required enormous amounts of water, and Yemen had little to spare.

There had been a time in Yemen when qat chews were reserved for important family occasions: the birth of a child, a wedding, even a funeral. Qat was the social glue that bound families and communities. Now, people chewed qat all day, every day. Cab drivers bustled around the city, their cheek protruding as if they held a tennis ball inside their mouth when, in fact, it was a wad of leaves that just sat there marinating, turning their teeth green, their saliva green, the spot on the street where they spat, green.

The fascination with the leafy plant was a bit difficult to identify. It provided an energy boost that was useful during the day, but that hardly explained the heavy usage at other times. Among themselves, Yemenis joked that a qat chew turned you into three different creatures all in the space of one night.

At the outset, you were like a bird. Your heart rate quickened, and so did the pace of conversation as your imagination started to take flight, carrying you along with it.

Then, as you continued chewing, you felt more powerful, and your ideas became more interesting. Slowly, everything seemed clear, solutions emerged to all that bedeviled you, and you grew more and more certain you had the strength to overcome any obstacle that might stand between you and the outcome you sought. You were a lion.

Finally came the crash as your body and mind grew weary, reminding you to sleep and eat and tend to all the mundane demands of the world you had, for a while anyway, left behind. The ridiculous bravado that consumed you for the past several hours evaporated, and the brilliant ideas you expounded on at length paled, leaving you in the same sorry state that you were in when the chew had begun. You felt like a jackass.

Abdulwahab chewed less and less now. But he had joined the chew last night because his son-in-law was having a group of friends over, and Abdulwahab thought it was important to know who these young men were, especially if he was going to be able to keep the promise he had made indirectly to the president himself—that Ibrahim would do nothing while living under his roof that would create any trouble for the Yemeni government.

Ibrahim hadn't made many friends since he and Abdulwahab's daughter Aisha moved back to Yemen. There were a couple of young men who had grown up nearby, but Abdulwahab knew their families, and they were not a source of concern for him. It was the others, the ones he had never seen before, that he worried about. There was one in particular, by the name of Saif. Abdulwahab was sure he was a Saudi. He was a longbeard, with dark, brooding eyes and a disconcerting habit of always speaking in hushed tones.

But last night Abdulwahab heard what he was saying, and it troubled him. Ibrahim, Saif, and two or three others had gathered in a corner of the mafraj, the top floor of the house where qat chews normally occurred. They were talking intently among themselves, oblivious to Abdulwahab, who approached to gather a fresh stem or two of the qat that was strewn over the floor near their feet.

"We're very close now," the one with his back to Abdulwahab had said. It was Saif. "In less than a month, we will have everything in place, and we will return to France and deliver another blow against the corrupt culture of the infidels."

"*Insh'allah*," the others had responded. God willing.

Now, lying in his bed as the morning light strengthened and the colored patterns shifted on the wall of his room, Abdulwahab grew increasingly troubled. He would have to decide what to do with what he'd overheard. But not right now. Now the daily obligations of his life beckoned: there were goats to feed and lambs to move to the higher pasture.

He thought of the young American reporter, the one with the red hair he had met in Sana'a at the minister's lunch. She had sent him several emails since she returned to the United States. He had read them all earlier in the week when he made one of his monthly trips to Ataq to purchase sacks of feed for his animals and other essentials unavailable at the small shops closest to his home. He also stopped into an internet café to check his email, which he was forced to do because there was no signal in his village.

In her last message, she told him of her progress looking into the case of his son.

> *I have spoken with his lawyer, who sends her regards and wants you to know she is working very hard to find a way to win his release. I am planning on returning to Yemen in a couple of weeks and hope we can meet again to continue our discussion. I think you and your family are essential elements of Ashraf's story, and I am looking forward to learning more about how he grew up. Perhaps I can travel to your home. By the way, I'm hoping to persuade a colleague to accompany me. He's also an American journalist. He has never been to Yemen but is working on a story of his own that is quite interesting. I will contact you when we arrive in Sana'a.*
>
> *My best regards,*
> *Kit Salem*

Abdulwahab would meet with her, but not in his home, and not in his village. That would raise too many questions that even he, a tribal elder, would find awkward. No, he would meet with her in the capital. Quietly. He would see if what she said in her message was true, that she was looking into his son's case. He would find out if she was someone he could trust, someone who would know what to do with a bit of troubling information that had just come to his attention.

Part Two

THE JOURNEY

Fall 2010

CHAPTER TWENTY-THREE

Approaching Yemen

There are cities in the world that appear out the window of your airplane seemingly hours before you land. Cairo, for instance. Or São Paulo. The lights on the ground begin to cluster and the massive sprawl of the city slowly takes shape beneath you while you're still miles above it. After some time, the lights thicken and brighten until the glow seems to exert its own gravitational pull, drawing you back to earth.

Sana'a, the capital of Yemen, is not one of those cities. Little is discernible until you start your descent and, even then, the lights seem dimmer than you'd expect—sparser, sadder somehow, as if to warn you that what awaits is not Yemen Felix, the Happy Arabia of old, but a conflict-riddled, poor, neglected corner of the world.

Hank felt the plane begin its descent, the engines throttling back ever so slightly, and he looked to his right to see if Kit had felt it too. But she was still curled up next to the window, wrapped in the blankets that were on their seats when they boarded, a light down jacket rolled up under her head, which was resting at an improbable angle against the fuselage. Hank studied her face, her flawless complexion, her long reddish-brown eyelashes, her perfect mouth. Sitting there, so close to her, he could imagine leaning over and gently kissing her. In his dream she would wake up with a smile on her face, and reach over and take his hand, happy to know he was close. But that was just a dream, nothing more.

For now, he had to be content just being with Kit. The past month had been the happiest of his life because she had become a regular part of it. The morning after their lunch in DC, while they lingered over coffee in the dining room of her hotel, he explained the story his grandfather had told him and showed her the note Marwan Darwish had translated. Before he even mentioned any thoughts of traveling to Yemen, she encouraged him to do just that.

"Hank, this is a wonderful story about a chapter in Yemen's history that very few people know. Perhaps by now the jewelry is on display in a museum somewhere in Yemen. Even if you can't hold it in your hand, you can say that you saw it, the work created by a man your grandfather flew to safety over sixty years ago, and it's safe and well cared for. There are very few Jews left in Yemen anymore, but what if one of those remaining is a descendant of your silversmith? What a connection that would be. What an incredible story you could tell."

Meanwhile, her own efforts to learn as much as she could about the young Yemeni imprisoned at Guantanamo for the past eight years continued. Carole Ann McAfee had agreed to speak with her for the story, and the two spent hours together. She met with officials at the Pentagon, although they continued to rebuff her repeated requests to facilitate her travel to the prison to see it for herself. She relied on Hank to provide as much detail about the facility as he could recall from his own visit. And she read. All the time. Hank knew his way around an internet search, but he was amazed at her ability to ferret official material, some that wasn't even declassified yet, from websites he'd never heard of, including transcripts of hearings, sentencing documents, first-hand accounts of life at Guantanamo from former prisoners, and, in some cases, former guards.

When she returned to DC two weeks later, Hank met her for lunch at a little French restaurant around the corner from the Library of Congress, her favorite spot to work in Washington. He took the Metro to the Capitol South station and rode the escalator to the street, stepping out onto a small plaza where a handful of hawkers were peddling newspapers, touristy T-shirts, and bottles of water.

Hank declined a newspaper that was thrust in his direction as he made his way to D Street. "Have a nice day," the heavyset man bellowed as Hank walked past, so insistently it sounded like a threat.

Kit was already sitting at an outdoor table as Hank approached the restaurant. She waved as he came across the street, and he pulled up a seat across from her. She described the progress she had made on her story, and then announced that she was going back to Yemen as soon as she could make all the necessary arrangements. "You should come with me, Hank," she said. "We both have stories to write, and we can help each other." She took a sip of her coffee, as if to give him a moment to decide.

Finally, he said, "I've been giving it a lot of thought but, truth be told, the idea is a bit scary. Yemen would be a really big leap for a guy like me who considers a week in Belize the height of adventure travel."

The corners of her mouth turned up in that smile that broke Hank's heart every time he saw it, and in an instant any doubts he might have had about going simply disappeared. And it all turned out to be surprisingly easy.

He reached out to Mort Connolly, who didn't hesitate when Hank asked him to write a letter to the Yemen Embassy on behalf of a former *Register* staff writer who was taking time off to research a bit of family history in Yemen. Hank took the letter to the consular section and walked out thirty minutes later with his visa stamped into his passport.

Kit departed first. She would spend a couple of days in Frankfurt meeting with a German colleague who covered counterterrorism issues for the daily newspaper *Die Zeit*. Perhaps he had developed some information from his own sources on Ibrahim al-Jubaili's whereabouts.

They agreed to meet at the airport in Frankfurt, where they would board the plane to Sana'a. That had been almost seven hours ago and now, as Hank sat studying the angles of Kit's face while she slept, he was still amazed that shortly he would be on the ground in a country about which he knew almost nothing, other than it seemed to have become the preferred refuge for a lot of guys who were heavily armed and bent on kidnapping or killing Western tourists. And beyond all the unknowns that came with terra incognita, he was traveling with a woman he quietly adored, chasing after what at times seemed to him something akin to buried treasure. His stomach started doing flips, and he had a strong feeling it wasn't just because the plane was encountering a bit of turbulence as it made its descent.

CHAPTER TWENTY-FOUR

Sana'a, Yemen

Haitham Batarfi was standing in his customary place in the arrival hall of Sana'a International Airport, and Kit spotted him immediately as she and Hank exited customs and immigration.

"*Ahlan wa sahlan*," he said, welcoming Kit before offering her a quick hug.

She introduced Hank to Haitham and the three quickly moved outside. On the way into the city, Hank explained the history of the note given to his grandfather by a Jewish silversmith in 1949.

"I know it's a long shot to think I can locate the jewelry, and to be honest, I had to think long and hard about coming to Yemen to find out. But in the end, I felt as though I had to make the effort. Even if I come up empty-handed, at least I will have tried, and maybe that will be sufficient for my grandfather to close the book on this episode. And, who knows, depending on the outcome, maybe there's a story here I'll be able to tell."

"I think it's got the makings of a great story," Haitham said. He was silent for a moment, and then continued. "As a practical matter, though, in a country like Yemen, I don't know how you go about what you propose other than through official channels. We could start with the director of the National Museum. I know him casually, and assuming the jewelry hasn't already come into their possession, he's in a position to get authorization from the Ministry of Culture to go to the address you have and conduct a formal search for it. And I'm sure he will be thrilled by the prospect of uncovering a trove of handcrafted

Yemeni jewelry that can be added to the museum's collection."

Hank sat back, deflated. "I suppose that makes sense," he said, "but let me sleep on it tonight before we decide to do anything." He could scarcely conceal his disappointment at the thought of inviting the Yemen government to claim ownership of the man's work, a man who had essentially been hounded out of the country. He understood that it had been a different time and a different government, but it still didn't feel right.

He turned his attention to the city they were entering while Kit explained to Haitham what her own research had yielded. A few people were moving about here and there, stopping into the small markets still open for business even though it was now approaching eleven at night. Many displayed fresh fruit and vegetables in crates piled on the sidewalk for passersby to examine. Kit was describing the emails she had exchanged with Abdulwahab and her suggestion that she travel to his home for a conversation.

Haitham was skeptical. "That seems unlikely, Kit. Too many questions would follow. *Why is Sheikh Abdulwahab bringing an American reporter into our village? Into his home?*"

"You're probably right. Well, insh'allah, we'll know soon enough," she said, and they rode the rest of the way into the city, making occasional small talk as the nearly twenty-hour trip to Sana'a began to take its toll. They declined Haitham's invitation to get a late bite to eat, and bid him farewell in the hotel lobby with a promise to regroup in the morning.

Minutes later, Hank and Kit were in an elevator en route to their rooms on the fourth floor, which Kit had insisted upon. "Car bomb protection," she said matter-of-factly, a prospect Hank realized he hadn't contemplated. "Anywhere above the third floor you're probably going to survive the blast, and from four you can make your way down the stairs quickly, if need be." At Hank's door they paused. "I'm glad you're here, Hank. I love coming to Yemen, and I've never had the chance to share it with anyone before." Then she reached out and quickly touched his arm. "Sleep tight. And bring your appetite in the morning. Breakfast here is fabulous," she announced with a smile as she moved down the hallway and disappeared into her room.

Hank fell asleep quickly, but at exactly 3:30 a.m. his eyes popped open. After flopping around for half an hour or so, he realized he was thoroughly jet-lagged and not going back to sleep. He got up and moved a small easy chair to a window that looked out onto the Old City of Sana'a, still shrouded in darkness. He spent some time reading his traveler's guide to Yemen, already dog-eared and heavily marked up. By now he knew legend claimed Sana'a was first settled by Shem, the son of Noah, of biblical flood fame.

He knew that Sana'a claimed to be the longest continuously inhabited city in the world, and that Marco Polo himself wrote about the ports of Yemen and nearby Socotra Island.

After a while he closed the book and thought of what Haitham had said about using official channels to try and locate the jewelry, rather than hunting for it on his own. He likely was right, but Hank decided that before he agreed to invite the Yemeni government to join his search, he would at least take the time to see if the house at 13 Hamdan Street was still standing. He clung stubbornly to the idea that if the Alloush family still lived there, they would be willing to abide by the promise Abdullah had made so many years ago to his childhood friend—to keep Moishe's jewelry safe until he could send someone to retrieve it.

That seemed like utter fantasy now, as the reality of being a complete stranger in a country unlike any he had ever known began to sink in. Of course, Haitham was right. Better to do this by the book. He had no claim on the jewelry, so he should be content with the opportunity fate had given him to put it in the hands of someone capable of sharing with Yemenis and others who wished to learn about Yemen's history. He also had to consider the distinct possibility that the government already had taken possession of the jewelry.

But at least now the story he would try to tell was beginning to take shape. Hank wanted it to do justice to the artistry of a man who felt obliged to leave his home country, but who left behind a legacy in the form of his beloved silver jewelry that forever tied him to that place. Remarkably, his grandfather was right in the middle of it. And, of course, there was Kit. She couldn't have known that Hank was so hopelessly in love that he would have walked to Yemen to be with her. He looked at his watch. It was now nearly five o'clock. He contemplated going back to bed but decided to sit a bit longer by the window and watch the city beneath him slowly stir, beginning its daily chores.

He dozed off in the chair, awakening just as the sky over Sana'a brightened and turned a shade of violet Hank had never seen before, lifting the veil of darkness from the Old City and revealing its unique shapes and textures. Slowly, the violet melted into a cloudless deep blue. From his hotel window, Hank looked out onto the thicket of the city's mud-brick houses, some of which he knew from his reading were hundreds of years old. Known as tower houses, there were over ten thousand of them in Sana'a, some as tall as nine stories. Here and there the skyline was punctuated by the round minarets of the city's many mosques. Hank thought he could make out the Grand Mosque of Sana'a, built on the site of an earlier one that dated back to the time of the Prophet Muhammad.

At that moment he decided it was time to stop admiring the city from his fourth-floor hotel room and get out and walk its streets. He dressed quickly, grabbed his phone, and made his way into the heart of the ancient city that for a moment in history had been at the crossroads of the world.

Boys pulling carts full of vegetables and other merchandise destined for the markets of the Old City were already moving along the cobblestone streets. Hank passed a large mosque just as dozens of men trickled out after morning prayer. They stopped to retrieve their shoes and went on their way. Hank stepped onto a sidewalk facing the mosque and admired the intricate patterns etched into the minaret.

A teenage boy came out of the mosque, slipped on his sandals, and walked directly over to Hank. "Hello, mister," he said. "You need guide?"

Hank looked at him. He must have been fourteen or fifteen. He looked like a miniature version of the men who had preceded him into the street, except his ankle-length thobe was blue instead of white. He had thick eyebrows and dark hair that looked as though it hadn't seen a comb in some time. Hank was about to dismiss him when the boy said, "I speak good English. I show you everything and you pay me what you wish. Yes?"

Hank smiled and surrendered. "Okay, yes," he said. "Let's start here," he said, pointing to the mosque across the street. "What is this?"

"This is Bakiriya Mosque, built by the Turks. Very old. Five hundred years. See the domes? Turkey, not Yemen. What else you like to see?"

Hank admired the boy's efficiency. "Can you show me the market?"

"The *suq*? Yes. Come." And off they went, the boy taking Hank by the hand, as if he were afraid to lose him. They walked down narrow streets, the tower houses of Sana'a looming over them.

Hank's crash course on Yemen had revealed that the houses' foundations were basalt and limestone, and that the upper floors were made of burned clay bricks. But it was the decorative touches that made them so unique: zigzag symbols and patterns that seemed sometimes random and sometimes carefully and intricately planned and executed. They ran horizontally across the facades of the houses, or sometimes in stair patterns that invited your eye to follow.

He took pictures of the houses, their doors, their windows, the neighborhood mosques. He took pictures of his young guide, who had introduced himself as Mustapha. They walked on.

Before they even turned the corner into the spice market, Hank's nostrils flared with the pungent aromas of cinnamon, cumin, cloves, fenugreek, and incense that hung heavy in the morning air. All around were enormous bins of coffee beans, raisins, corn, and grains.

"*Suq al-milh*," Mustapha said, and Hank looked at him, puzzled.

"Salt market," one of the merchants helpfully interjected. Hank thanked him, and the pair moved along, past small stalls where merchants were setting up to sell all kinds of housewares, packaged foods, woven baskets, clay pots, and brassware. Hank had the impression you could probably find anything you needed somewhere in the warren of streets that seemed to wind around the Old City like a skein of yarn.

It suddenly dawned on Hank that Mustapha might be able to show him something else he wanted to see. He paused at a street corner and fished a pen from the bottom of his backpack. He flipped open his reporter's notebook and wrote carefully on a blank page, *13 Hamdan Street*. He ripped it out, handed it to Mustapha, and asked, "Can you take me here?"

Mustapha looked at what Hank had written, then lifted his head to look around. He seemed puzzled. "Wait," he said, and he ran back into the suq. Minutes later he returned. "Come. Not far." They walked a couple of blocks, down narrow streets that were now filling with children on the way to school and women emerging from their homes with brooms and buckets of steaming hot water to wash down the sidewalks.

They crossed a wide intersection and Mustapha raised his arm in front of Hank, signaling him to stop. "There," he said, pointing to a building across the street and halfway down the block. Hank turned to face it. The building, at least seven stories tall, looked to be very well-maintained. As they approached it, a brass plaque to the right of the front door came into view. In Arabic and English, it read: *Department of Antiquities, Ministry of Culture*. Above it was a small tile square with the number thirteen on it embedded in the plaster.

Hank laughed quietly. "Well, Haitham, I guess you were right. Looks like we'll have to go through official channels."

"You happy, mister?"

"Hard to say, pal," Hank replied. "Hard to say."

He took more photographs, and then he asked Mustapha to walk him back to his hotel. He realized he hadn't changed any dollars into Yemeni rials, so he offered him a twenty-dollar bill as payment for his services. "Okay?" he asked.

Mustapha took it and smiled broadly. He gave Hank a thumb's up. "Okay," he said. He turned to go and stopped, looking back at Hank. "*Shukran*, mister," he said. "*Masalaama*," thanking Hank and bidding him farewell.

CHAPTER TWENTY-FIVE

Sana'a, Yemen

The hotel lobby was bustling when Hank returned, a far cry from the almost deserted space he had walked through earlier in the morning. The clock behind the front desk read 7:30 a.m. He had been out wandering for nearly two hours, and he was ready for breakfast. He went upstairs to his room, showered, shaved, and put on fresh clothes. He called Kit, but got no answer, leading him to conclude she had already made her way to the dining room. He hurried downstairs and spotted her sitting at a small table in the corner. She waved when she saw Hank, smiling, and he once again experienced that ridiculous sense of joy that swept over him every time he saw her.

"You look all bright-eyed," she said as he sat. "Sleep well?"

"Hardly at all," Hank replied. "But I went out for an early morning walk around the Old City. Very invigorating. And educational." He leaned forward. "Kit, I saw the building that the silversmith mentions in his note. I stood right in front of it."

"I'm impressed, Mr. Amato. How did you manage that?"

"I fell into the hands of a very resourceful tour guide by the name of Mustapha. He led me there. But here's the thing. It's no longer a family home. In fact, it belongs to the Yemeni Department of Antiquities. Is that fitting or what?"

"Oh my God, Hank, how ironic that would be," Kit said, chuckling at the prospect of Yemen's historical artifacts custodian unwittingly storing on its premises the handiwork of a man who felt compelled to leave it behind when he departed his homeland over half a century ago.

Hank told Kit what he had said when he first laid eyes on the building, that Haitham had been right about going through official channels to see if the jewelry was still where it was supposed. "I'm going to call him as soon as we finish eating and see if he can arrange a meeting for us. But right now, I've got to eat. That early morning walk left me with an appetite."

CHAPTER TWENTY-SIX

Bayt Baws, Yemen

Haitham arranged a meeting with the director of the National Museum at ten o'clock in the morning later in the week, so Hank had a day free while Kit went off to work on other stories she was trying to finish when she wasn't busy running down the whereabouts of Ibrahim al-Jubaili.

Hank wanted to visit Bayt Baws, a largely deserted settlement on the outskirts of Sana'a that he'd read about as he prepared for his trip to Yemen. The village dated back several thousand years and, throughout virtually all its history, had been home to a sizable Jewish population. The exodus of Jews from Yemen to Israel in the years following World War II dramatically shifted its demographics, and subsequent migrations further depleted the population. But for Hank, it was a link to the story that had brought him to Yemen, and the hotel concierge was more than happy to arrange for a car and driver to take him there.

By midmorning he was on his way. The driver said it would take them about thirty minutes to reach the village, all of it spent winding through the streets of Sana'a, which had slowly crept outward over the years and now nearly enveloped the tall promontory upon which Bayt Baws had been built. The stone formation was impressively steep, inaccessible from three sides. The only road into the village approached from the south, which is where Hank's taxi fell in behind a small bus belonging to a company called Sheba Tours.

"Europeans," his driver said. "They keep coming, as if nothing can happen to them. That's what the Belgians and the Spanish before them thought until Al Qaeda killed them. And for what? To walk around a pile of stones in the middle of the desert? Stay home, I tell them. But they keep coming. Why?"

"Well, I'm a journalist," Hank said, as if coming to Yemen for reasons other than tourism obviated the risks. "I'm researching a story on the Jews of Yemen."

"Then you've chosen a good place to visit, my friend," the driver said as he pulled into a small car park where the road narrowed and a cobblestone street led into the village. "Plenty of Jews have lived here, although not now. Now they've all left. Gone to Israel, gone to America. Ask the old man sitting over there." He pointed to his right, where a small, elderly man sat alone. "His name is Saleh. He speaks English and can tell you anything you need to know about Bayt Baws."

Hank stepped from the car and watched as a handful of people from the bus stretched their legs before forming a circle around their tour guide. They were swarmed immediately by half a dozen young boys intent on persuading the visitors that they alone could reveal the village's hidden secrets.

"*Bienvenue!*" they shouted in unison as soon as they realized the new arrivals were French, followed by a chorus of "*nous parlons francais.*" The guide made a desultory effort to shoo them away, but it was clear the boys were going nowhere, an outcome that, as far as Hank could tell, pleased the French tourists almost as much as the boys themselves. He watched the gaggle form until it disappeared behind the village walls. Then he walked over to where the old man sat on a large stone, a roughly hewn cane in his right hand.

"*A salaam aleikum*," Hank said, happy for a chance to use his meager Arabic.

"*Wa aleikum a salaam*," came the reply.

The man motioned for Hank to sit, and he did, on a large flat stone so they were facing one another. The man looked at Hank carefully. "The way you walk and the way you dress makes me think you are an American," he said in English.

"You are correct. My name is Hank Amato."

"I am Saleh."

"I'm very glad you speak English. I just exhausted my Arabic."

"I was a schoolteacher for forty years. Many of the things I wanted to learn about, that I wanted to teach, were found in books in English. It made sense to become familiar with the language."

"Did you teach school here in Bayt Baws?" Saleh nodded but said nothing. "Did you teach Jews or Muslims?"

The old man shot Hank an indignant look. "I taught everyone who wanted to learn," he said, "and they learned together. We were a small village. We had one classroom, and one teacher. If you wanted to go to school, you went along with everyone else, or you didn't go. No one complained. Not like now." He slowly tapped the ground with the tip of his cane.

"My driver said you are a good man to speak with to learn about this village."

The old man continued tapping his cane on the rocky earth in front of him. "I can tell you more than those boys, or that tour guide," he said, and Hank smiled.

"But an old man sitting quietly by himself is invisible to most people. Perhaps this is because people look at me and see what awaits them, and it is something they would rather not contemplate." He nodded, as if agreeing with himself. "Still, invisibility is not always a bad thing. You can learn much when people pay you no mind. Three days ago, late in the day, when the tourists had all returned to their hotels, two large black vans came up this hill. The people inside were not tourists. They came with sniffer dogs, and with equipment to allow them to detect metal. They were treasure hunters. I believe they were Turks, from what I heard of their language. They paid the local boys to go away and not bother them. Then they separated into two teams and each walked slowly through a different part of the village.

You could hear the dogs when they came upon something, and the beeping of their machines, and the sounds of picks and shovels digging through the rocks. And you could hear their voices calling to each other." Intrigued by the old man's story, Hank scarcely moved.

"They spent an hour digging and shouting to one another. I was sitting right here when they left, carrying whatever it was they found in small bags. Silver, I imagine. The Jews of Bayt Baws were silversmiths. Perhaps they hid their work in the stone walls of their homes when they left here. Perhaps they thought they'd return. But no one returns to Bayt Baws. As you can see, there is nothing to return to."

"Why do you stay here?"

"Where would I go?"

"To Sana'a?"

The old man laughed. "No need. If I wait just a bit longer, Sana'a will come to me."

"How do you survive?"

"Once a month people come with food for the few of us who still live here. They sit and talk and then they leave. And I find things in the village that I sell to visitors like you. I found these after the Turks came and dug their holes." He reached inside his thobe and pulled out a small cloth bag. He unknotted the top, opened its mouth, and poured the contents onto the flat rock where he sat. It was a small collection of silver jewelry, earrings, necklaces, and several rings.

One of the rings caught Hank's eye. It was delicate and small, and when he rubbed it on his jeans to clean it off, the clear amber stone mounted on its face seemed to come alive in the midday sun. "If you wish to sell this, I'll be very happy to buy it. What would be a fair price?"

"Whatever you think is fair will be fine with me. As you can see, it is a buyer's market." Hank looked up from the ring to the old man's face and saw a hint of a smile. He stood and reached into the pocket of his jeans. He had exchanged money at the hotel that morning and he peeled three bills from the handful of Yemeni currency he was carrying, each of them a ten thousand rial note. He handed them to the old man.

"You must be unfamiliar with our currency. This is too much," he said.

"I don't want you sending the police after me, saying I tried to cheat you."

The old man looked at the three bills, rolled them up, and stuck them into the small sack with the jewelry.

"That is a lovely ring. It will make your wife very happy."

"Not my wife. Not yet. But I will ask her someday. And if she agrees, I will give her this ring."

"She will say yes," the old man said.

"I wish I had your confidence, my friend. But I will carry this with me and one day, if it turns out you're right, I will think of you, and the day we met here. But right now, I'm going to excuse myself and return to the city."

"You haven't learned much about the history of Bayt Baws," the old man said.

Hank stood and looked around him at the neglected settlement of slowly disintegrating mud houses and shook his head. "No, you're right," he said, "Guess I'll have to return for that. I'll look for you when I do." He started to walk away.

"Don't wait too long," called the old man. "This stone grows less comfortable each day. Soon, I think, I will need to lie down for a long rest."

Hank paused and looked back at the man. "I hope to see you again."

"*Ahlan wa sahlan*," Saleh said, assuring Hank he would welcome his return.

"*Ahlan bik*," said Hank, and he walked back to the waiting taxi.

CHAPTER TWENTY-SEVEN

Sana'a, Yemen

It was midafternoon when Hank returned to his hotel, and the lobby was so busy he had to hunt to find a place to sit and observe the activity. He made a beeline for a small swivel armchair near the front desk, not far from the stairway leading to the guest rooms upstairs. A group of well-dressed travelers chattering excitedly in Italian waited at the front desk. To his right, a group of Yemeni men in traditional garb had pulled a handful of chairs together, smoking water pipes and drinking steaming coffee from small demitasse cups. There were even people in Western-style business suits huddled together in conversation. What caught his attention, though, was an animated discussion taking place in English just behind him. While he couldn't hear everything that was being said, it was clear that the people engaged in the conversation were very unhappy about something.

Hank resisted the temptation to see what was going on for as long as he could, then he casually stood up and motioned to a waiter who was weaving his way around the small knots of people in the lobby. He asked for a cup of tea and sat back down again, rotating the chair as he did so it faced the other direction, toward the small group whose conversation had piqued his interest.

Three people stood close to one another about six feet away from Hank. A man in a dark suit and tie was doing most of the talking. He was tall and slender, with thinning hair that might have been blond at one point, but now was turning a color that Hank thought would likely be described as ash. He was agitated, gesturing energetically with his hands to emphasize what he was saying.

The other two looked nothing like him: one was a younger man, maybe Hank's age and stature, with short brown hair and a light beard. He wore a pair of scuffed black rubber-soled shoes and jeans, and a blue crew neck sweater. Next to him was a woman perhaps ten years older, dressed more carefully in khaki slacks and an untucked white blouse. She was trying to get a word in edgewise.

"Look, David, this is a terrible situation," she said to the man in the suit. "I understand that. We both do. But do you think you might be overreacting just a bit? How are we supposed to leave the country tonight? We have none of our possessions. Nothing."

"You have no idea what these people are capable of," David replied, fumbling with the buttons of his suit jacket, apparently trying to corral his necktie, which flapped as he gestured. "That child was the daughter of Amr al-Shami. He is one of the president's closest advisers. They are not people known to forgive and forget. They are going to want someone to pay for what happened today, and the two of you are at the very top of the list.

"For your own safety, you need to get out of Yemen. I say this both as chairman of the school board, and on behalf of the ambassador, who takes her obligation to protect American citizens very seriously. This is not open for discussion. I want you both to stay here, as inconspicuously as you possibly can. We have staff en route to your apartments. They'll call each of you when they arrive, so keep your phones handy. You can tell them what you need to take with you and where they can find it. One carry-on bag is all. We'll pack up the rest of your things and forward them to you back in the States once this whole mess blows over."

The woman and the young man next to her looked distraught at the news. At first, Hank thought it might be some sort of family crisis, but the more he watched, it was clear this was no family emergency. A cell phone rang, and the man in the suit reached into his pants pocket, withdrew his phone, and put it to his ear. His eyes darted in the direction of the door leading from the street into the lobby.

"They're coming now?" was all he said, and then he hung up quickly.

He looked up at the man and woman, and continued. "That was my security officer. Police have started searching all the hotels. A car just pulled up out front. They're on their way in." Hank swiveled around in his chair. Two men in shabby suits and white shirts open at the collar had just come through the door, followed by a pair of uniformed officers. They stopped and began scanning the lobby.

Hank stood up and walked quickly over to the small group. "Sorry to jump in here unannounced," he said. "I'm an American journalist, and I've been eavesdropping on your conversation. Occupational hazard, I guess." He reached into his pocket and pulled out his room key card, extending it to the woman. "There's a staircase behind you. Take it up to the fourth floor. My room is 402." The three looked at him, puzzled. "It's up to you. I've got no beef with these guys."

He started to put the key card back in his pocket when the man in the suit jumped in, "What's your name?"

"Hank Amato. I work—well, I worked—for *The Des Moines Register*. I'm here freelancing an article." He could hear the commotion behind him as the police officers began spreading out in the lobby. For a moment, no one moved.

Then the man in the suit said, "Do as he says." Hank handed the card to the woman and she and the younger man turned quickly, disappearing behind the stairway door.

"I'm David Leslie. I'm the Deputy Chief of Mission at the US embassy," the man in the suit said. He held out his hand.

Hank shook it. "Pleasure."

He turned just as one of the plainclothes officers approached. "*Amrikyeen?*" the officer asked.

Leslie replied in Arabic, confirming that they were indeed Americans, after which he identified himself and introduced Hank as an American journalist with whom he had just finished an interview. The information seemed to satisfy the officer, and he continued his sweep through the lobby.

"*Mukhabarat*," Leslie said. "Secret police, although there's not much secret about them." He exhaled. "That was close. Your intervention probably kept two good people from an experience I wouldn't wish on anyone." He looked at his watch. "I have to get back to the embassy. Our military attaché keeps a small plane at the airport, and we want to get those two folks on it and safely out of the country as soon as possible." He paused and looked closely at Hank. "I seem to be telling you a great deal. But I guess at this point I've already decided to trust you."

"Look," Hank said, "I'm glad I was nearby and able to help. But I have to ask. What did they do?"

Leslie started to describe the day's events, and then seemed to think better of it. "I'll let them explain." He reached into the breast pocket of his jacket and extracted a business card. "My cell phone number is on the back. Give me a call. Maybe we can have a drink or something before you head home. And someone will be coming to take these folks off your hands as soon as possible. Thanks again, Mr. Amato."

"Hank is fine."

"Got it. So long, Hank." And he moved to the door.

CHAPTER TWENTY-EIGHT

Sana'a, Yemen

The three of them crowded into Hank's room, which he was relieved to see had been made up by the housekeepers in his absence. She was Cheryl DiLuca, the director of the American School in Sana'a. He was Brian Murtagh, a fourth grade teacher. That morning, he had piled the fourteen students in his class into the bed of a Toyota Hilux pickup truck and instructed them all to sit down and not get up until they reached their destination. They were going on a field trip to the Dar al Hajar. Known in English as "The Rock Palace," it was built in the 1930s atop an imposing rock formation as a summer home for Imam Yahya, who, at the time, ruled Yemen's Muslim imamate.

After getting his students settled, Murtagh climbed into the front seat of the pickup truck with the driver, and off they went. Just outside the city, the truck slowed as it approached a stoplight. As it did, a boy snatched the cap off the head of another and tossed it onto the roadway. The truck came to a stop and one of the girls, who had no brothers and couldn't understand why boys were so stupid, stood up and looked over the rear of the truck to see where the hat had gone. At that moment, the light changed, the truck lurched forward, and she tumbled over the tailgate onto the road. The children screamed, the truck screeched to a stop, and Murtagh dashed around to see what had happened. He gasped when he saw her. She had fallen on her head and was bleeding profusely. They wrapped her head as best they could in his shirt, he scooped her up in his arms, and they rushed to the nearest hospital, but she never regained consciousness.

It fell to David Leslie to address a hastily organized meeting of frightened, angry parents that afternoon. By virtue of his position at the embassy, he chaired the board of the American School. Suddenly, he was expected to explain how one of their children's classmates had gone off on a field trip that morning and never come home. The parents were a mix of wealthy, well-connected Yemenis who could afford the school's five-figure tuition, US and foreign diplomats, UN officials and international businessmen. Deeply shaken by the knowledge that it could just as easily have been their own son or daughter who died that morning, they had come for answers, and a few wanted more. They wanted someone to punish.

From their children they had learned that no adult was in the back of the truck with them, that Mr. Murtagh was seated up front with the driver. How could this be, they demanded to know. What adult leaves a group of ten-year-olds by themselves in the open bed of a moving truck? And what kind of school allows students to travel like that in the first place? Doesn't our tuition cover the price of a bus? They wanted to know why neither the teacher nor the school director was present at the meeting. They wanted to speak with them directly.

Leslie could understand their outrage. He was a father, too. But Brian Murtagh was going home. So was Cheryl DiLuca. The US government was not going to abandon its citizens to a criminal justice system that bent unfailingly to the will of the nation's leader, especially in a case like this, where that leader would come under enormous pressure from his inner circle to claim the moral high ground and strike a blow against the arrogant United States, in the person of a thirty-three-year-old elementary school teacher from Albany, New York, and a forty-five-year-old school principal from Rochester, Minnesota. This would come down to scoring political points and revenge, and neither had anything to do with justice.

Leslie had been around long enough to know that if this had happened in France or Germany or another state with a strong tradition of judicial independence and a modern penal system, decision-makers in Washington would likely see things differently. But they were in Yemen, and if either of the two people now being sought were apprehended, the question was not whether they would be found guilty, but how many years it would take the US government to negotiate their release from prison, and what condition the two would be in when they got out. No, both would have to disappear as quickly as possible.

CHAPTER TWENTY-NINE

Sana'a, Yemen

Brian Murtagh paced back and forth across Hank's room, still visibly shaken. He seemed to be on the verge of tears. Hank thought he could see traces of blood on his jeans. "I just never thought the kids would be in any danger," he said, running his hands through his hair and shaking his head over and over. "We do this all the time on field trips. Nothing ever happens. And then all of a sudden . . ." His voice trailed off as he once again ran headlong into the reality that a young child was dead as a direct result of decisions he had made.

In comparison, Cheryl DiLuca was just plain pissed. Angry at Murtagh, angry at the small group of parents who decided she should shoulder an equal measure of the blame, and angry at David Leslie for deciding so quickly that the only way to resolve this situation was to uproot them from the lives they had constructed in Yemen and ship them stateside under the cover of darkness. Like criminals, which she most certainly was not. And that pissed her off, too.

"What happened today was a tragedy," she fumed at Hank, as if he had suggested otherwise. "But it was an accident. Preventable? Maybe. But an accident nonetheless. And why blame me? Was I there?" She caught herself and looked at Murtagh. "Sorry, Brian. I know this is awful for you, but this was just a colossal screwup."

Hank didn't know what to say. So he asked if they were hungry or thirsty. They both looked at him as if he was speaking a foreign language, but then each agreed that, yes, something to eat and something cold to drink might be good. Ten minutes later, there was a knock on the door.

"Room service," the bellhop announced. Hank asked them both to step out of sight, and he rolled the cart into the room himself.

They had barely started eating when there was another knock at the door. Everyone froze. Hank walked to the door. "Who is it?"

"It's me, Hank." He opened the door and Kit entered the room. She looked at the two strangers, and then at Hank. "Well, hello, everyone," she said. "Hank, you're making friends?"

Hank wasn't quite sure where to begin. He started with introductions. "Kit Salem, this is Brian Murtagh and Cheryl DiLuca. They both work at the American embassy school, but there was an accident this morning, and a young girl died, and now the police are looking for them, and the embassy is making a plan to get them out of the country before they're found, and I just happened to be in the lobby when the police came in, and I offered my room as a place for them to hide." He took a breath. "So. How was your day?"

Cheryl DiLuca jumped in before Kit could answer. "Are you a journalist, too, like he said he is?"

Kit said she was, and DiLuca pounced. "Then why don't the two of you write an article about what's happening here, about how two professional educators are being railroaded out of this country because there's no such thing as a fair trial for an American expatriate whose only real crime is having become so acculturated that even he transports children in the back of a pickup truck—just like everybody else in this country." In the silence that followed, she seemed to collect herself. "Sorry," she said. "I'm not . . . I didn't mean . . . Oh, Christ. This is a fucking nightmare." And she returned to her chair and sat down.

Hank wished he could be of some help, but he couldn't imagine writing a story that could possibly absolve these two people of some degree of guilt for the ten-year-old girl's death. Even an honest judge guided only by the law would likely conclude they were culpable—Murtagh directly, and DiLuca as the school director who failed to exercise sufficient oversight and safe transportation means.

He explained this, and when he was done, Kit simply said, "When you're safe at home in America, you may choose to tell your story, but I would encourage you to keep Hank's words in mind."

They ate in silence after that, until DiLuca's cell phone began to ring. She spoke quietly to someone for several minutes, then looked up. "That was David Leslie. They think it's safe for us to leave and want to move us to the ambassador's residence. We'll go to the airport from there. Someone from the embassy is coming upstairs now to escort us to a van that's waiting outside." She had tears in her eyes. "You were very kind to intervene downstairs," she said to Hank, "and I fear I haven't thanked you properly for what you did. I'm not sure either one of us will ever be able to do so." And with that, she walked over and embraced Hank. She even embraced Kit. Murtagh followed suit, just as there was a knock at the door.

"Who's there?" Hank asked.

"I'm here to make a pickup, sir. I believe David Leslie called to say you should expect me."

Hank opened the door to a beefy young man wearing tan cargo pants and a navy-blue polo shirt. Next to him was an older man who looked like he might be Yemeni. They both stepped into the room long enough to introduce themselves. He was the embassy security officer and the older man was his senior local investigator. DiLuca and Murtagh quickly collected their things and followed them into the corridor, offering final goodbyes. Hank watched them disappear down the stairwell at the end of the corridor before he shut the door.

"Jesus," he said to Kit. "I know a little bit about how quickly your world can collapse, but those two folks are going through hell."

"Didn't you say a little girl died? What must her family be going through?"

"I can't even imagine," Hank said, shaking his head, bereft of any good answer to Kit's question. Kit looked at him, and slowly her face softened. "I'm sorry. I know you can't relieve everyone's suffering at a moment like this. You did what you could. You're a good soul, Hank Amato. Come on, let's clean up this mess."

CHAPTER THIRTY

Sana'a, Yemen

The following morning Hank and Haitham were moving through the traffic-clogged streets of Sana'a en route to a meeting with the director of the National Museum. Still suffering from jet lag and unnerved by the day's events, Hank had slept poorly, and the seemingly random nature of the traffic moving around him simply added to his discomfort. Haitham, meanwhile, was busy trying to explain that there was a discernible pattern to the chaos that surrounded them. "You have to think like water flowing, Hank. Avoid the eddies. Be the current and feel your way around the rocks. Which in this case are the other cars."

"You make it sound very Zen, Haitham, but it looks like bumper cars on steroids."

"Bumper cars?"

Hank started to explain and Haitham interrupted. "Oh, you mean dodgems. At least that's what they call them in the UK. And yes, I can see the similarities. Except here, at least in theory, the objective is to avoid bumping into the other car. Sometimes easier said than done," he said, downshifting as he changed lanes behind a taxi that had accelerated into an open bit of road.

Hank turned the conversation back to the meeting Haitham had arranged. "So, the museum director said he wanted to meet us, but not in his office?"

"That's what he said. It may have something to do with the fact that I told him you were interested in the immigration of Yemeni Jews to Israel after World War II." Haitham steered quickly away from a truck that had just materialized to their right. "Yemenis are proud of the fact that there have always been Jews here, and sensitive to criticism that they have been mistreated. This housing complex we're going to is where virtually all the Jews who remain in Yemen have been moved to assure their safety. This time the threat comes from Muslims who adhere to an increasingly intolerant strain of Islam, one that blames Israel for all the problems that afflict the region.

"There's even an armed movement called the Houthis that has been giving the government fits in the northwest of the country. They have a lovely slogan: Death to America. Death to Israel. Curse the Jews." Haitham turned the car sharply to the left, pulled up a short driveway, and stopped at the checkpoint. "Here we are."

He explained to the soldier peering into the car that they were to meet the director of the National Museum at ten o'clock that morning. The soldier, who looked all of sixteen years old, told his companion to lift the drop bar and let the car pass. Hank noticed the sign in English and Arabic as they entered the compound: *Tourist City*. He wondered if any tourists had ever visited the complex.

Inside, a police car was waiting to lead them through a maze of small streets badly in need of repair, past shabby two-story apartment blocks to a location where a small cluster of people had gathered around a shiny, late-model Mercedes E-Class Coupe that could hardly have appeared more out of place.

"Looks as though the director brought company," Haitham said as he slowed to a stop. "Maybe he decided speaking to an American reporter was bad for job security."

They stepped out of the car, and the small crowd parted, creating a path leading to two men in suits standing a short distance away, talking quietly.

The National Museum director made introductions, revealing the mystery guest to be Hisham al-Maeli, the director general of antiquities, a youngish man with a neatly trimmed beard and a decidedly unbureaucratic manner. Greeting Hank like a long-lost friend, Maeli took his arm and walked him away from the crowd, inquiring about his experience in Yemen, what he had seen and who he had met, all in very clear and only slightly accented English.

"Your English is superb," Hank said, leading Maeli to happily disclose that he was a proud alumnus of the University of Central Florida.

"Perhaps the best years of my life, I might say."

"And yet you decided to come back to Yemen."

"Yes, I did. Living in Orlando, surrounded by theme parks and make-believe worlds made me really miss this place. Here, you turn a corner and stumble into a world that dates back a thousand years. And it's all real." Maeli glanced back over his shoulder. "But we have other business to attend to this morning, no? I hesitated to come along, but I was excited to learn that there was an American reporter in Sana'a with an interest in something other than terrorism or child brides. So I invited myself to the party." He gave Hank a slightly sheepish smile. "Not that this is much of a party. But still . . ." He slowly began to steer Hank back toward where the small group of people waited.

As they rejoined the small circle, Maeli seemed to gather himself. When he spoke again it was in Arabic, and his tone of voice was more subdued. Hank leaned toward Haitham, who quietly translated.

"He's saying how pleased he is to be able to help today's distinguished visitor—that's you, Hank—understand that Jews have been part of Yemen and its culture for fifteen hundred years. He's saying that, sadly, Jews often have faced mistreatment and, as a result, many have departed, and that is Yemen's loss."

Maeli paused, as if to give Haitham enough time to finish his translation. Then he resumed his remarks, and Haitham continued: "We must acknowledge the presence in our country of extremists who target Jews because they are opposed to the existence of the state of Israel, or they carry a distorted idea of Islam. Our president is committed to protecting those Jews who have chosen to remain here, in their homeland, and he has taken extraordinary measures to ensure their safety." There was a polite smattering of applause.

"Today," Maeli continued, "we are going to hear directly from a family that has experienced the dangers posed by these extremist groups." He nodded to the museum director, walked over to where Hank stood, and said quietly, "I'm going let Jamal handle this part of the program. He is a big supporter of our president. Of course, we all are." He smiled.

Jamal Ezzi, the director of the National Museum, beckoned with his right hand, and a man with long sidelocks and what appeared to be a permanent expression of resignation stepped forward from the crowd with two boys. He had the hands of a working man and wore a dark blue T-shirt, sandals, and a pair of gray pants that had seen better days. Hank guessed he was in his mid-thirties, although he just as easily could have been ten years older.

The older boy, who never left his side, was likely twelve or thirteen. His features were rounder and softer than those of his younger brother, who was the spitting image of his father. Same angular face and dark eyes, but brighter somehow, as if his spirit hadn't been extinguished yet.

The museum director spoke in Arabic to the man, who listened without expression and nodded. The man with the sidelocks looked at Hank and, in rudimentary but passable English, said: "I am Yahya Habib. These are my sons, Yousef and Soliman."

He paused for a moment, until the museum director said, "Please, continue."

"I am a furniture maker. Life had become very difficult in the village where I was born."

The museum director interjected quickly. "He is from Raydah. It is twenty-five kilometers north of Sana'a. *Alhamdulillah*, thanks to the concern of our president, all the Jews who wished to leave Raydah have been brought here and given apartments of their own." He looked at the father and his two sons. "And do you feel safe here?"

"*Nam*," Yahya replied in Arabic, nodding his head in the affirmative.

The museum director, satisfied with his intervention, motioned again for the man to continue, which he did. "In Raydah, we would only leave our homes to go to work, or to market. And many of the men trimmed their peyot," he said, pointing to his long, curly sidelocks. "Myself, I concealed them under a headscarf." He paused, as if deciding what to say next. "We have always lived among Muslims. But now, things feel different. We used to trust one another, but now, people we don't even know come and accuse us of building our homes on their lands. With them come the police. So we have left our homes and come here, *alhamdulillah*," he said, offering thanks to God.

"*Shukran*, Yahya," said the museum director. "We hope you will remember this family when you return to America," he said to Hank. "They are Jews, but they are Yemenis. We are all family."

Hank felt as though he was expected to respond. Before doing so, he turned quickly to Haitham. "Please give Habib your cell number and ask him to call you. I would like a chance to speak to him without the crowd."

Then he turned back to his Yemeni hosts and said, "I'm very grateful for this opportunity to learn about the efforts of your government to ensure that all Yemenis are able to live in peace and raise their families without fear. Thank you for inviting us." He bowed deeply, although no one returned the gesture, and he wasn't sure where the idea to do so had even come from.

The Yemeni officials each handed Hank their business cards, Arabic on one side, English on the other, and invited him to be in touch if they could be of any further assistance during his visit. Hank glanced at the cards and saw something that made him look a second time. Hisham al-Maeli's business address was 13 Hamdan Street. He pocketed the cards. Haitham approached and gave Hank a quick thumbs-up.

Hank walked over to Maeli and shook his hand. "Yemen is very lucky you decided to come home. If you don't mind, I may take advantage of your kind offer of assistance. Could I call on you at your office?"

"*Ahlan wa sahlan.* I would be pleased to continue our conversation," Maeli said, as he walked Hank back to Haitham's car. "Call the number on my card and my staff will set up a time for us to meet." Hank could scarcely believe his good fortune. He had just received a gold-plated invitation to visit the very building where he was almost certain Moishe Azani's silver was still hidden. What he had imagined was going to be an unhelpful occasion with the museum director had suddenly turned into a game changer.

CHAPTER THIRTY-ONE

Sana'a, Yemen

"You have asked me to describe my son to you so you might know who he is and why he left us. I will explain as best I can."

Kit sat across a heavy oak table from Abdulwahab. The table was enormous, surrounded by twenty-four chairs, all of which fit comfortably into the formal dining room. French doors at either end were closed now so that Kit and Abdulwahab could speak privately. The house belonged to Abdulwahab's brother, Sufian, who had accumulated a tidy fortune exporting Yemeni Sidr honey throughout the Middle East. Prized for its medicinal properties, Sidr honey was often described as liquid gold, given the price it often demanded on the world market.

Sufian's villa in the upscale Hadda neighborhood of Sana'a left little doubt as to the success of his export business. Like virtually every other house in the enclave, it was surrounded by an eight-foot-high wall with coils of razor wire strung across the top, a disincentive to uninvited guests. Vehicles entered the compound via a large double-doored steel gate painted a bright sky blue. On a clear day, when the industrial haze and smog had burned off, it almost replicated the color of the sky over the capital.

Kit arrived in a taxi; she had negotiated with the driver to wait and return her to the hotel. As she walked to the house gates, a guard carrying an AK-47 stepped out of a small booth that hugged the exterior wall of the gate. She explained in Arabic that she had come to see Sheikh Abdulwahab, and the guard nodded. He knocked on a door cut into the vehicle gates, and it opened from within. Another armed guard escorted her to the house, which stood tall and imposing on a large tract of land. To the right was a parking area with a carport capable of sheltering multiple vehicles from the elements. Kit could see two Mercedes, a Land Rover, and two small Toyota trucks. A group of men hovered around: drivers, bodyguards, household staff. They watched as she ascended the broad concrete staircase that led up to the front door, which opened as she approached, allowing her to enter the house without breaking stride.

A man who identified himself as Mahmoud greeted her in the foyer, and they went quickly to the dining room, where Abdulwahab was seated. He motioned to a seat across from him, and she settled into the chair. Plates of fruit and small cakes were on the table, and Kit was served hot, sweet tea in a small glass cup.

Then the room was theirs.

"Sheikh Abdulwahab," Kit began, "thank you for agreeing to meet me."

Abdulwahab nodded but said nothing.

She went on. "When we last met I said I would look into your son's case on my return to America. Unfortunately, I was unable to visit Ashraf. Only the lawyers of the prisoners can do that. But I did meet with his lawyer, whom I know you have spoken with yourself. She was able to arrange a phone call with your son while I was in her office, and I told him that I was going to see you on my next visit to Yemen. He was very pleased to hear that you are well and that you are thinking of him. He misses you and his family terribly. He said he especially misses the times you and he would go hunting together, and he longs for the day when he can return home and do so once again."

Kit could see the emotion in Abdulwahab's face as he recalled happier times with his son. She hesitated for a moment before continuing, sipping her tea slowly. It was hot and sweet and comforting. Nothing she was about to say would be comforting in the least to the man sitting across the table from her.

"Sheikh Abdulwahab, Ashraf's lawyer is trying her very best to win your son's release. She visits him as often as she can and is permitted to bring food, but lately he has refused to take meals. He says he will not eat until he appears before a judge and is given an opportunity to present his case. His lawyer is worried that if he doesn't resume eating soon, the prison authorities will force-feed him. I must tell you, that is painful and often leads to severe health problems. Ashraf's lawyer believes that if you send word to him to resume eating, he may change his mind and avoid being force-fed."

Abdulwahab looked at Kit and slowly shook his head. "I will not do that," he said. "My son is being held unjustly and I cannot urge him to cooperate with those who are responsible for the terrible wrong that has been inflicted on him, and on his family."

Kit could see the determination and the sadness in his eyes. It was why she had only described to him a small bit of his son's suffering at Guantanamo. She and Carole Ann had talked about how to convey the reality of Ashraf's situation to his father, knowing how painful it would be for him to hear the truth. And now, sitting with Abdulwahab, Kit couldn't bring herself to reveal that his son wasn't just contemplating a hunger strike, he had been refusing to eat for over six weeks. He wasn't just about to be force-fed, it was happening to him every day. His nostril passages were now swollen shut from the tubes forced down his nasal cavity during the feeding process. At the age of twenty-nine, he was suffering severe and chronic back pain from being forced to sit shackled to a chair for hours each day while being force-fed. How could she tell his father all this? It would itself be a form of torture.

And yet Kit couldn't help but wonder how much of her silence was because of her desire to shield the older man across the table from a brutal truth, and how much of it was because she was afraid that he might react to the news by refusing to cooperate with her on the story she so badly wanted to write. She believed it was the former, and yet the thought that she was being driven by ambition and not compassion gnawed at her.

And then, almost as if he could read her thoughts, Abdulwahab said, "Perhaps the story you have said you will write for your newspaper will make people aware of what is happening to my son and convince your government to release him."

"I would like to think that is true, Abdulwahab, but I must say, it is very unlikely. Still, I would like to write about Ashraf. And about you, and your son-in-law, about how a family living far from the seats of world power finds itself at the heart of what is being called the Global War on Terror. I want the world to understand how decisions made in Washington and London ripple outward, to homes and villages thousands of miles away, changing families' lives forever. For me to be able to do this, I would like to know what led your son to leave home, to travel to another country." She stirred her tea with a tiny silver spoon. "I also am still hopeful I will be able to speak with your son-in-law. He is a part of this story, as well, and his actions have drawn you and your family deeper and deeper into what I know is a very painful and complicated situation."

Abdulwahab sat quietly for a moment, weighing what Kit had said. He wasn't a man given to deep reflection or soul-searching. He made decisions and he lived with them. But if there was a chance that Kit might be able to bring his son back home, he was prepared to acknowledge his own misjudgments, and how they contributed to his son's decision to leave home, a journey that eventually led him to a US military prison halfway around the world. And so, he began:

"Ashraf was our second-born. He came three years after Walid, my oldest son. Walid died of cholera when he was twelve. The well in our village had become contaminated, and many people took sick after drinking the water. The children suffered the most. Walid grew weaker, but the hospital is in Ataq, a three-hour drive over very poor roads. We thought it best to treat him at home. He died in a matter of days.

"Ashraf was nine when his brother died. He was always a serious boy, but he had never displayed much interest in religion before that moment. Not many young boys do, I suppose, but he became deeply interested in the Quran and went to the mosque daily to sit with the imam and study the hadith of the prophet, peace be upon him. We didn't object to this change in him because at the same time he became much more dutiful. He didn't have to be coaxed to help his mother tend the animals or sweep out the stalls. He took care of his sister. We thought he was happy."

Abdulwahab slowly sipped from the glass of tea. He seemed to be composing himself. Then he continued. "But he wasn't happy. He was mourning the loss of his brother. And now, looking back, I think all that time he was preparing to leave us. And eventually he did. When he was seventeen he enrolled in university in Taiz. He said he wanted to become a pharmacist. I have no idea where this idea came from. I should have seen that he was searching for direction and, most importantly, he was searching for someone who could become the older brother he had lost. Unfortunately, the boy he chose took Ashraf's sadness and twisted it into anger. Anger at the West, at a world that was content to see Yemenis living in a place where they drank water from their village well and died.

"One day he announced he was leaving university and moving to Hodeidah to study at the Azzam Mosque. He was nineteen by then. He was able to make his own decisions. I think he must have been there for a year or so when he came home unexpectedly to say he was going to Afghanistan.

"I asked him what he intended to do when he got there, and he said he didn't know. All he could say was that it was important to defend Islam. I grew angry with him. I asked if he thought joining the Taliban or going to live with Osama bin Laden was the proper way to show respect for our faith, the very name of which means peace. But he wasn't thinking clearly. He said Islam was under attack by the West and he had an obligation to stand with his fellow Muslims.

"So he left, and I didn't hear from him for almost a year. And then one night he called. He said he and several others he had met in Afghanistan were getting ready to leave. Al Qaeda had carried out a devastating attack against America and now US soldiers were flooding into the country and the fighting was growing more intense every day.

"I asked him if he was fighting. I asked him if he had killed anyone. He said he had not. He said that because of his studies at the university he had been working in a dispensary, helping to treat fighters, yes, but also people from the nearby towns. He said he was afraid that if he stayed he would be forced to fight, and he didn't want to do that. He said that he wanted to return to university and study to become a doctor. He was going to cross into Pakistan and from there he would make his way to the Yemeni embassy in Islamabad and arrange to fly home. We haven't spoken since that night."

Abdulwahab reached into a pocket of his jacket and withdrew a small leaflet. He unfolded it carefully and passed it to Kit.

"It is written in Pashto. The smiling Afghan is saying, 'You can get rich. You can receive millions of dollars if you help catch Al Qaeda and Taliban murderers. With this money you can take care of your family, your entire village.' The Americans distributed these flyers all over Afghanistan. Do you think Ashraf might have been captured by bounty hunters and delivered to the Americans?"

Kit studied the leaflet. "This is how a lot of the prisoners at Guantanamo were captured, Abdulwahab, so yes, it is very possible that your son was one of them. May I take a photograph of you holding this?"

"No, no photographs. We will talk." She returned the piece of paper, which he folded back up and returned to his pocket. He looked very tired.

Kit hated to ask him to continue, but she didn't know if or when she would have another chance to meet with him alone.

"Can you tell me about your son-in-law? Can you describe how he came into your family?"

Abdulwahab chuckled quietly. "My daughter Aisha is very headstrong. My wife insisted on encouraging her to be this way from the day she was born. Otherwise, she said, our daughter would never find her way in this world that is run by men. So, when Aisha became a young woman, she declared she was going to leave our village with its goats and mud bricks and move to London. Or perhaps Paris. I told her that was impossible. But she kept insisting until I relented and said I would let her go to Kuwait and live with my brother and his family there. That way she would be able to see what the world was like outside of Yemen, and her mother and I would know she was safe.

"That is where she met Ibrahim. His father is a business partner of my brother's. They run a small mining company. My brother vouched for the family. He told me it would be a good marriage, that Aisha would live a comfortable life. What we didn't know—what no one knew—is that Ibrahim had already fallen in with a small group of young men who decided it was their obligation to resist the American presence in Arab lands. Ibrahim had a particular talent. He was familiar with explosives, a skill he had learned working in the family business. Which is why no one thought twice when Ibrahim said he wanted to study at Saint Petersburg Mining University. Do you know of it? It's one of the most prestigious in all of Europe. Vladimir Putin himself studied there. Aisha was thrilled, of course. She was finally getting to Europe, even if it was Russia."

Abdulwahab paused as the door opened and his assistant asked if they needed anything more. He shook his head no, waited for the door to close, and continued. "So they left Kuwait and moved to St. Petersburg. Ibrahim was a good student, and they traveled sometimes to Germany and the Netherlands, where he seemed to have a group of friends, although Aisha told me later that Ibrahim always went to see them alone. Then, last August, Aisha called to say she and Ibrahim were coming home to visit. We were happy. It would be our first chance to see our grandson, even if their return to Yemen was unexpected. And then we heard the news of the bombing at the museum in Paris and the suspicion that Ibrahim was responsible. He denied it, of course. He even traveled to Sana'a to be interviewed by the intelligence service. That's when the interior minister invited me to his office and relayed the president's message: Ibrahim could remain here with us if I promised he would not become involved in any activities that would bring unwanted attention to Yemen and force the government to take action. Of course, I agreed."

Abdulwahab paused and looked around the room slowly, as if to reassure himself that he and Kit were still alone. "But I have failed, and I fear that Ibrahim is using the safety of our home to prepare another attack."

He made the statement so matter-of-factly that it took Kit a minute to realize what he had just revealed. Her surprise must have been apparent, because Abdulwahab said, "I am telling you because this knowledge has become a burden I can no longer carry on my own. I must trust someone with this information. I believe I can trust you. Ibrahim is part of my family now, whether I am happy about it or not. But he is abusing this privilege by bringing people into my home who are intent on causing harm to others. I cannot permit this to happen. If I tell the authorities in Sana'a, they will arrest Ibrahim and I am certain he will learn eventually that I was the one who alerted them to his activities. Aisha will be furious with me, and I fear she will take baby Hamid and leave. She is the only one of my children still with me. I don't know what I would do if I lost her, too."

Abdulwahab seemed unable to continue at that moment, so Kit said, "I can help. I know the relevant authorities in Europe, and I can quietly contact them, pass along the information you wish to share. They will be able to stop another attack from happening."

"Yes," he said, "that is what you must do, but you must do it quickly. I fear I have waited too long. Ibrahim has not been at our house for a week. He told my daughter he had to return to Kuwait to attend to a family matter and would be back at the end of the month."

He passed her another piece of paper, on which he had written his account of the conversation he overheard at his house the night Ibrahim and his friends chewed qat and talked until the early morning hours. He included the names of those he recalled as having been part of the group.

"This information," he said, pointing to the paper Kit held, "could cost me my life, because it reaches well beyond my family and leads directly to Al Qaeda. You must protect it. Now you must go. Is your car waiting for you?" Kit said it was, and Abdulwahab said he would have Mahmoud walk her to the front gate. "We will say farewell here. I am grateful for whatever you can do to help Ashraf. If you can get a message to him, please tell him we love him and pray each day for his safe return home. As for the other business, I believe you will do what you must, just as I have."

CHAPTER THIRTY-TWO

Sana'a, Yemen

It was after nine o'clock at night when Kit returned to the hotel. She picked up her room key at the front desk and the clerk handed her an envelope at the same time. Inside was a note from Hank.

> *Kit: I waited for you but I'm exhausted after a long day, so we'll have to catch up tomorrow. I hope your day was fruitful. I missed not seeing you. H.*

Kit stood in the lobby wondering if Hank was still awake. She felt as if she would burst if she couldn't share the newest developments with someone. But she couldn't draw Hank into this. She had encouraged him to come to Yemen to pursue his story, not hers, and certainly not one that might place him at risk. No, what she had learned was a matter she would have to resolve herself. She glanced at Hank's note. She had missed seeing him, too. It was an unfamiliar sensation, one she would have to think about a bit more. In the morning, along with everything else she had to sort out.

In her room, instead of sleeping, Kit made a reservation to fly to Paris the following morning and wrote a long email to her editor in London on the progress she had made with her story, omitting any mention of Abdulwahab's claim that his son-in-law was engaged in another plot to attack a European target. She simply wrote, *I think it unlikely that Ibrahim al-Jubaili will agree to an interview. So, I have struck out there. But I have spoken at length with his father-in-law and am confident this story will come together. Meanwhile, I have come across an unexpected thread that's going to require a quick trip to Paris. I know I am testing your patience, and your budget, with this constant travel, but I'm closing in on an important piece of the story. I can come to London to share details if you wish. Please advise. Salut.*

Kit slept fitfully that night and went downstairs for breakfast as soon as the dining room opened. Hank was already there, midway through a bowl of *ful*—cooked fava beans with lemon, garlic, olive oil, and tomatoes. He had discovered the dish on his first day in Sana'a and it immediately became daily fare, along with a basket of warm pita bread.

He broke into a huge smile when he saw Kit enter the dining room and, before he even knew it, was on his feet. Then, not knowing what to do while she walked to the table, he decided to pull her chair out so she could be seated. It was an awkward gesture, and Hank wished he had just stayed where he was, but Kit accepted his offer with a warm smile and a "good morning, how'd you sleep?" as she settled into her chair.

"Better than the night before," he said as he returned his napkin to his lap and idly tore off a piece of pita, folded it in half, and dipped it into his bowl. "How did your meeting with the father go?"

Kit described her conversation with Abdulwahab, finishing with the news that something had come up and she was leaving for Paris at noon.

Hank made no effort to conceal his disappointment. "I'll only be gone a day or two," Kit said, "and Haitham will be here to help you get where you need to be, Hank."

"Haitham's great, and he's been really helpful," Hank agreed. "But I'm not sure I'll ever spring to my feet when I see Haitham coming across the room." He hesitated then, feeling as though he had stumbled into a conversation he wasn't sure either one of them was ready for just yet.

Still, he continued. "Which brings me to something I've been waiting to tell you, Kit. Although, honestly, I'm pretty sure that first thing in the morning may not be the best moment to try. But the truth is, I came to Yemen as much to be with you as to chase down any story." He picked at the food in front of him. "I hope that doesn't come as a total shock." He tore off another piece of pita, dipped it quickly into a bowl of hummus that sat untouched in the middle of the table, and then just held it in his hand, as if he had forgotten it was to be eaten. As if his ever eating again depended entirely on her response to what he had just said.

Kit wasn't oblivious to Hank's feelings for her, she was just a bit unfamiliar with the territory and uncertain how to respond. For longer than she wanted to admit she had denied herself the luxury of developing an emotional attachment to anyone, focusing her energies on her career, content to define herself by each rung of the professional ladder she climbed successfully. Hank's entrance into her life was totally unexpected, and so was the pleasure Kit allowed herself to feel when she was with him.

Still, his boyish, fumbling declaration caught her off guard. So, she deflected. "You two will be fine motoring around Sana'a together. He can show you all the sights. Adventure travel, remember?" And then she said something that even surprised her. "But since we're speaking candidly, Hank, I wish you were coming to Paris with me. I'm happier when I know you're nearby. And that's my little bit of breakfast truth."

Having startled herself, Kit closed that door as quickly as she had opened it. "But you have work to do here, and I will be back before you know it. A quick stop in Paris and then off to London for a sit-down with my editor, whom I need to assure that all the money I'm spending is going to produce a blockbuster of a story. And then straight back to Sana'a. Promise."

Hank nodded in agreement, content that Kit hadn't fled the dining room in the face of his declaration of affection. They made small talk while they ate and walked out of the dining room together. In the lobby, after a quick hug, Kit returned to her room to begin packing for her flight, and Hank walked outside to begin his day. Haitham had already pulled up to the front of the hotel and was waiting in his small white Peugeot.

"Habib said he wants to meet us in the Old City, in the furniture shop where he works," Haitham said as he pulled into traffic.

Hank thought they might walk to the Old City, but Haitham seemed content to drive, even as the streets narrowed and grew increasingly congested with foot traffic. He found a spot in a small car park, and they walked the last couple of blocks, ending up in a corner of the suq populated by hardware stores and metal and woodworking shops. They found Habib's shop at the end of a street next to a welding and sheet metal supply store. They walked in the front door, into a large space littered with pieces of furniture in various stages of assembly. Habib was hunched over in a corner, carefully using a router to scroll a design into the headboard of a bed. Hank didn't immediately recognize him, and realized it was because he had tucked his ringlets under a scarf that was wrapped tightly around his head.

They waited for Habib to finish and the router to go silent. He looked up as it did and smiled when he realized he had visitors. He greeted them in English. "My father said it was not enough to speak just Hebrew and Arabic," he explained, "although he would be unhappy if he heard how little progress I have made. Come, I will make tea. I am the only one here. We can talk."

Sitting on what appeared to be dining room chairs that were stripped and waiting to be refinished, Hank explained Moishe Azani's brief exchange with his grandfather on the airport runway in Tel Aviv, omitting details about the note, saying only that he had come to Yemen to see if the silver jewelry Moishe had left behind had come into the possession of the Yemeni government.

"When he was a young man, the silversmith seemed to have struck up a friendship with a boy who lived at 13 Hamdan Street," Hank said. "The family name was Alloush. I walked by the house yesterday, and it looks like it belongs now to the Department of Antiquities."

"Yes, I know the house," Habib said. "It is one of the oldest tower houses in Sana'a. From what you say, the Alloush boy would have been about the same age as Moishe Azani. I know of an Abdullah Alloush—he ran a very successful jewelry shop for years in the suq. He was always generous with the craftsmen of our community, especially the silversmiths. He paid well for their work. His son, Hassan, moved to Dubai some years ago and opened his own shop. He seems to have done very well selling to rich tourists. He returns to Sana'a from time to time to purchase silver jewelry and other traditional pieces, although with so few Jews left, very little high-quality jewelry is being produced anymore. Abdullah passed away a few years ago and I believe the family sold the house to the Ministry of Culture. Then they all moved to the Emirates."

"Do you know if the government did much to change the interior after they bought it?" Hank asked.

"I don't know," Habib replied. "Why do you ask?"

CHAPTER THIRTY-THREE

Paris, France

Kit sat on a park bench sipping a café au lait. She had placed another, along with a croissant, next to her in a paper sack, which was slowly losing its warmth from when she walked out of the patisserie a block away. She was waiting for Bernard Duplessy, a longtime contact at the French intelligence service, commonly referred to as RG, the acronym for its formal title, Direction Centrale des Renseignements Généraux. That name had gone away after a bureaucratic merger a couple of years earlier, but Kit thought the old acronym was perfectly serviceable.

The bench was located on the west bank of the Île de la Jatte, a small island in the Seine just a short walk from Bernard's office. The pedestrian path in front of her was quiet and the river calm on a Tuesday morning, but Kit was having a hard time sitting still.

Bernard had invited her for coffee in his office, but she declined. She disliked having to enter the RG building. Too much security, too many people poking around in her things.

"Bernard, please, you know how unhappy it makes me to have to come to your office. Let's meet at the usual place. I will even bring you coffee and a croissant."

Behind her, Kit heard footsteps. A moment later, Bernard appeared, wearing a tailored dark blue suit, white shirt, silk necktie, and, as always, brown shoes. The combination drove Kit mad, but she had stopped asking Bernard how an otherwise perceptive Frenchman could make such a fashion mistake.

"*Bonjour*, Kit," Bernard said. "*Ça fait trop longtemps.*"

"*Vous etes toujour tres gentil*, Bernard," Kit replied before switching to English. "And for that you receive one coffee and a croissant, each of which was warm twenty minutes ago."

He took the paper bag Kit offered. "Your French doesn't seem to have suffered from all the time you are spending with your Arab friends," he replied in English, which was his preference with Kit because, he said, it gave him a chance to practice.

"And what do you know of my time spent with my Arab friends?" Kit asked, not entirely in jest.

"Not much," Bernard replied vaguely as he opened the paper bag. "*Merci beaucoup*," he said, lifting the cup in a small salute.

"It's good to see you again, Bernard. Thanks for agreeing to meet me."

"When the famous Kit Salem calls to say she is coming to Paris with information so sensitive it requires a face-to-face meeting, one would be foolish to say no."

They made small talk while Bernard went to work on his croissant. Then Kit got to the point. "Ibrahim al-Jubaili has been staying with his wife's family in Yemen. I went there hoping to speak with him, but no luck. I spent a long time speaking to his father-in-law, though. He doesn't think much of his daughter's choice in husbands and shared with me some information he overheard in a conversation Ibrahim had with some other, shall we say, like-minded individuals."

Bernard returned the lid to the top of his coffee cup. Kit's mention of Jubaili's name had clearly piqued his interest.

She continued. "According to Abdulwahab—that's the father-in-law—Ibrahim and two or three others are planning to return to France to conduct another operation. The target isn't clear, but he's worried the attack may be imminent. Two weeks ago, when he overheard their conversation, Jubaili and his friends agreed they should be ready to travel in less than a month. And now the father-in-law says that he hasn't seen Jubaili for almost a week. His daughter told him that he had gone to Kuwait on family business. I think he may be heading back this way."

She reached into her handbag and withdrew a reporter's notebook. She extracted the piece of paper Abdulwahab had given her, on which he had written his recollection of the overheard conversation and the names of those involved. She handed it to Bernard. "These are notes Abdulwahab passed me, with names. It's all in Arabic. I was going to translate it for you, but I thought you might prefer to have your own people do that." Then, anticipating what was almost certainly going to be her friend's next question, she said: "I believe him, Bernard. He's promised the Yemeni government that Jubaili will not be a problem as long as he is living under his roof. His honor is at stake."

"If I'm not mistaken," Bernard replied, "this Yemeni family you've taken such an interest in has another distinguished member, no? One who is now enjoying the hospitality of your government?"

"Yes, Bernard. Ashraf al-Akli has been held at Guantanamo for nearly eight years. He's never been charged with a crime, although that hardly makes him unique. According to his father, he was just a troubled young man who was convinced that he could defend Islam by going to Afghanistan. By the time he came to his senses it was too late, and he got caught at the Pakistan border trying to get home."

Bernard seemed to be processing what he had just been told. "Was your friend Abdulwahab any more specific about the time frame? It would help if we had a better fix on when Jubaili and the others might be traveling."

"Understood, but no."

"This is a bit like, what do you Americans say, looking for a noodle in a haystack, no?"

"I think it's a needle, Bernard, but I take your point. There are only a handful of flights from Sana'a to Europe each week, though, so that will shrink the haystack a bit. And I would imagine your counterparts in Yemen could be helpful flagging individuals on the manifests of flights that might merit extra attention. Same with the Kuwaitis, if

Jubaili actually went home and intends to depart from there. But why am I telling you all this? You're the intelligence professional. I'm just an itinerant journalist with an interest in preventing mayhem on the streets of Paris."

"For which I am deeply grateful, Kit," Bernard said as he wiped his mouth with a small napkin.

"There is just one thing I have to ask, Bernard. Well, two things. You must keep the source of this information confidential. If it becomes known that Jubaili's father-in-law revealed these names, his life will be in jeopardy."

"I understand. I'll restrict it to a very small circle. Only those who need to know." He paused for a moment. "And the second request?"

"That you let me know if you manage to detain Jubaili."

"That may be more difficult, Kit, depending on whether we round up his companions at the same time. We wouldn't want to alert them to what we know and risk having them go to ground."

Kit smiled. "Bernard, your English surprises me sometimes—you know that, right?"

He laughed. "I watch a lot of your country's spy movies. And you know, I'm just desperate to impress you."

"Then you must stop wearing brown shoes with dark blue suits, Bernard. I'm beginning to think you're not listening to me."

Slowly, Bernard got to his feet. "Not so, Kit. I take your fashion advice seriously. But I have learned over the course of a long life to be kind to my feet, given how much I depend on them. These shoes that you so admire do a very good job of that. And now, while I hate to be the one to end this lovely interlude, you'll have to excuse me. I must attend to some urgent business. Thank you for making the trip, Kit. I hope to be in touch soon with good news."

He took a step and then paused. "Oh, and while I am always delighted to see you, should you decide that shuttling to Paris to share information is a bit tedious, you'll be interested to know that your old friend Marsh Ridley has returned to Sana'a. You can call on him at your embassy and save your newspaper a lot of money on airfare. Of course, you will miss my charming company, and I will miss the coffee service you provide, but *c'est la vie. À bientôt.*" And he walked off, his soft-soled shoes squeaking ever so slightly on the paving stones that led from the park to a pedestrian bridge and off the island.

CHAPTER THIRTY-FOUR

Paris, France

Kit sat on the bench absorbing the news that Marsh Ridley was back in Sana'a. Not that it came as a big surprise. He had saved the life of the Yemeni president some years back when he was deputy station chief, the number two CIA case officer at the US embassy, although officially declared to the government of Yemen as a State Department political officer. Ever since that moment, the Yemeni president had lobbied hard to keep him in Sana'a, insisting he slept better knowing Marsh was nearby.

The incident in question transpired in the middle of a large Ramadan reception the president hosted every year in the gardens of the presidential palace. Hundreds of people were milling around, and Marsh was standing off to one side speaking to a German diplomat when he noticed a man making his way through the crowd wearing a topcoat, although it was an eighty-degree day in July. The man was walking awkwardly in the direction of the president, who was in a receiving line greeting guests.

Marsh watched the man, who was reaching inside his coat and fumbling with his midsection, as if his trousers were about to fall. Without pausing, Marsh made a beeline across the garden, grabbed the man by the collar, and hauled him single-handedly away from the crowd, followed closely by several very alarmed members of the presidential security detail. What they discovered beneath his topcoat was a fully armed explosive belt, which the man intended to detonate as he approached the president to wish him "*Ramadan Mubarak.*" He simply had lost the detonator in the folds of his clothing and had been furiously trying to locate it when Marsh spotted him.

The breach in palace security triggered a sweeping investigation that led to the arrest of several members of the Presidential Guard, the elite unit whose sole mission was the well-being of the head of the Yemeni state. Two of them, including the senior officer on duty the day of the Ramadan reception, were discovered to have links to AQAP. They were tried, found guilty of treason, and executed before the week was out.

Marsh's heroics made him something of a local celebrity, although he tried to laugh it all off, describing the incident as just one more game-saving tackle he had made in his life. This one came years after he walked away from a promising career as a middle linebacker at the University of South Carolina, a decision he attributed at the time to his parents, "who raised me to use my head as something other than a battering ram against two hundred-pound running backs." So, after two seasons that brought him national attention and talk of being a first-round draft pick when the time came, Marsh just called it quits. He entered a prelaw program with a focus on international relations.

When he graduated he was still heavily recruited, although instead of the NFL, the CIA came calling. So Marsh signed on, putting aside his plans for law school and going instead to Jerusalem as a case officer, studying Arabic each day and developing relationships with Palestinian activists at night. The appointment to Sana'a station came next, and his subsequent heroics convinced the Yemeni president that Marsh should serve out the remainder of his career right there.

The Agency had other plans, however, and Marsh moved on to Doha, where he was expected to keep tabs on representatives of the Afghan Taliban, Palestinian Hamas, and other unsavory types who had started turning up in the Qatari capital. Marsh's assignment irked the Yemeni president, who continued to make very clear his disappointment that Washington was unwilling to grant him this one small favor, especially at a time when the two countries were deeply engaged in joint counterterrorism programs, the success of which depended heavily on the Yemeni government's continued cooperation.

Within the CIA, there was considerable debate as to whether the president was willing to make good on his implied threat to slow-roll the joint counterterrorism programs that had become the centerpiece of Washington's relationship with Sana'a. Some argued it was foolish to turn the issue into a test of wills, especially at a moment when Al Qaeda seemed to be reconstituting itself in Yemen. Others took the view that the Agency should never put its assignments process in the hands of a foreign leader. In the end, the institutional view prevailed, and the standoff continued.

Kit had known Marsh since the late '90s, when both were developing contacts within the Palestine Liberation Organization, she was an Associated Press reporter resident in Beirut, and he from his perch at the US consulate in Jerusalem. They developed a good working relationship, the way journalists and embassy reporting officers often do, comparing notes on leadership figures and up-and-comers in the organization. Even then, it was clear to Kit that Marsh was good at his job, and careful with his cover. He never revealed his Agency connection, although it didn't take too long for anyone familiar with the world of diplomacy to conclude that Marsh almost certainly was employed, not by the Department of State, but another government agency.

It wasn't just the hours he kept that gave him away. It was also the questions he asked, and the issues in which he took a particular interest.

Certainly the hours were hellacious—Kit couldn't count the number of times she had asked to meet him and he had invited her for a "late" bite to eat at a local hotel's all-night coffee shop, which usually meant sometime after midnight. In Kit's experience, traditional diplomacy was rarely conducted at such hours.

Had Kit heard the rumor that the wife of a certain Palestinian official was having an affair with a young Moroccan diplomat? Was it true that the infant son of a prominent cabinet member had been born with a severe heart defect? Just the sort of information an American intelligence officer would find useful in his efforts to recruit a new source.

Kit couldn't remember the last time she had seen Marsh, although this seemed like an excellent moment to get reacquainted. She still had his State Department email address and made a mental note to send him a message from the airport.

CHAPTER THIRTY-FIVE

Sana'a, Yemen

Hank stood across the street and looked at the handsome stone house looming over him. He crossed to the other side and stepped around the freshly painted black parking bollards, which seemed to be one of the few concessions made to the fact that the building now housed government bureaucrats rather than an extended Yemeni family.

He was about to call on Hisham al-Maeli. He phoned him the day after the Tourist City event, explaining that he wanted to learn more about the architecture of the Old City. Maeli suggested there was no better place to start than the building that housed his own office, which was exactly what Hank had hoped to hear.

He looked at his watch. It was five on the dot. He was right on time. Switching on his brightest, I'm-so-glad-to-be-here smile, he pulled open the door and stepped inside. A uniformed soldier holding an AK-47 eyed him warily and motioned to a small room that seemed to be a combination reception area and office. Three desks occupied the space and behind each one sat a clerk in traditional dress. The desks were covered with papers, and a telephone sat prominently on each one, but there wasn't a computer in sight.

"*A salaam aleikum,*" Hank said, directing his Arabic greeting to the young man at the desk closest to the door.

"*Wa aleikum a salaam,*" the seated man replied and then, switching to English, said, "Mr. Amato?"

"Yes," Hank replied, a bit surprised his arrival had been anticipated. "I'm here to see the director general."

"Of course. He said we should expect you." He lifted a phone handset with one hand and pointed to a chair with the other. Hank took a seat. Moments later Maeli came wheeling into the room, all smiles and handshakes, just as Hank recalled from their initial meeting.

"Hello, Hank. *Ahlan wa sahlan*," he said. "How nice to see you again. Come." He led Hank down a corridor toward the rear of the house, where it was noticeably darker and cooler. They stopped at a heavy wooden door, which Maeli pushed open with some effort. The late-afternoon sunlight filled a small courtyard, and Maeli motioned to Hank to step outside. It was paved with large irregular stones, and in the center stood a small tree surrounded by a low wall. "In case you're wondering, this is an olive tree, and it's not native to Yemen. Agronomists searching for alternatives to qat cultivation started experimental planting of olive trees about thirty years ago. Now the focus has shifted to resurrecting Yemen's traditional coffee industry. The experts have decided it will be more lucrative. Everything takes time, though, doesn't it?"

Hank couldn't tell if it was a rhetorical question or if Maeli expected an answer, but he was itchy to get on with the business at hand. "I really appreciate you letting me come by so late in the day, Dr. Maeli."

"Please, call me Hisham. Frankly, I was very happy to hear from you. As I said the other day, we don't get many American visitors these days. So this is a treat for me."

"Well, for what it's worth," Hank said, "I was grateful for the way you managed what I suspect was a bit of a complicated situation at Tourist City."

"The price of doing business in my beloved Yemen," Maeli said. He sighed and tugged gently at the cuffs of the white shirt he wore under his suit jacket. "Sometimes I wonder what I might be doing today if I had stayed in Florida and not come back. I wasn't unhappy there. I had a good job working the front desk at a Hilton Garden Inn right in the world capital of the hospitality industry. And then, out of nowhere, I got a call from an old friend who told me the Yemeni government was going to make a big push to revive the tourism industry, and he was leaving his job with HSBC to take a position with the Ministry of Culture and he wanted me to come back and work with him.

"He was just so sure that if we got the right people together, we'd be able to create something truly special that would put this country on the map in a positive way. It wasn't until I returned that I realized just how far Yemen is from being able to showcase its history properly. The Old City of Sana'a is as magical a place as I have ever seen, capable of transporting you back through time in a heartbeat, but it has been neglected for so long that just deciding where to begin its revival is a monumental task.

"I feel like we sometimes lose sight of the fact that people still live here in the Old City, that they work here every day. It's a living, breathing place. It's not a theme park. We need to be respectful of that. But doing nothing is the least respectful thing we can do." He looked away and quietly wiped flecks of dust from his trousers.

"You have such a strong connection to this place," Hank said. "That's a pretty remarkable thing these days with people uprooting themselves and moving around the world without so much as a thought."

Maeli laughed. "That was me, Hank. At least for a short while. But you've got me talking about myself again. You want to learn about Yemeni architecture, so I suggest we begin here on the ground level and work our way upstairs." He opened his arms, seeming to embrace the space that surrounded them. "Here we can see hints of the genius of the engineers and architects who built this marvelous city. No matter the temperature outside, the ground level of the house was always cool. The stone construction and careful ventilation guaranteed it. A perfectly suitable environment in which to store meat and vegetables year-round. And, of course, surrounding the courtyard we can see the remains of the stalls where goats and other small animals would have been kept."

He stood up, straightened his jacket, and invited Hank to join him. They walked back inside and down the corridor they had initially traversed, back toward the front of the building. "We believe the house was built sometime in the early 1900s. As you can see, we tried to preserve as much of its original design as possible during the renovation. Fortunately, the family that used to live here understood its historical value and made few changes, which was one of the reasons we wanted to buy it, to ensure its preservation."

They approached a staircase. "I hope you wore your walking shoes. These old houses are very vertical." As they proceeded, Hisham pointed out architectural features. "Gypsum and lime were applied to the walls to brighten the interior of the house. We still mine it here in Yemen, so you'll see it everywhere," Maeli said without looking back at Hank.

The first upstairs level of the house was dominated by what appeared to be a sparsely furnished and very large reception area, the floor of which was covered with well-worn, hand-woven carpets. The next floor was devoted to family living spaces, small sitting rooms, and bedrooms. On the third level was the kitchen, with ample storage areas for foodstuffs, "now mostly used as supply closets by the housekeeping staff," Maeli said as they passed. Living and sleeping quarters for the women were on the fourth floor. Maeli went straight to an intricately carved wooden screen that looked out onto the street below. Cushions were strewn on the floor behind it.

"This is the *mashrabiyyah*. The women of the household could sit comfortably up here, enjoy the breeze, and observe the neighborhood without fear of being seen by strangers passing in the street below."

As they made their way up another flight of stairs, he explained that the many windows set into the walls of the staircase provided both light and steady cross-ventilation throughout the house. "No need for air-conditioning," he said triumphantly as they continued to climb to the fifth floor. There, a large drawing room had been converted to a library. "We wanted to be able to accommodate scholars and researchers who need workspace and access to relevant journals and other materials." Hank looked inside. The room was divided by three rows of bookcases that ran front to back and reached almost to the ceiling. Desks and chairs were scattered around the room.

Offices occupied most of the next level, "including my own," Maeli remarked. "Selfishly, I took the office that looks out over the silver market, which we call the suq al-fidha in Arabic. Have you visited?"

"Yes, I did, and I'm looking forward to going back," Hank said, his legs starting to feel the steady climb up six flights of stairs.

"Almost to the top now," announced Maeli as he led Hank up one final stretch. "And here we are, the jewel of every Yemeni home, the mafraj." Maeli walked to the middle of the room, with large windows on three sides, and spun in a slow circle, taking it all in. "This is where the family would gather with friends for social occasions, especially qat chews. You're familiar with our tradition of qat consumption, Hank?"

"Yes, I've read about it. Haven't tried it yet." He took in the space around him. "This is quite beautiful," Hank said as he pulled his cell phone from his pocket and began to take pictures of the stained-glass half-moon windows. "These are qamariya, correct? I have seen some elsewhere in the Old City, but these are really lovely. Judging from the light this time of day, I'm guessing this would be north," Hank said, turning toward the rear of the house.

"Yes, that's correct. Saudi Arabia lies just about a hundred fifty miles away in that direction. Our big brother," Maeli added, laughing quietly.

Hank walked around the mafraj for a few minutes, looking out onto the surrounding buildings and neighborhoods below, but his mind wasn't on the view. All he could think about was the fact that the room appeared undisturbed, and it was possible that he was standing just a few feet from Moishe Azani's collection of silver jewelry. He'd come all the way to Yemen just to get to this place, and now he was here.

He realized he had never anticipated this moment actually arriving, and hadn't given any thought to what he would do if it did.

In that instant, he decided that he was not going to leave the building empty-handed. He didn't know how he was going to accomplish that, but he simply couldn't see himself walking away with a handshake and a handful of photos.

"May I show you anything else?" Maeli's question startled him.

"I'm sorry," Hank said, "I guess I was daydreaming. I could almost imagine what it was like when friends and family would gather here, relaxing on these cushions. You've done a great job preserving the house as it must have been all those years. I kind of hate to leave."

"Well, you don't have to. Why don't you spend some time in our library? You can browse through our collection. I think it's quite a good one."

Hank couldn't help but smile. "Hisham, that's a wonderful suggestion. I can even take some notes while everything is fresh in my mind. I just don't want to impose any further. You've been such a terrific guide and so generous with your time."

"Not a problem at all, Hank. Come, I'll walk you downstairs." As they entered the library, Maeli walked around the room, turning on the lights. Hank chose a desk and assured his host he would make his way out of the building when he was done.

"What time do your offices close, Hisham?" he asked.

"Our schedule is a little different from what Americans are used to," he said. "We work from ten to eight."

Hank looked at his watch. It was just after six. "That gives me plenty of time," he said as he chose a desk and began rummaging through his backpack in search of his notebook.

He spent the next hour idly paging through books and journals specializing in urban design and civil engineering while he wrestled with the question of where and how he was going to conceal himself when the offices closed. He glanced at scholarly articles on mud-brick architecture and traditional multistory house construction in Sana'a. One came with multiple drawings of a typical Old City tower house. Hank zeroed in on the kitchen, as he recalled the storage closets they had passed in the kitchen two floors beneath him.

He considered packing his things and going there directly but decided it was better to stay where he was. In the library he could hide in plain sight until the office was about to close. No one would bother him and, if they did, he was there at the invitation of the director general. So, he sat and leafed aimlessly through books on the morphology of buildings in Yemen and principles of sustainable architecture.

At 7:50 p.m. he decided it was time. He returned all the books to the shelves, collected his notebook and pens, and started down the stairs at a deliberate pace. A couple of people passed him but paid little attention, likely concluding he was just another Western academic wrapping up a long day of research. The third floor was deserted, and he went directly to the kitchen and opened the door to a small windowless storeroom. It looked big enough to accommodate him, so he ducked inside and closed the door behind him.

He let his eyes adjust to the darkness and made out a small pile of boxes on a pallet. He sat and willed his heart rate to slow down. A bit of light from the kitchen seeped through small cracks where the door no longer squared against its frame. Along with his heart, his mind raced. He wondered what he would say if someone discovered him. He thought of the soldier downstairs with the AK-47. He thought of Maeli, whom he genuinely liked, and who had been only helpful, and felt a momentary twinge of guilt at the thought that this was how he repaid his generosity. But he had made up his mind. He was going to sit quietly and wait until everyone left, and then he was going back upstairs.

The minutes passed and, slowly, his thready breathing subsided. He noticed a strong odor and realized that the closet was storing cleaning equipment and supplies. He moved closer to the door to try and capture some fresh air. Outside, he could hear footsteps and occasional voices, although fewer now than before. He hoped that meant people were leaving for the day.

He held his wristwatch up to a thin shaft of light that penetrated the darkness of the closet. It was ten minutes after eight. He sat back down and listened, waiting.

Twenty minutes later, the building seemed to go silent. Hank opened the door and stepped through the kitchen toward the staircase. From there, he could hear voices drifting up from below. *Oh, shit*, he thought. There were still people in the building. He didn't move. He didn't even want to breathe. He wanted to be outside, in the street, a tourist wandering through the Old City, haggling with shopkeepers over souvenir trinkets.

Instead, he was standing on the third floor of a government building that was now closed, with no good explanation as to why and no obvious way out. He took a deep breath. An exit plan would have to wait. He needed to get back upstairs. As he climbed, he heard more voices, this time from the direction of Maeli's office on the sixth floor. Jesus, Hank thought, why aren't they all on their way home? He quickly made his way up the final flight of stairs to the mafraj and began to move the cushions out of the way, exposing the wooden floorboards.

The sun had already disappeared behind the surrounding buildings and the room, which had been so bright earlier in the day, was now almost dark. Hank couldn't immediately see the outlines of the small trapdoor, if it was even there. He couldn't risk turning on the overhead light, so he leaned closer and waited for his eyes to adjust to the darkness. He ran his hand across the floor slowly, relying more on touch than sight to detect any variation in the surface beneath his fingers.

When he felt an almost indistinguishable edge, he stopped and used both hands to trace a small square that was barely visible in the low light. He tried to recall Moishe's instructions but couldn't remember anything specific about how to remove the trapdoor, so he ran his hands over the surface again and again, trying to detect an irregularity, something he could grip. The first pass yielded nothing. He tried again, inching his hands along the edge more deliberately, applying pressure each time he felt a change in the contours of the wood. Then he felt it: a small, carefully carved indentation. He leaned in and pulled. It didn't budge. He thought the wood might have expanded over the years, so he adjusted his position and pulled harder. Suddenly, the piece came free, sending him backward onto the floor, and the square of wood he had just liberated sailed across the room, clattering mercilessly as it went.

Hank lay on the floor and listened. No alarms were sounding, no footsteps were racing in his direction, so he returned to the now-exposed opening in the corner of the room. What he saw was a woven sack, just as Moishe's note had promised. He picked it up, wiped off the heavy layer of dust that had accumulated, and undid the knots.

Inside were bracelets, pendants, necklaces, and rings. His heart pounded. It was exactly like finding buried treasure. He shoved the sack into his backpack and set about returning the trapdoor to its original location. The fit was so tight he had to strike it a couple of times with the heel of his hand. He replaced the cushions, stood up, and tried to compose himself.

He walked as quickly and as quietly as he could to the stairs and started down, intent on returning to the kitchen storeroom until he was certain the building was empty. He had almost reached the third floor when, once again, he heard the voices below him, only clearer now than before, at least two, perhaps three people. Their voices echoed in the stairwell. They were coming toward him. He couldn't go down any farther; he had to go up. On the fourth floor he passed the decorative wooden screen he had admired during his tour, which felt like ages ago. He peered through it. The street below was quiet. But the voices kept approaching. Someone must have heard the racket he made when he fell, or perhaps when he was forcing the trapdoor back into place. Perhaps it had been Maeli himself, and he had called downstairs and instructed his staff to come up and see what had caused the noise. What if they were coming with the gun-toting guard?

He had to get off the staircase. He climbed to the fifth floor, to the library level, and entered the room he had left less than an hour ago. He could hide behind the tall bookshelves, but he would be exposed if anyone decided to walk around. Then he thought, why hide? He was an American journalist conducting research into Yemeni architecture who just lost track of time. He turned the lights on, ran to the stacks, and grabbed a handful of books. The voices were getting closer. Hank raced back to the desk where he'd been sitting earlier, opened the books, and scattered them around. He laid the biggest on its spine against a leg of the desk as if it had fallen. He grabbed his notebook from his backpack and flipped it open, shoving the backpack under the desk. The voices had reached the landing and were just steps away from the library. Hank sat down, folded his arms on top of the desk, and laid his head down, feigning sleep.

There were two men, one a special assistant to Hisham al-Maeli and the other his chauffeur. They never left the building until the boss was ready to go. They turned the corner into the library and stopped at the entrance, puzzled by what they saw: someone sleeping at one of the desks.

They walked over, and one of them shook Hank by the shoulder. "Mister, wake up. You can't be here."

Hank slowly raised his head, squinting into the light. "I'm sorry . . . did I fall asleep?" He glanced at his watch. "Gosh, I guess I did. Dr. Hisham invited me to use the library after our tour and I found all these books that I had never seen before, and at some point I think I just laid my head down to rest for a minute, and gosh, I'm so sorry." He looked down at the floor. "Oh, it looks like a book fell." He picked it up. One of the staffers extended his hand and Hank gave it to him.

"You have to leave now, mister. We are closed. Come back tomorrow."

"Oh, that's very kind of you. I'm sorry if I caused any trouble. Let me just return these books to the stacks."

"No. Leave them."

"Okay." Hank stood up, flipped his notebook shut, and reached under the desk for his backpack. He pulled it toward him and was instantly reminded of the added weight of the jewelry. Quickly, he sat, opened the mouth of the pack, and dropped his notebook and pens inside. He closed it, swung it up, and inserted his arms into the straps as casually as he could. The two men never took their eyes off him.

He adjusted the weight of the pack on his back, smiled, and said, "Well, I know I've said this already, but I really do apologize if I startled anyone by overstaying my welcome. It's just such a lovely library. I expect I'll take advantage of your kind invitation to return before I head back to the States. But for now, I'll just bid you both a good evening and be on my way."

The two men escorted him downstairs to the door he had used to enter the building earlier in the evening. Hamdan Street was busy with pedestrian traffic, but no one paid any mind to the young Westerner exiting the building belonging to the Ministry of Culture. Hank heard the door latch behind him and breathed a deep sigh of relief. Then he adjusted the shoulder straps on his backpack and walked to the hotel.

CHAPTER THIRTY-SIX

Sana'a, Yemen

Kit and Hank sat facing each other, so close their knees almost touched, she in a small upholstered chair in the corner of his hotel room, and he facing her in the desk chair he had carried from its place by the window. Despite the physical proximity, there was an enormous distance growing between them, and it seemed to radiate directly from the jewelry Hank had dumped from his backpack onto the bed.

He didn't expect Kit to return to Yemen for another couple of days, but she had surprised him with a call from Charles de Gaulle Airport shortly before he left for his appointment with Hisham al-Maeli. "I'm coming back to Sana'a first thing in the morning, Hank," she said. "I've done what I needed to do here. I spoke with my editor, and he agreed a trip to London wasn't necessary. Besides, everything that's important is in Yemen, so that's where I need to be." Hank didn't dare imagine that one of those important things might be him, and he was afraid to ask, for fear his question would prompt an answer he simply didn't want to hear.

As usual, Haitham met Kit at the airport, and Hank stayed behind, waiting for her in the lobby of the hotel. He glanced at the revolving door each time someone entered, wanting it to be her, wanting to be near her, excited to show her what he had found. When she finally came through the door, he was checking his phone for messages and didn't even see her until she was standing in front of him.

"Is this seat taken?" she asked.

Hank, flustered as usual, blurted out, "Oh my God, you're here.

How did I not see you?" He came around the small table to where Kit stood laughing and gave her a hug, and it didn't seem unusual or awkward. "I know you only left two days ago, but it seems much longer than that," he said as Kit stood her roller bag on end and settled into a chair. He ordered tea from a passing waiter while Kit briefly described the business that had taken her to Paris. She said that she needed to follow up on the museum bombing and had met with one of the gallery curators to see how restoration efforts were coming along, and then with an old contact of hers, a French counterterrorism official named Bernard Duplessy, who was leading the investigation.

"But what about you?" she asked as the waiter placed a small glass teacup on the table before her. "What have you been up to?"

"A lot," he said. "I'll show you when we go upstairs." Kit looked momentarily puzzled, then returned to her tea, which she sipped slowly while recounting how happy she had been to return to Paris, even if briefly, and how she really hoped to show Hank the city one day. When she was finished, they went up to his room, where he dumped the contents of his backpack onto the bed.

"This is the jewelry that Moishe the silversmith described in the note he handed my grandfather sixty years ago on the tarmac of Lod Airport in Tel Aviv," Hank said triumphantly.

Kit shook her head in disbelief as she picked up each piece and examined it. "These are beautiful, Hank. Just beautiful. But how did you ever locate them?"

Hank explained how he had called one of the Yemeni officials he had met at Tourist City earlier in the week and arranged a visit to his office, which happened to be in the house at 13 Hamdan Street. He described his guided tour of the building, including the mafraj that Moishe Azani had mentioned in his note, and the spur-of-the-moment decision to stay behind after the ministry office closed to search for the jewelry.

He could feel Kit stiffen in her chair as she asked him to explain, and immediately he wished he had thought more carefully through the story before rushing into it the way he did. He described the time he spent in the library before quietly walking downstairs and concealing himself in the kitchen storeroom.

"You did what?" she asked.

Hank took a breath and tried to ignore the sensation that he was digging a deep hole from which he would never be able to extract himself. "I hid in a kitchen closet until the building was empty. Then I went up to the top floor and located the hiding place Moishe described in his note. And the jewelry was there, just as he said it would be. So I put it in my backpack and I left." Hank sat back in his chair, a deep uneasiness creeping over him. Instead of feeling triumphant, he felt embarrassed by what he had just acknowledged doing. Not to mention that he had chosen to omit all the uncomfortable details, including how close he came to being discovered. He was being less than honest with Kit, and that troubled him. Even more troubling was the way she was looking at him.

"So you stole it," she said. It wasn't even a question.

"No, no, Kit," Hank protested. "Who did I steal it from? The Department of Antiquities?" He swept his hand over the jewelry strewn on the bed. "They don't own this. They don't even know it exists. This all belongs to a Jewish silversmith from a little town north of here who left Yemen six decades ago."

Kit shook her head as if trying to fend off an unwelcome thought that was determined to intrude. "This is why you came to Yemen, Hank? To live out some crazy Indiana Jones-goes-to-Arabia fantasy? You had this in mind all along, didn't you? You just decided to not tell me. You lied."

Kit's words were like shards of glass that embedded themselves under Hank's skin.

"I never lied to you," he insisted, although the assertion immediately rang hollow and false to his ears.

"There are sins of commission and sins of omission, Hank."

"Oh shit, am I going to confession now?"

Kit didn't smile. Her mouth was taut, her bright green eyes unflinching.

Hank could feel his desperation growing. "Kit, please, listen to me. Of course, I dreamed up all kinds of scenarios where I managed to retrieve the jewelry, but I never in a thousand years thought I would actually end up in that house, in that room, and that the jewelry would still be right where Moishe left it. And then, there I was. It just . . . happened."

"And what if you had been caught? I suppose you would have expected me to rush to your rescue, to make myself an accomplice in the eyes of the Yemeni government? Did you ever once think about that?"

"To be honest, Kit, I never thought about what would happen if I got caught. I think I acted totally on impulse."

"What impulse prompts you to enter a government building under false pretenses and extract property that is not yours? What is that impulse called, Hank? I'm curious."

"I don't know what to call it, Kit. It's something I've lived with my whole life. I'm not trying to trivialize it, but it's always felt like a game to me. Can I snatch something from right under your nose? Will you notice? Most of my life the answer has been no."

Hank got up from his chair, hoping it might release some of the tension in his body. He walked to the window, wishing the room was bigger. He needed space to move around, space to collect his thoughts. "When I was younger, I almost convinced myself I didn't have to worry about getting caught, or if I did, I didn't have to worry about being punished, that I would just skate right out of it. I know that's not true now, because I did get caught not long ago, and it cost me my job, a job I really loved. It was like a punch to the gut that took my breath away, and when I finally was able to breathe, I realized I'm not twelve years old anymore lifting paperback novels from the corner drug store." He looked back to where Kit was sitting. He realized he'd never seen her this angry before.

"Kit, there's so much I want to share with you. I came to Yemen hoping there would be time to do that. Hoping that you would want to do that. But we get here and you've got a purpose and a direction and a story you're trying to tell, and I'm supposed to have my own. So I started acting like that was the case. And I've shared everything with you. When I first located the house. My trip to stupid Tourist City. Everything. I didn't tell you I was going to take the jewelry because I didn't even know that myself until I was standing literally a few feet from where I thought it must be and something switched on in my head. I had come too far and gotten too close to just walk away. That's the impulse in me that is both deeply familiar and, at the same time, very, very hard to understand. And, I fear, impossible to explain."

Hank sat down in his chair, then stood up, unable to be still. "I never met Moishe Azani and I almost certainly never will. But sixty years ago on that tarmac in Tel Aviv he trusted my grandfather enough to ask him to find something important he couldn't take with him when he left Yemen. And my grandfather never did. But I thought I could, Kit. Am I sorry? I wasn't until right now. Now I feel awful because you're angry and hurt, and it's my fault. And I'm really, really sorry about that."

Hank realized he had been pacing back and forth. He stopped. "Kit, look at me. I'm stumbling, falling down, dead drunk in love with you. That's the absolute truth. When you called from the airport in Paris, you said that everything that was important to you is here, in Yemen. You can't imagine how badly I want to be included in that universe, Kit. I just hope that what I've done isn't going to drive you away." He looked at Kit, who sat with one hand over her mouth, as if to keep herself from responding. "Look, I'll do anything you say. I'll go back to the house on Hamdan Street tomorrow and I'll return the jewelry if you want. I'll go back to Cedar Rapids, to Mr. Babbitt's drug store and pay for the paperbacks and the chocolate bars I lifted from his store. I'll . . ."

"Stop, Hank." Kit leaned forward, put her head in her hands and took a deep breath. So much had happened in the last forty-eight hours, and now this. She looked up at the ceiling, at the blades of the fan that rotated quietly above their heads. She didn't speak for what seemed like an eternity. And then she said, "Hank, you are the reason I came back to Sana'a. I'm almost afraid to admit it, because I can't remember the last time I felt this way about anyone. Which is why I'm so confused by what you've done. It makes me wonder if I know you at all. I'm worried, Hank, that I'm falling in love with a ghost. Someone who doesn't even exist, someone I've conjured in my mind."

Hank walked back around the chair and sat down. He didn't want to crowd Kit but, at the same time, he desperately wanted to be close to her.

"Kit, I'm not a ghost. I'm simply an imperfect human being. And maybe my imperfections and my failings are more than you bargained for. If that's the case, I won't be surprised, and I won't make it difficult for you. You can just tell me, and I'll be on my way. I won't love you any less. But I'll hate myself for being so stupid and so clumsy that I wasn't able to persuade the one woman I've ever truly loved to trust me."

Hank gripped the seat of the chair to keep himself still. He felt like his body was about to explode. "Do you know I've just told you twice in the span of two minutes that I love you?" He reached across to where Kit's hands were folded in front of her and gently wrapped his fingers around them. She didn't pull away. He held them for the very first time, felt the sensation of her skin against his own. "This is me, Kit. Clumsy, a little aimless, profoundly thoughtless sometimes, but I hope you'll believe me when I say that you're the last person on earth I ever want to hurt."

Kit didn't speak right away, and then said: "I don't want you to leave, Hank. But I'm frightened. It's as if there's a side of me I've kept closed up tight, afraid my career would suffer, afraid I would suffer if I let someone in and allowed myself to become vulnerable. I just tucked all those emotions away and went about my business. But with you I can imagine things being otherwise. I can imagine *us*. This is scary,

Hank, because I am willing to trust you not to hurt me. I'm willing to see if what I'm finally able to imagine can be real. But I need to understand what makes you tick, Hank. You have to explain that to me. And I need to tell you all the same truths about me. I won't be afraid, Hank, not this time. But we have to be honest with each other, and careful, so that neither one of us ends up broken if all this doesn't work out."

Hank stood up slowly and drew Kit to her feet. He put his hands on either side of her face. Her skin was warm. He kissed her and wrapped his arms around her.

"I feel like I've been tied up in knots forever, and they've just started to come undone," he said. Kit embraced him, releasing her breath at the same time, a deep exhale that seemed to settle her into his arms. They stood motionless in his hotel room, holding each other, breathing quietly.

Then, without moving, Kit said, "So, what do we do now?"

"Well," he answered, drawing his head back so he could see her clearly, "as far as right now goes, I have an excellent idea. But it is going to require moving this jewelry. And while I know you're going to cringe when you hear me say this, as far as next steps go, I have a plan. But first things first."

CHAPTER THIRTY-SEVEN

Sana'a, Yemen

It was nearly midnight when Kit stirred from a light sleep and glanced at her watch. She turned to Hank, who was lying on his side facing her, and said, "I'm starving. The last thing I can remember eating, and it seems like days ago, was a croque monsieur at de Gaulle Airport. If I don't eat immediately I will die." They ordered room service from the hotel's twenty-four-hour coffee shop: two omelets with toast, a pot of tea, and a bowl of ful, because Hank insisted. They played rock, paper, scissors to see who would get dressed to answer the door when the food arrived. Kit won two out of three, and Hank crawled out of bed in search of his clothes, complaining bitterly about the loss.

Hank watched in amazement as Kit attacked the food, which they ate from the cart while sitting at the foot of the bed. They showered and went back to bed after they ate, making sure to hang the *Do Not Disturb* sign on the doorknob.

It was midmorning before they stirred again. They debated the merits of breakfast in bed before deciding the civilized move was to get dressed and make their way to the dining room.

Kit returned to her own room after they ate to unpack her bag, check email, and finish some work she'd been neglecting. They agreed to meet for dinner. Hank decided to give David Leslie a call and see if his offer to grab a drink was genuine. Leslie answered his cell phone on the third ring.

"*Sabah al khair*," he said, "David Leslie here." After a week in Yemen, Hank recognized the Arabic phrase for good morning.

"David. Hank Amato here. From the hotel the other day. Hope I'm not disturbing you."

"Oh, hello, Hank. No, no. Good to hear from you. Just a busy day. The ambassador's gone back to Washington for meetings, so I'm trying to keep a lid on things while she's away. Say, thanks again for your help the other day. It was most appreciated."

"Glad I could do something useful," Hank replied. "Did you get those folks out safely?"

"Yup. As tragic as it was, that episode is closed. Except, of course, for the lingering suspicion on the part of every senior Yemeni official I've spoken with in the last three days that we orchestrated their disappearance. But that, too, will pass. What are you up to?"

"I was wondering if I could take you up on your kind offer for a drink before I head back home?" There was a moment of silence, and Hank wondered if he had overstepped.

Leslie came back on the line. "Sorry, Hank, just checking my calendar quickly. How about if I do you one better and have you over here for lunch the day after tomorrow? The ambassador's residence is on the compound and her cook is idle while she's away. Might you be free?"

"I'm sure I can make that work," Hank said.

Leslie said that the taxi drivers at the hotel were familiar with the embassy, and any one of them would know where to drop Hank off. He said his secretary would alert the security guards at the front gate to escort him to the residence. They bid farewell and Hank tucked his phone back into his pocket.

Pleased with himself for having developed a new contact, Hank decided to take a walk through the Old City while Kit was out making calls of her own. Back at the hotel he read for a bit, napped, and relished the unfamiliar sensation of calm that seemed to be settling over him. At seven o'clock that evening, Kit knocked on his door and waited while he laced up his shoes.

"I've done all the work I can do for one day," she said. "I'm declaring this evening an official no-work zone." They walked downstairs to the dining room and found a small table next to a window overlooking a park, in front of which was a sign that Kit identified as saying "for women only." Small children played on a set of swings under the watchful gaze of two women wearing black abayas.

They ate slowly and contentedly, making small talk, reaching for each other's hand from time to time.

Almost an hour later they stepped back into the lobby, and Kit could feel the chill that crept into the air each evening in the Yemeni highlands. She was wearing just a cotton sweater over jeans and her running shoes. She would put on something heavier when she got back upstairs, and maybe she and Hank would take an evening stroll.

A man approached, wearing a traditional Yemeni thobe and a sport coat that still bore the Joseph Abboud label on the sleeve.

"Miss Kit, I am Mahmoud. I work for Sheikh Abdulwahab. Do you remember me?"

It took her a minute to place him from the meeting she had with Abdulwahab at his brother's house. "Ah, yes, of course, Mahmoud. *Keifak?*" she asked, inquiring as to his health.

"*Alhamdulillah,*" he replied. "Sheikh Abdulwahab was summoned to a meeting here in the capital today and is going to spend the night at Sufian's before he heads home, but wanted to stop by quickly to see if you have any news on the matters you discussed with him when you met recently. He's outside in his car if you have a moment to speak."

"Why doesn't he come in? We can have a coffee. It will be much more comfortable than sitting outside in the dark."

"He's in a bit of a hurry. It's been a very long day. But you can invite him if you wish, Miss Kit. His car is right out here."

Kit looked puzzled, and Hank asked, "Do you want me to come with you?"

"No, no. It's fine. I'll just be a minute." She smiled and followed Mahmoud outside. Several vehicles were lined up in front, but he led her past them.

"It's just over here. There was no place to park when we arrived."

Kit barely detected the two men who had fallen in behind them as they moved down the line of cars toward the large SUV parked thirty or so yards ahead near a small stand of acacia trees. As they approached the car, Mahmoud moved quickly to the right rear door and swung it open. At that moment, the two men behind Kit each took her by an arm and shoved her effortlessly into the back seat of the vehicle. One got in behind her, the other came around quickly to the other side, trapping her between them. They didn't look at her or speak. Mahmoud climbed into the driver's seat, the SUV roared to life, and they drove off into the evening traffic.

"Mahmoud, what is going on here?" Kit tried to sound as indignant as possible, but she was having a hard time keeping her voice steady.

"Not to worry, Miss Kit. Everything will be fine. No more talking now."

Kit was tightly sandwiched between her two captors. She took a deep inhale, as much to try and calm herself as to create a bit of space, but they didn't budge. Her mind raced with possible scenarios, all of which seemed bad. She realized she was without her phone. Before she and Hank had come downstairs, they agreed to leave their phones behind so that they wouldn't end up sitting at dinner absorbed by emails and texts. She could see it on the night table in his room.

They drove quickly along darkened streets, through neighborhoods Kit didn't recognize and would never be able to identify. The SUV stopped in front of a large compound gate that appeared a gloomy steel gray in the glare of its headlights. The gate swung open, and the car drove into a small parking area next to a typical newly constructed suburban villa. The gate closed quickly, Kit was pulled from the car, and the two men, their hands tightly on her arms, led her up a short flight of stairs into a darkened entryway, and from there to a sitting room where a small wiry man in a freshly pressed thobe sat in an easy chair, fingering a set of polished prayer beads. Kit didn't recognize him.

"Miss Kit Salem. Have a seat." Kit thought she heard traces of a British accent.

"I prefer to stand," she said with as much resolve as she could muster. "I don't expect to be here very long."

The man in the chair chuckled. He crossed his legs and smoothed his thobe. "Excellent. Suit yourself. Let's get right to it then, shall we? You may not have heard the news, but a good friend of ours, Ibrahim al-Jubaili, was arrested at Schiphol Airport in Amsterdam earlier today. That was disappointing, but even worse, two other good friends were detained after they landed in Frankfurt. A very bad day for traveling to Europe, wouldn't you agree?"

The news that the three Al Qaeda operatives had been intercepted emboldened her. She said, "Do I look like a travel agent?" and immediately regretted it. The man sitting across the room wasn't large, but Kit had the uneasy sensation that he could uncoil like a snake and kill her on the spot if provoked.

"No, of course not. You look like someone who spent a great deal of time last week meeting privately with Sheikh Abdulwahab al-Akli. And you look like someone who flew immediately to Paris after she did. Oh, and now you look surprised. Don't be. Information is not hard to come by in Yemen if you know who to ask. So, I've invited you here this evening because I would like to know if there is any connection between your meeting with the sheikh, your French excursion, and the, shall we say, complications I have just described with my associates' travel plans."

"Well, first of all," she said, "I don't think we've been introduced."

"You can call me Abu Salim. Of course, that is not my birth name, but you were raised in an Arab home, and I'm sure you understand what a *kunya* is."

Kit was indeed familiar with kunyas, nicknames formed with the Arabic word for father, abu, and the name of the individual's first-born child—in this case, Salim.

He leaned forward just a bit. "And I do wish you'd sit down."

Kit did. "Your English is quite good," she said. "You must have studied abroad."

"Ah, there's the journalist in you, always hunting for information. Well, in this case, you are correct. My father was a Yemeni diplomat. We traveled quite a bit. Spent a lot of time in South Asia, a bit in London. It was an interesting life. So, may we get back to my question?"

Kit looked at him carefully. He had fine features, a slender face, and dark eyes. "Abu Salim, as you have noted yourself, I am a journalist, not a law enforcement officer. I spoke with Abdulwahab at some length because I am working on a story about his son, Ashraf. I presume you know he has been held at Guantanamo for the past eight years."

"And your interest in Ibrahim al-Jubaili is also quite clear. You're very keen to speak with him, no?"

"You are well informed, sir. Yes, I did. I believe my portrait of Ashraf will be incomplete if I fail to describe his family, and that includes his sister and her husband. Sadly, I was told that Ibrahim was unavailable. So I stopped asking. However, perhaps you would be willing to speak with me for this story. I would love to learn more about what it was like to grow up the way you did, how that experience shaped your beliefs and your—"

Abu Salim lifted his hand, palm out, as if he were a traffic cop commanding a line of cars to come to an immediate halt. "Enough of that. Tell me about your trip to Paris. Just a quick visit to your favorite patisserie?" The comment startled Kit, who thought for a minute he was referring to her meeting on the Île de la Jatte with Bernard Duplessy. She thought it unlikely, and she certainly wasn't going to volunteer that she had met with a senior French intelligence officer.

"I flew to Paris because I am doing a follow-up story on last year's attack on the Musée de Montmartre, and I had a meeting with the director of the Islamic art collection to see how restoration of the damaged wing of the building is proceeding. I had planned to stay for a couple of days, but I had second thoughts and decided to return to Sana'a. A friend is here researching a story of his own, and he's unfamiliar with the country. It didn't seem right to leave him alone."

"Ah, yes, Mr. Hank Amato. Looking into the fate of Yemen's Jews. How interesting." Kit quietly exhaled. In her eagerness to return to Sana'a she had almost decided to skip the meeting at the museum but was grateful now that she kept the appointment.

Abu Salim stood up. For a second time he smoothed the wrinkles in his thobe. "So, I am to believe that everything that has happened is pure coincidence? That your interest in the museum bombing in Paris and the al-Akli family has nothing to do with the arrest of Ibrahim al-Jubaili, the man French authorities claim is responsible for the incident?" He shook his head. "I'm having a hard time with that. So, while I think on this further, let me invite you to spend a bit of time thinking yourself. My colleagues here will escort you to your room."

Kit felt a sharp jolt of fear. "Abu Salim, I really don't know any more than I have already told you."

He waved her away without a word, and she was led to the rear of the house, into a small room that contained a metal-frame bed on top of which rested a thin mattress. The sole window in the room was a small rectangle six feet from the floor covered with a heavy wire mesh grate. The only source of light was a bare bulb in the ceiling. Her escorts locked the door behind her. Kit shuddered, not sure if it was from the damp chill of the room or the realization that she had just been taken prisoner by Al Qaeda.

At the hotel, Hank lingered in the lobby, expecting Kit to return once she spoke with Abdulwahab, but after twenty minutes, he wandered around outside to see if there was any sign of her. The doorman said he hadn't seen Kit. Nor had the cab drivers hanging around idly waiting for a fare to exit the hotel. Hank walked back upstairs and sat on the bed, a deep uneasiness growing in his chest. He looked at both cell phones. No missed calls. No texts.

Just as he put Kit's phone back on the nightstand it began to vibrate. He picked it up quickly. "Kit?"

There was silence on the line. Then, a voice speaking English with a distinct French accent. "No, this is Bernard Duplessy, a friend of Kit's. I'm calling from Paris. Might I speak with her please?"

Hank recognized the name as the contact Kit said she had met in France. He felt a rush of relief. "Bernard, this is Hank Amato speaking. I'm also a friend of Kit's and I'm worried that she's in trouble. She left the hotel a half hour ago to meet someone outside and she never came back. She's just gone. I don't know what to do."

"Ah, yes, Monsieur Amato. Kit told me you were traveling with her in Yemen when we spoke last week. You also are American, yes?"

"Yes."

"And where are you at the moment?"

"In my room at the Ghamdan Hotel in Sana'a. Kit left her phone here when we went for dinner. We were on our way back upstairs when a man approached us in the lobby. He said he worked for a contact of Kit's named Abdulwahab. His boss was outside in his car, he said, and wished to have a word with her."

"The name was Abdulwahab?"

"Yes, that's what the man said. His name was Mahmoud. Kit's been meeting with Abdulwahab for a story she's working on. I looked outside for her but she's not there, and no one's seen her, so I came back upstairs and that's when you called. Do you think something's happened to her?"

The line was silent. Hank waited. Bernard said, "Monsieur Amato, let me make a phone call. I will be back in touch. Excuse me, please. *Adieu.*" And the line went dead. Hank sat heavily on the bed, staring at the phone, willing it to ring again, but there was only silence.

CHAPTER THIRTY-EIGHT

Sana'a, Yemen

Bernard Duplessy quickly dialed a US area code and telephone number. It was the operations center at CIA headquarters in Langley, Virginia. He identified himself and asked that Marsh Ridley in Sana'a return his call as quickly as possible. His instincts and training told him to arrange for the call on a secure line, but that would have required technical support from the CIA station at the American embassy, and that needed time, a luxury he just wasn't sure he had. Still, he waited. Ten minutes went by, then twenty. Finally, his phone rang.

"Marsh, *sa va?*"

"*Oui*, Bernard. Living the dream here in Happy Arabia. *Comment allez vous?*"

"I'm fine, Marsh. But I may need your help. A friend of ours, Kit Salem, came to see me earlier this week with some important information."

"So I heard. She emailed me out of the blue. Said she'd seen you and you told her I was back in town. We're supposed to have coffee."

"I fear Kit may be in danger, Marsh. I'm sure by now you've heard of the arrests earlier today of Ibrahim al-Jubaili and two others as they landed in Europe. Kit came to see me with information about their plans she had gotten from Jubaili's father-in-law. About forty-five minutes ago Kit walked out of her hotel in Sana'a to speak with him, and now she seems to have disappeared. I'm worried the two events are connected."

"You think Jubaili's network has gone after Kit?"

"Yes, I do."

"Damn, Bernard. How do you know all this?"

"I just called Kit because I promised to inform her of the arrests and spoke with a young American she's traveling with. His name is Amato. Hank Amato."

"Yeah, she mentioned him in her email."

A lengthy silence followed, prompting Bernard to ask: "Marsh, are you there?"

"*Oui*, sorry, Bernard. Just thinking. Let me see what I can find out. And thanks for the heads-up."

Marsh returned the phone's handset to its base. He picked up his cell phone and scrolled through his contact list, stopping at the name of the man who served as director of Yemen's intelligence agency, the National Security Bureau. He pressed the call button and waited.

After two rings a connection was made and the voice at the other end of the line said, "*Nam?*"

"Bassam, my brother, it's Marsh Ridley. I hope I'm not disturbing your dinner."

Bassam al-Badawi laughed. His wife, Dima, had just placed a large platter of food on the table and was sitting down to join her husband.

"*Ya ahi*, your timing is perfect. It's almost like you could smell the food being carried from the kitchen. What do you need?"

"Bassam, I have a very urgent situation on my hands that requires your immediate attention. I was going to speak directly with the president but knew he would only call you himself."

Marsh never tired of reminding senior Yemeni officials of the special access he enjoyed to the president, although it wasn't really necessary. They knew that Marsh's access likely exceeded their own, and that knowledge alone was sufficiently motivating for them to offer assistance whenever he asked for it. He explained quickly what had transpired at the hotel, and his concern that Kit had been abducted by associates of Jubaili, likely believing that she had played a role in Jubaili's arrest and that of the other AQAP operatives.

"We need to move very quickly on this," Marsh said. "This is an American citizen. If she is harmed, it will be very bad for your country. Very bad for the president himself."

"I understand," Bassam said. "I know these people, and there is only one man who would do this." He ended the call and looked at his wife, who glared at him across the dinner table. "One phone call. Ten minutes," he said, and he rose from the table, where steam drifted lazily from the serving platter heaped with lamb and rice.

He walked up the marble staircase that led to the second floor of their home, past the bedrooms on either side to the end of the hall. He unlocked the door to his private office and went directly to a leather chair. Before he sat down, he switched on a lamp next to him, opened a drawer in a small table, and extracted another cell phone. His fingers moved quickly over the keypad. He lifted the phone to his ear and waited.

Abu Salim hadn't moved from the chair in which he was sitting when Kit was brought into the house over an hour ago. He was in no hurry to go anywhere. Kit was secured, no one knew where she was. In a couple of hours he would bring her back and they would have another conversation. And then another. And as many as it took for her to tell him the truth. And then, he would kill her. Mahmoud, too. He had paid him handsomely to lure the American from the hotel, but he would crack like an egg if the authorities applied even the slightest pressure on him.

A cell phone on the table next to him began to vibrate. He picked it up. "*Meen?*" he asked. "Who is this?"

"Abu Hamza," Bassam replied, using his own kunya.

A chill made its way down Abu Salim's spine. Yemen's intelligence chief was literally the last person he wanted to hear from at that moment.

"Abu Hamza, what a pleasant surprise," he said, with as much cordiality as he could muster.

"Perhaps not. An American journalist seems to have gone missing, and I think you know where she is. In fact, she may even be with you right now. Either way, she must be released immediately, unharmed. If she is not, I will be forced to take steps that we all will regret."

"Habibi," Abu Salim said good naturedly, addressing Badawi as he would a friend, "why would I have an American journalist in my home?"

"Abu Salim, do not try my patience, or that of the president. He has been faithful to our agreement. He has not pursued you or Jubaili. He has not taken any steps to disrupt your organization or dismantle the training camps you are operating. He has assured the Americans and their European friends that Yemen will not be the staging ground for attacks against their citizens.

"In return, he expects you to keep to your agreement, to not engage in activities that risk provoking the Americans into taking action on their own. You have failed to do this. I know about the arrests today in Europe of Jubaili and the others. And now you kidnap an American journalist. I am telling you only once that if the woman is not released immediately, the arrangement we have is over. We will have no choice but to declare war on your organization and the Americans will be more than happy to join us. They will hunt you down. You'll never enjoy another night of peaceful sleep. Am I being clear?"

Abu Salim didn't speak. He held the phone very still.

"And if I am able to locate this woman and she is released unharmed?"

"We'll consider this matter closed."

Abu Salim took a moment before he replied in a tone devoid of emotion. "Then it will be done."

"I'm sending a car to your house. It will be there in twenty minutes. I expect the woman to be waiting. She will get into the car and be returned to her hotel. You will have nothing to do with her again. Do you understand?"

"Yes."

"There is still the matter of Jubaili and the others returning to Europe, and we will discuss that at another time, after I have spoken to the president." And then the line went dead.

Abu Salim sat quietly in his chair. Twenty minutes passed. Mahmoud took a call from the guard station in the street saying a car had just arrived. He relayed the message to Abu Salim, who said, "Bring the woman to me."

The two men who had seized Kit outside the hotel escorted her back to the study, where Abu Salim was standing by a window. He said, "There appears to have been a misunderstanding, for which I apologize. You are free to leave. A car is waiting outside." Kit didn't move immediately, confused by the unexpected turn of events. "Go," Abu Salim pressed. "And thank your God for his intervention."

Kit walked to the front door of the house, down the steps, across the small paved parking area. The guard opened the gate, and she stepped out into the street. A black Mercedes was waiting, the driver holding open the left rear door. Kit hesitated. Should she run? Where would she go? The streets were dark and unfamiliar.

The driver was holding a cell phone. He extended his hand, inviting her to take it.

"Hello?" she said tentatively.

"Kit Salem, is that you?" It was an American voice. Kit felt an enormous wave of relief wash over her.

"Is this . . .?"

"Yes, it's Marsh Ridley. Who else arranges for a Mercedes to pick up a wayward journalist in the middle of the night?"

"Oh, Marsh, it is so good to hear your voice."

"Likewise, Kit. You can get into the car. The driver will take you back to your hotel. We can talk while you ride."

Kit got into the car and settled into the soft leather seat. The door closed and it was quiet and warm inside. "Marsh, how did you ever find me?"

"I didn't. A friend did. Mighty glad too. I must say, Kit, I never took you for the damsel in distress type."

"Marsh, I am so sorry. My brain just switched off."

"Well, you're in good hands now, Kit. I might suggest, though, that in view of this evening's events we meet a bit sooner than we had planned. Why don't you call me tomorrow, after you've had a chance to rest?"

"Yes, of course. That's fine, Marsh. And thank you."

"Easy day, Kit."

CHAPTER THIRTY-NINE

Sana'a, Yemen

Abu Salim was furious. A self-important government bureaucrat had issued an ultimatum, and he had obeyed. It was humiliating. And yet, the more he thought about it, he began to see there was still a path forward to extract revenge for what had happened to three of his most valuable operatives. He had been told that he must leave the American woman alone, but nothing had been said about Jubaili's father-in-law.

And since he was convinced that Abdulwahab and the American had connived to alert the Europeans of Ibrahim and the others' travel plans, one of them would have to pay. Getting to Abdulwahab would not be easy, though. He was a tough old man who could assemble a small army of tribal fighters if need be, although as Abu Salim had learned with Mahmoud, there were limits to the loyalty of those Abdulwahab commanded. Still, his home was well protected, not least of all by the surrounding geography, so the element of surprise would be essential.

Abu Salim sat in his chair, brooding deep into the night. When he finally made his way to bed, he still hadn't come up with a plan—but he was certain there was a way to get retribution. He just had to keep thinking on it.

CHAPTER FORTY

Sana'a, Yemen

Kit lay on the still-made bed spooned with Hank, who had finally fallen asleep, his left arm draped over hers. It was after four in the morning. They had held each other and talked for hours. She was physically exhausted but still buzzing with adrenaline. She couldn't seem to stop replaying in her mind everything that had happened. It was a constant loop. She felt like there were a million exposed nerve endings in her body tingling, firing, sounding alarms. You're not safe, the messages said. You can't trust yourself to know when you're in danger.

Was Hank the difference? Had her feelings for him, the welcome sense of comfort in the company of another, dulled the instincts she had so carefully honed working in unfamiliar, hostile places? She curled herself deeper into his arms and drew his body closer. She wanted a place to hide, somewhere her own thoughts wouldn't be able to find her. Somewhere she could rest. But she knew it was futile. So, slowly, she disentangled herself and got out of bed.

She realized she was still wearing the same clothes she had on when she'd walked out of the hotel with Mahmoud, the same clothes she had worn while sitting on the small metal bed in the poorly lit room inside the house where she had met Abu Salim. She needed to shower, to wash away as much of what had happened as physically possible. Then she needed to reach Abdulwahab. He was in danger. How she would do so eluded her. Minutes later, as she stood in the shower rinsing her hair, the answer came to her: Marsh Ridley. Surely, he would see the need to keep Abdulwahab from harm and, with his network of contacts, he had the means to do so. She and Marsh were going to meet in just a couple of hours, and she would ask him to intervene. She felt calmer as she toweled off, slipped on a pair of sweatpants and a long-sleeved jersey, and walked to the small desk where her computer waited. She didn't yet feel as though she had regained control of her life, but maybe she could stop it from unraveling any further.

CHAPTER FORTY-ONE

Sana'a, Yemen

Hank stirred in the early morning chill and reached down to pull a blanket over himself when he realized he had fallen asleep on top of the bedspread, in his clothes. He'd fallen asleep with Kit. And now she was gone. He sat up quickly.

She was sitting in a chair with her back to the bed, facing the window Hank favored, through which the sunrise was just beginning to announce itself. Hank looked at his phone. It was 5:30 a.m.

He didn't want to surprise her, not after last night, so he rustled around in the bed before he said, "Hey, good morning."

Kit didn't turn around. "I couldn't sleep," she said.

"I get it. Do you want to go downstairs for breakfast?"

"A bit early, don't you think?" she asked, turning toward him from where she sat.

He fell back onto his pillow. "Yeah, I guess so. What have you been doing all night?"

"Beating myself up for being so obtuse that I didn't see a trap before stumbling right into it. When I got tired of that I thought I would get started on my profile of Abdulwahab and his family, even though I feel like so many pieces are still missing. I thought the arrest of Jubaili and the others in Europe would be the perfect hook, but what if they go after Abdulwahab? I need to warn him, but I can't reach him. Marsh can, though."

"Well, based on his performance so far, I wouldn't bet against him."

"What about you?" she asked.

"I've cleared my calendar today, Kit. I'm here for you if and when you need me, which I hope will be often throughout the day."

He tried to coax a smile from Kit but what he got was a slightly perplexed look as if she was having difficulty understanding what he was saying. So he walked across the room, leaned over the back of the chair where she sat and put his arms around her. She still smelled fresh from the shower.

"Kit, this hurts—I know. You've been through an awful scare, and it's not going to go away easily. Maybe you're right to focus on the work that brought you here. Maybe telling Abdulwahab's story will help you make sense of everything you've just been through. Please, though, tell me that after we're done here we'll go someplace quiet and warm where we can sleep on the beach and worry about nothing more than whether we've applied sufficient sunblock." He couldn't see her face from where he stood, so he waited for some indication she had heard him. After a bit she reached up, and he could feel the pressure from her hands tighten on his arms. For the moment, Hank thought, that was enough.

They entered the nearly deserted dining room shortly after it opened at six thirty. They ate quickly, and thirty minutes later they returned to Hank's room. Kit was having a hard time sitting still, so Hank suggested they take the walk through the Old City they had planned the previous evening, before everything went haywire. He goofed around playing tour guide, pointing out the few landmarks he had become familiar with over the course of the week, but it was clear that Kit's attention was elsewhere. Every few paces she seemed to glance at her watch. Finally, it just got to be too much for Hank.

"Oh, for God's sake, go ahead and call him," he said.

Kit nodded, withdrew her phone from the pocket of her jeans, and punched in a number.

"One moment, please," said the operator at the US embassy after she asked to speak with Marshall Ridley. After a minute of subdued music, another voice came on:

"Political section. This is Trevor." Kit explained who she was and asked for Marsh. "Hang on for a second; let me see if he's come in." Another wait, another musical interlude.

"Kit," said Marsh in his big voice. "You're up early."

"Never went to bed, Marsh. Little wound up. You know."

"Of course. Are you ready for a coffee?"

"As soon as you can get here."

"My gosh, Kit, you only have one speed, don't you?"

"I'll treat," she said.

"The hell you will. I'm the home team, I treat. I'll swing by your hotel in an hour. There's a small café on Zubairy Street I want to show you. It has the best strudel this side of Munich, but it doesn't open for a bit. You remember what I look like, right?"

Unexpectedly, Kit laughed—a good, healthy sound that came up from deep in her belly. "Yes, Marsh, that much I remember."

CHAPTER FORTY-TWO

Sana'a, Yemen

It was nearly eleven o'clock, the sun reaching midday, by the time Marsh returned Kit to the hotel. He watched her disappear inside and then he put his Toyota Land Cruiser into gear and headed back to the embassy. They had sat and talked for two hours, sipping coffee and eating pastries, including the strudel he had promised. The coffee shop was an anomaly in traditional Sana'a, a place where young men and women could sit together without incurring the wrath of conservative Yemenis who believed they shouldn't mingle.

They sat at a table on a small patio near the rear of the café, the outdoor space dotted with trees in ceramic pots. The owner, a handsome Yemeni woman wearing a brightly colored hijab to cover her hair, took their order. She had gone to Germany to study economics but discovered that baking was her true passion. She left school to work in a shop run by an Austrian family who jealously guarded a traditional recipe that produced paper-thin layers of pastry, which reminded her of the baklava her father would bring home from the neighborhood bakery when she was growing up in Sana'a.

She also found a husband, a Bavarian agronomist who was fascinated by Yemen's history of coffee cultivation and determined to help engineer a renaissance of the industry. While he went off every day to the surrounding highlands to work with coffee farmers, she baked and oversaw operations at the small shop that was her pride and joy. Her husband was making steady progress with the coffee growers, she said. Already, they used only locally grown beans in their coffee, and soon, perhaps even before the end of the year, they would begin to package the beans for retail sale, especially to Europe, where they hoped authentic Yemeni coffee would find a receptive market.

Marsh invited Kit to walk him through the events of the past twenty-four hours, which she did in as much detail as she could recall. She described being spirited away from the hotel. She recalled her conversation with Abu Salim, her surprise at how much he knew of her meetings and her travels. "He knew everything, Marsh. He even knew about Hank's research into the emigration of the Jews."

"It's information, Kit. It's all for sale," Marsh said in response.

She explained the circumstances of her long conversation with Abdulwahab, what he had revealed to her about the travel plans of Jubaili and his companions, and how he was now the most likely target for Abu Salim's retaliation. "Marsh, he saved lives. Who knows, possibly hundreds of lives. We can't let him die for that."

Marsh nodded in agreement but was noncommittal. "I'll make sure folks back home understand what he's done and the danger he's in, but the decision as to how we respond, or even if we do, is not mine to make, Kit."

"But you can alert him to the danger he's in, right? We have to warn him. You can do that, right?"

Marsh could see how deeply invested Kit was in Abdulwahab's well-being. He'd seen that same loyalty surface years before with contacts in Jerusalem. If you took Kit into your confidence, you became more than just a source of information to her, you became like a family member, someone she would never betray or knowingly expose to danger. Marsh had no doubt that if he told her he didn't know how to get in touch with Abdulwahab, she would find herself a car and drive directly to his home, figuring out how to get there as she went, certain of just one thing: she had put him at risk and that had to be remedied.

"Yes, Kit, I can get word to people who will be able to alert him. I'll take care of that." Marsh could almost see the tension leave Kit's body as she accepted his assurance. She sat back in her chair and nodded.

"Thank you," she said.

CHAPTER FORTY-THREE

Sana'a, Yemen

As he weaved his way through the late-morning traffic, Marsh formulated the ask he would make of his superiors back home at Langley: redeployment of an armed surveillance drone for the next couple of weeks to put eyes on Abu Salim. It wasn't a given that the Agency would agree—drones were in short supply and high demand. Marsh could make a case, though, that if Abu Salim had it in his mind to go after Abdulwahab, he would have to surface. When he did, they might be able to get a clear shot at him and some of his most-trusted fighters, perhaps on an otherwise empty stretch of highway where there would be no risk of collateral damage. Taking him off the board would be welcomed by virtually everyone who had watched him rise through the AQAP ranks to become a senior operational planner, a man who thought civilian targets—like European tourists visiting Yemen or art lovers strolling through museums in the French capital—were fair game.

Marsh knew putting that option on the table would prompt discussion at the highest levels of the interagency on Abu Salim's threat, and whether it warranted a lethal operation.

The fact that he was the subject of an Interpol Red Notice issued in the wake of the Paris attack would strengthen the argument of those pressing the Agency to go after him. It would be easy enough to put an armed Reaper drone up in the sky and, with a single Hellfire missile, make the world a safer place. There was, of course, the pesky issue of conducting an operation of that sort on Yemeni soil without the concurrence of the government, which could easily bring an end to much-needed cooperation on other counterterrorism initiatives Washington cared about.

The problem was, just one man could authorize such an operation, the president of Yemen himself, and Marsh was all but certain that he would refuse to do so. There already had been too many missteps, one of them just eighteen months earlier. The president had given the green light to an aerial strike after receiving assurances from the US intelligence community that a secluded Al Qaeda training camp in the eastern province of Hadramout was populated only by fighters preparing to spread out across the country to kill Westerners and Yemenis alike.

Two days later, five Tomahawk cruise missiles armed with cluster munitions were launched from a US Navy vessel anchored in the Red Sea two hundred miles to the west. Twenty-eight minutes later they slammed into the training camp, obliterating the immediate area. Initial reports that thirty-four AQAP recruits and trainers were killed were quickly revised down to fourteen, and when local and international media arrived on the scene, they were told by residents that at least forty-one civilians living in a nearby Bedouin camp also had been killed, including nine women and nineteen children. The civilians had been working at the camp as drivers, cooks, and housekeepers, not because they sympathized with AQAP, but because they were desperately poor and needed the money. The blowback was fierce, as photos of grieving family members in an impoverished Yemeni village made their way around the world.

The president was apoplectic. He summoned the American ambassador to his palace the next day and gave him a thorough dressing down, at the conclusion of which he made clear that all counterterrorism cooperation with the United States was suspended because it had proven itself incompetent and untrustworthy.

Washington moved quickly to mitigate the damage and get the counterterrorism relationship back on track. It authorized the payment of one hundred thousand dollars in blood money to the families of those Yemenis who had been killed while working at the camp. The money was funneled through the National Security Bureau, which declined to disclose the source of the funds to the Yemeni lawyers representing the surviving family members, although it was easy enough to figure out.

Over the next six months, a half dozen or more senior defense and intelligence officials made their way to Sana'a to assure the president that there would be no repeat of the incident.

After much cajoling, two things got the president to relent. The first was a six-million-dollar counterterrorism aid package for his most-trusted security forces, each of which, not coincidentally, was commanded by a close family member. There were armored personnel carriers, advanced assault weapons, night vision optics, and lightweight body armor, some of which only Yemen's much wealthier neighbors could boast having received from the US, a point of pride for the president.

No one in Washington believed for a minute that Yemen's counterterrorism forces would ever put all that expensive gear to any meaningful use. Despite their best efforts, US military advisers had yet been able to field an effective strike force, even a small one. They had tried for months with elements of the supposedly elite Central Security Forces, preparing them for a nighttime assault on an AQAP compound in the desert east of the capital.

During a dress rehearsal, the CSF team boarded a Huey helicopter just after midnight in Sana'a carrying fully loaded backpacks and their assault weapons. To avoid detection, the helicopter put them down about three miles from the target, in this case, a deserted residential compound. The plan was for the Yemenis and their American trainers to hump it across the desert for an hour to a location overlooking the compound, from where the assault would be launched. It didn't go well. To begin with, one of the Yemenis was nearly decapitated as he made an ill-advised leap from the helicopter as it touched down and came within inches of its rotors.

The trek across the desert proved to be the biggest obstacle. All but a handful of the Yemenis were unable to carry their gear the required distance, so everyone returned to Sana'a and the mission was scrubbed. Despite such failures, the feeling in Washington was that six million dollars was a small price to pay to ensure that specialized American units would be able to continue operating inside Yemen.

The second thing the president got was Marsh's return to Sana'a, as the argument that a foreign leader shouldn't be allowed to influence the CIA's assignments process suddenly fell out of favor.

Marsh's familiarity with the complicated history of counterterrorism cooperation between the US and Yemen led him to quickly conclude that the president would not agree to a strike on Abu Salim—or anyone else, for that matter—on Yemeni territory. The other option, conducting the operation without his okay—even if it went off without a hitch and with no civilian casualties—was fraught with risk, although Marsh felt obliged to propose it to policymakers back home, simply because he didn't know when such an opportunity might present itself again.

He pulled up to the staff vehicle entrance of the embassy just as the car before him was moving through the second of two gates, allowing it to enter the inspection area. A wedge barrier rose from the pavement in front of him; he popped the hood and tailgate of his SUV and waited while the guards conducted a quick search to make sure no one had planted explosives on the vehicle while it was unattended outside the coffee shop.

While he waited, he added a call to the head of the Political Security Organization to the running to-do list he kept on his cell phone. The PSO was Yemen's sprawling internal security service with a network of officers and agents all over the country. Marsh had promised Kit that Abdulwahab would receive a heads-up that Abu Salim might be heading his way with ill intent, and that the PSO could send someone to deliver that message faster than anybody else. That would be his second call. First, he needed to call the NSB chief to thank him for the assist last night. While he was at it, he would send flowers to Bassam's wife, to apologize for dragging her husband away from the dinner table—knowing full well it was not likely to be the last time.

It was nearly two in the afternoon by the time Marsh had taken care of all the tasks on his list. He had sent out his cable to headquarters proposing the drone surveillance on Abu Salim. He had spoken to the NSB chief and asked his office manager to arrange for the flower delivery. Finally, he had a long conversation with General Qassem al-Saif, the commander of the PSO, explaining his concern that AQAP might be contemplating an attack against Abdulwahab al-Akli.

All that done, he walked down to the small cafeteria in the basement of the embassy and lingered over the last of the day's lunch special talking to a pair of marines, part of the detachment providing physical security for the embassy. From there he went to the gym for a quick workout. He showered and was on his way back to his office when Sarah Hilliard, the NSA rep at the embassy, caught up with him.

"Marsh, I need a word," she said, reluctantly following him up the stairs to the third floor, because Marsh never took the elevator. They walked to the end of the corridor and he tapped a code into a cipher lock on the door. They wove their way through the cramped workspace that housed the CIA station to a windowless room in the rear. Marsh sat down at his desk and motioned for her to sit as well. "I saw your cable on Abu Salim," she said. "Headquarters just sent us the readout of a conversation you're going to want to see."

"Abu Salim?"

"Yup. And guess who he's talking to—your good friend and head of the PSO, General Saif."

Marsh threw his hands in the air. "For Christ's sake, you can't trust anybody to keep a secret anymore. I'll bet Qassem couldn't wait to tell that little weasel what I shared with him when we spoke."

"Well, he does make specific mention of your conversation."

"What a peckerhead." Marsh rocked forward in his chair. "Give me ten minutes and I'll come over. I just need to check my email."

A short while later, Hank was sitting in Hilliard's office carefully reading the cable she'd just received. The conversation between Abu Salim and the PSO chief started out with the usual Arabic pleasantries. Then the two got down to business.

"Habibi, you are causing the Americans a great deal of distress," General Saif said, with what Marsh thought was an excess of good humor. "I received a call from the CIA director at the embassy asking me to send a man to alert Sheikh Abdulwahab that you may wish to do him harm. Why would they think that?"

"Because Abdulwahab has been talking to an American reporter and now three of my best men are in European jails. The old man needs to be taught a lesson."

"Is this the same American reporter you picked up from the Ghamdan Hotel on Friday night?"

"I'm surprised the activities of a humble man such as myself are of such interest to you."

"Oh, I'm interested in many things, although your weekend adventures are a matter for others to concern themselves with. I'm calling to discuss the sheikh, and the Americans' desire to alert him to potential danger. You know how unreliable cell phone service is in the eastern part of the country. It's hard to say when I'll be able to speak with the chief in Ataq and arrange for him to pay a visit to Abdulwahab. I can't imagine it happening before next week."

The phone line was quiet as the tacit assurance to Abu Salim seemed to sink in. When he replied, it was simply to say, "I understand. I am grateful for your call."

Marsh shook his head. "Well, one less bottle of Johnnie Walker to give away this Christmas," he said, and he quietly walked out.

Back in his office, he dialed a number he used only on the most urgent occasions.

CHAPTER FORTY-FOUR

Sana'a, Yemen

The uniformed guards at the presidential palace always looked sharp: red berets, English-tan khaki uniforms, and creased trousers tucked into polished black boots. The one peering into the back seat of the embassy SUV where Marsh sat had epaulets on his shoulders. He moved with the efficiency of a good officer, confirming quickly by radio with the palace that Marsh was expected, even as the clock slipped past 11:00 p.m. Not that it was unusual for the president to receive guests late into the evening. He was known to be a night owl and, as a result, traffic in and out of the palace was often heaviest after midnight.

The officer stood back and gestured to let Marsh's car pass. The heavy drop bar slowly swung up until it was at a ninety-degree angle, and the SUV moved ahead quietly, along a tree-lined promenade that ended in a circular drive with an enormous fountain at its center. The car continued around the circle to a small parking lot adjacent to the palace. Marsh stepped out of the car.

He approached an ornate set of doors and waited. There was no reason to knock; he knew cameras had tracked him since his vehicle entered the palace grounds. The door swung open and Marsh stepped into an elaborate foyer with Italian marble floors and mahogany wainscoting. He was greeted by the president's chief of staff, who accompanied him down a flight of circular stairs that Marsh knew from previous visits led to the swimming pool.

The president liked an evening swim followed by a glass or two of

Macallan 12 Year while he was drying off. He was sitting near the pool in a heavy white terry cloth robe, combing his wet hair, which was still jet black, even though the president was well into his seventies. He smiled when he saw Marsh and motioned him over.

"It's not too late for a swim," he said.

"I forgot my trunks, Mr. President."

"Pity. Then perhaps I can persuade you to have a drink with me."

"That would be a pleasure, sir." The president raised his hand to signal another drink was needed, and Marsh looked around the pool. The president's chief of staff, who had walked him downstairs, was seated at the far end of the room with a notebook on his lap, talking quietly on a cell phone. The only other person nearby was a white-jacketed waiter who approached just long enough to place a glass of scotch on the table next to Marsh's chair, after which he quietly withdrew.

"To your health, Mr. President," Marsh said, lifting his glass, a gesture his host reciprocated.

"These quiet moments late in the evening are to be treasured," the president said. "So much noise during the day. Everyone moving about. Being disagreeable. It gets tiring." He brought his glass to his lips, sipped the whiskey, and said, "What about you, Marshall? I understand you've been very busy lately. Do you ever tire of it?"

"Sometimes, sir. I think we all need to find moments of peace and quiet in the course of our day, when we can collect our thoughts and remind ourselves that the jobs we've chosen to do make a difference in people's lives—hopefully for the better. At least that helps me get through the days when, as busy as I might feel, little seems to get accomplished."

The president nodded his head in agreement. "We're navigating treacherous waters, and powerful currents are working against us. It's easier when you have strong partners, Marshall." The president always called him by his full name, fascinated by the fact that Marsh had been named for Thurgood Marshall, the great African American jurist, a bit of family history Marsh had shared with him.

"I hope you'll always consider me one of those partners, Mr. President," Marsh said, raising his glass slightly. The president nodded enigmatically, and said, "So what is it that brings you here this evening, Marshall?"

Marsh knew the president kept close tabs on him; he liked to think it was out of personal concern, but he was a realist and had concluded long ago that it was more likely because of his professional capacity as the embassy's chief intelligence officer.

"Mr. President, you know I rarely call on you directly, even though you have told me that I may. It is a privilege I don't ever want to abuse. But as you said a moment ago, this is a dangerous moment, and I wanted to convey my concern to you in person."

"And what is your concern, Marshall?"

"My concern is that people who kidnap foreign journalists from their hotels in Sana'a are jeopardizing your standing with important countries, including my own. My concern is that these same people have very close ties to others who were planning to conduct an attack on civilian targets in Europe for the second time, which undermines confidence in your government. Speaking frankly, sir, and with all respect, it raises questions as to who is in charge of Yemen."

The president bristled visibly at Marsh's comment, his dark eyes flashing in anger, but he let it be. Marsh had warned him in one of their first meetings after his return to Sana'a that "I will always speak to you with the candor the close ties between our two nations demand." That honesty had become yet another quality in Marsh that the president admired, even if it wasn't one he'd ever tolerate in his own advisers.

"Ah, yes, you are speaking of Abu Salim. He is a bit of a thorn in my side. And now yours, as well. I have tried to come to terms with him, but he is, as you say, very determined. This is a problem I will have to address."

"There is another problem, Mr. President. The chief of your PSO seems to be a close confidant of Abu Salim."

The president seemed unsurprised by this observation. "General

Saif performs a very important function for me, Marshall. He stays in close contact with unpleasant people like Abu Salim who can make my life difficult. And sometimes he must do small favors in order to maintain his influence with them. It's an unsavory business. At the end of the day, everyone's hands are a little dirty. Given your line of work, I would imagine that you may feel that way yourself from time to time."

Marsh couldn't disclose to the president what the two men had discussed during their recent phone conversation without revealing it was acquired through signals intelligence, so he sipped his scotch and said nothing. For a moment, the two sat in silence.

"Let me just say, Marshall, that you shouldn't always believe everything you hear."

Marsh looked at the president, impressed once again by the old man's ability to seemingly read his thoughts. It was as if he was reminding Marsh that he was quite aware the United States routinely eavesdropped on conversations of senior officials from governments around the world, including his own. The president's face betrayed nothing, however. He finished his scotch and tightened his robe, a subtle signal to Marsh that the visit was over.

"That's good advice, as always, Mr. President." Marsh drained his own glass. "I won't take up any more of your time. Thank you for seeing me and thank you for listening to my concerns."

"Marshall, I owe you that and much more." They both stood and shook hands. "Faisal will show you out," the president said as he turned toward the door leading to his private quarters. "Next time, bring your bathing suit, Marshall. A good swim helps you unwind after a busy day. It's very therapeutic." The president adjusted his robe once more and walked away slowly, disappearing through a doorway at the far end of the pool.

CHAPTER FORTY-FIVE

Shabwa, Yemen

The headlights of the oversized pickup truck pierced the darkness, illuminating the uneven contours of the packed dirt road ahead. It was a Ford F-550 and it weighed nearly seven thousand pounds. It was the only truck of its kind in Yemen. Two Al Qaeda operatives had traveled to Saudi Arabia, purchased it with cash, and driven it back to Yemen earlier in the year.

Abu Salim was sitting in the front seat of an SUV trailing the truck, growing increasingly impatient with the pace at which they were traveling. The sun would be rising in less than thirty minutes and they still had to pass through one more village on the way to Abdulwahab's compound.

The lead truck had a crew cab and a heavy frame attached to its front bumper. It went by many names around the world: cow catcher, moose bumper, nudge bar. In this instance, its purpose was to ram the truck through the gates of the perimeter wall surrounding Abdulwahab's house, at which point the five men inside would leap from the truck and lay down suppressing fire with the automatic weapons they carried. They would use the hand grenades attached to the tactical vests they wore to create more havoc. As soon as the truck opened a path into the compound, the other vehicles in the small convoy would follow: the SUV in which Abu Salim was sitting, and another one behind him that was transporting an additional four men, all experienced fighters. They had timed their arrival to coincide with daybreak, when the majority of those inside the compound would be at morning prayer, without their weapons.

As they passed through the village below Abdulwahab's house, they saw no one but drove slowly just the same. No reason to kick up a lot of dust and draw the attention of a local who might—if he were ever asked by the police—remember a detail or two about the three vehicles that passed through the village just before Abdulwahab's house went up in smoke. Once the village was in their rearview mirror, Abu Salim pressed the transmit button on a radio clipped to his vest to issue a command, and the drivers of the three vehicles extinguished their headlights, navigating only by the light of the slowly approaching dawn.

Four hundred miles away, in a dimly lit conference room at the US embassy in Sana'a, Marsh sat with a half dozen others around a large computer screen and watched the images of Abu Salim's convoy transmitted from a surveillance drone some five miles above the earth.

They'd been watching since the vehicles departed Ataq almost three hours earlier, virtually alone on the small road that eventually would lead them to Abdulwahab's compound. The drone had been tracking Abu Salim's SUV since it drove away from his residence in Sana'a four days earlier. It followed him to Ataq, where he holed up in what appeared to be a safe house on the outskirts of the city. That in itself was a very helpful find, and Marsh made sure someone added the coordinates of the house to a list of potential targets they kept.

Over the next two days, the other vehicles and the remaining fighters arrived. Marsh was afraid the drone would be out of range when they went operational, but it was on target and captured the three vehicles departing the safe house just after three in the morning. He was sleeping on an office sofa much too small for his large frame when a knock on the door alerted him that the vehicles were on the move and about an hour out.

The Agency had denied Marsh's request to conduct a lethal operation against the occupants of the vehicles. Too many individuals involved, they said, some they hadn't even identified yet, and others about whom they had insufficient intelligence to order a lethal strike against. Besides, conducting such an op at this moment without the consent of the Yemeni government was risking another rupture with the president, and the counterterrorism relationship was just recovering from the previous episode. American assets were not at risk. Abdulwahab was on his own.

The truck accelerated as it approached the house. Everyone sitting with Marsh seemed to lean forward at the same time, anticipating the moment it would make contact with the vehicle gate. When it did, it barely slowed. The left panel of the steel gate buckled under the impact, came free of its hinges, and sailed backward toward the house. The other half also spun free, tipping up on its edge before falling flat onto the ground in a large cloud of dust. The truck came to a halt inside the compound and five men leaped out, their automatic weapons ablaze in all directions. The two SUVs followed closely behind.

As soon as all three vehicles entered the compound, the screen lit up as the intruders came under withering fire. The vehicles jumped with the impact of heavy-caliber bullets that riddled their chassis, blowing out headlights, windows, and tires.

"Holy shit," someone behind Marsh said. "They drove into a fucking ambush." The gunfire continued for another thirty seconds or so, and then as quickly as it erupted, it stopped. A thick haze filled the screen. Marsh and those around him didn't move, didn't speak. They'd just witnessed an execution.

Nothing moved on the screen for a moment and then, slowly, figures drifted into view from the left and right. They wrenched open the doors to the vehicles and threw bodies to the ground, checking for any sign of life. When they were satisfied, one of them signaled to the house. Three men emerged and walked down the stairs.

"Abdulwahab," Marsh said when he saw the sheikh approach the car with an AK-47 slung over his shoulder. "I'll be damned. 'Don't believe everything you hear,' the president told me, and I didn't know what he meant. They set him up."

Marsh leaned back in his chair and shook his head. "That's one way to get rid of a thorn in your side."

CHAPTER FORTY-SIX

Sana'a, Yemen

Kit sat alone in her hotel room in Sana'a. She told Hank she needed time without any distractions to finish the piece on Abdulwahab and his family. Hank reminded her that he had been invited to lunch at the US embassy and expected to be there for hours, sampling fine wine and exotic hors d'oeuvres, and she would be lucky if he made it back for dinner.

Kit worked straight through lunch. London was waiting for the story; her editor had already called to ask when they should expect it. She told him it was all but done—she just wanted to make sure it was right before she hit send.

In a simpler world, it began, *without the sadly familiar cycle of terrorist violence and government retaliation that is a hallmark of our age, Sheikh Abdulwahab al-Akli would almost certainly lead the life he once imagined. He would tend to his tribe in the remote Yemeni governorate of Shabwa, offer advice and counsel, arbitrate disputes, and dispense the wisdom he has accumulated over a lifetime. He would, in other words, do his best to ensure the cohesion of his community in spite of the centrifugal forces that threaten to undo everything he holds dear.*

Abdulwahab doesn't know with certainty when he was born. Like many Arabs conceived during periods of unrest and institutional upheaval, his exact birthdate wasn't recorded, so he chose January 1. He believes the year was 1947. He is tall and sturdy by Yemeni standards, a nation where men tend to be slender and small of stature. Unlike many Yemeni families who number children in double digits, Abdulwahab fathered three: Walid, Aisha, and Ashraf. Walid died of cholera when he was twelve. Aisha, the most headstrong of the three, went off to Kuwait at eighteen to attend university but abandoned her studies after she met Ibrahim al-Jubaili, a young Kuwaiti she later married. And while Abdulwahab still mourns the death of his oldest son, and rues his daughter's choice in a husband, it is the fate of Ashraf, his youngest child, that brings Abdulwahab such sadness each time he thinks of him.

Ashraf's official designation is ISN 1453. He is one of nearly two hundred prisoners still held at the US Naval facility at Guantanamo Bay, Cuba. He has been in custody for eight years without ever being charged with a crime or appearing before a judge to contest his detention. In that respect, he is like virtually every other man imprisoned at Guantanamo.

"Every day is another form of torture for these men," says Carole Ann McAfee, who has represented Ashraf since 2002, when he was brought to Guantanamo after having been detained as he tried to cross into Pakistan from neighboring Afghanistan. "In some cases, that is literally true. The methods used in the interrogations they have endured are criminal.

"Ashraf weighed a hundred thirty pounds when I met him. Today, he weighs scarcely a hundred pounds and has difficulty standing for any more than a few minutes because of injuries he has suffered. Three months ago he stopped eating to protest his continued imprisonment with no opportunity to prove his innocence. He is now force-fed every day while strapped to a chair. This supposed humanitarian gesture is literally killing him."

Kit paused. She knew those words would cause Abdulwahab unmerciful pain. She also knew that if her words were going to have any impact whatsoever, if she had any hope of drawing attention to Ashraf's case, she needed to paint a picture in the starkest terms possible.

At least Abdulwahab was alive. Marsh had called and described the failed attack by Abu Salim, without revealing to Kit the circumstances that led to its failure. He simply said that the attackers had underestimated Abdulwahab, and it cost them their lives.

Kit turned her attention back to the open page on her laptop.

> *And while Ashraf's ordeal in Guantanamo is a poignant reminder of how America's so-called Global War on Terror has crept into homes in the most remote corners of the world, it is not the only one with which Abdulwahab must contend.*
>
> *French authorities claim that his son-in-law, Ibrahim al-Jubaili, led the attack on a Paris museum last year that damaged priceless pieces of art in its Middle East collection and wounded a security guard. Jubaili evaded capture in the wake of the attack and made his way back to Yemen, living with his wife at the family compound, off the grid and out of the reach of Western authorities. That all changed last week, when Jubaili and two others attempted to enter Europe again, arriving at airports in Germany and the Netherlands. All three were detained as they disembarked. Authorities believe they were planning to conduct another attack against an undisclosed target. The men have now been extradited to France, where they will stand trial on a variety of terrorism-related charges.*
>
> *It is not lost on Abdulwahab that his family has become inextricably linked to a world that has overlooked Yemen in almost every respect other than counterterrorism. He doesn't answer immediately when a visitor asks how he thinks this neglect became a seemingly permanent condition. Instead, he looks away, as if imagining an existence where it was not the case.*
>
> *"Even here," he says, "the world intrudes. We, too, become*

witnesses to events happening in places that most of us will never visit. Images of our brothers and sisters suffering stir the anger of our children, no less than that of young Muslims in Germany or France. But perhaps in those countries children are taught to believe they have the power to change the structures around them without resorting to violence."

He laughs softly, although he doesn't appear amused. "Of course, young people in Europe don't grow up with an AK-47 in their arms the way our sons do, so perhaps it should be no surprise that some of our children are drawn to those who would use guns and bombs to solve the problems they see in the world."

Abdulwahab has encountered first-hand people like those he describes, whose preferred tools of conflict resolution are automatic weapons. His home was attacked last week by a group of fighters identified by authorities as belonging to Al Qaeda in the Arabian Peninsula (AQAP), the Yemen-based franchise of the international terrorist organization. They were seeking retribution for the arrests of Jubaili and the two others, apparently convinced that Abdulwahab bore some responsibility. The attack on his home failed, and the assailants all died in the furious response mounted by the armed fighters whose job it is to protect their tribal sheikh.

Kit pushed away from the desk, stood up, and began to pace around the small hotel room. It was time to leave Yemen. She had become too much a part of the story she was telling. If there were ever lines between her role as observer and those she observed, they were now hopelessly blurred. She had finally spoken with Abdulwahab, expressed her relief that he had escaped Abu Salim's attack, and had promised to stay in touch with his son's attorney. "I'll make sure he knows you think of him often, and that you love him, Abdulwahab." Kit choked back tears at that moment, pained by her inability to promise a grieving father anything more than that.

"That is fine, Kit. I will hope to hear from you, perhaps with some good news someday."

"Abdulwahab, nothing would make me happier than to be able to call you with good news. Perhaps I will even return to Yemen to deliver it personally."

"*Ahlan wa sahlan*, Kit," he replied. "It will be a pleasure to see you whenever you decide to return. I hope you will be well. *Masalaamah*." Go in peace.

"*Allahyusalaamak*, Abdulwahab," Kit replied, wishing him God's care. "*Allahyusalaamak*."

CHAPTER FORTY-SEVEN

Sana'a, Yemen

Hank's first glimpse of the residence of the American ambassador to Yemen revealed a surprisingly inelegant two-story brick construction tucked into the corner of a large walled compound that also housed the embassy itself and a residential apartment block for mission staff.

Getting onto the compound had been surprisingly easy, given the daunting level of security outside: concentric circles of Yemeni police and paramilitary forces, all heavily armed and seemingly bereft of any English-language skills. The US passport Hank carried moved him through the security maze with welcome alacrity, and before he knew it, he was inside the compound and on his way to the residence, accompanied by an embassy guard.

David Leslie was sitting alone in a small alcove next to a large formal reception space when Hank entered. A tall glass of what appeared to be iced tea sat on a table in front of him. "Glad to see you under less dramatic circumstances," Leslie said as he stood to welcome Hank, motioning him to sit in a yellow wicker chair with flowered cushions. As he did, a waiter appeared, and Hank asked for a glass of whatever his host was drinking.

"I have to say, that was an unexpected introduction to American diplomacy," Hank said. "I mean, is spiriting Americans out of the country a common occurrence in your life as a diplomat? I always thought you guys negotiated treaties and kept wars from breaking out and stuff like that."

Leslie laughed. "We do that when there's time, Hank. But protection of American citizens is a responsibility we take very seriously. In a country like Yemen, that can sometimes be complicated. But what about you? What led you to this confounding corner of the world?"

Hank explained in brief what had brought him to Yemen, although in this version, he came up empty-handed in his search for Moishe Azani's silver jewelry. "It was always a stretch to believe I would actually find it," he said. "But it's been a great experience, and I'm pretty sure I can mine it for a good story. Without mentioning the incident in the hotel, of course."

Leslie smiled. He seemed relaxed, not at all the man Hank had encountered in the hotel lobby days earlier. "This is probably a good moment to confess that I googled your name when I got back to my office that afternoon. Call it due diligence. Was it hard for you to leave the *Register*? Or was Iowa just too tame for you?"

Hank hated to lie to Leslie but didn't want to disappoint him with the truth. Instead, he offered something that he had honestly felt from time to time, even if it hadn't figured into his sudden departure from the newspaper.

"Small-town journalism can sometimes make you feel like a gerbil on an exercise wheel. Stick around long enough and the same events that you were covering last year are right back in front of you. Johnson County Fair? Check. Heated discussion over the mayor's budget proposal? Check. The girls' soccer team losing a heartbreaker on their way to the state finals? Check. I guess I needed a change of pace."

He paused then, uncertain if he should follow his impulse to reveal a bit more. But Leslie had a manner about him that put Hank at ease, so he continued. "If I'm being candid, I also met a woman. She's a journalist too, and turns out she was on her way to Yemen, and suddenly I had a good reason to join her. Well, two, in fact. The spoken one was to try and write an ending to my grandfather's unfinished story, and the other was that I couldn't imagine letting her get away from me. So here I am."

"Well, I wish you the best of luck with both, Hank—the story and the young woman. I'm a little jealous, in fact. Was a time when my life was just unfolding, and . . ." Before he finished his thought, an explosion rattled the room. It seemed very close.

Hank looked at Leslie, who himself seemed to be trying to sort out what had just happened. Seconds later, another explosion brought him to his feet. He reached into his pocket for his cell phone, which, at the same moment, began to ring. "My apologies, Hank. I need to take this. Have your tea. I'll be back in a second."

It was five minutes before Leslie returned. "Hank, I am terribly sorry, but we're going to have to cancel our lunch. It seems that someone fired two small mortar rounds in the direction of the embassy, but they fell short. One landed in an empty lot next door, but the other landed in the playground of a girls' school just south of us. Some students have been injured. I'm going there now with our embassy nurse to see if we can offer any assistance. One of my bodyguards will escort you out to the street and wait until you can get a taxi back to your hotel." Leslie looked regretful. "Not exactly the lunch either one of us had in mind. Come. I'll walk you outside."

As they stepped out the door, Hank suddenly said, "Would you mind terribly if I tagged along? I've done it before. Not like this, of course, but with EMTs when I was at school. I know how to stay out of the way." Leslie appeared to be listening, so Hank kept at it. "Look. This is a good story. Nobody back home has the foggiest idea what diplomats actually do, or the dangers you face. Let me be the one who tells this story. Your story."

Leslie looked at him. "Not my story. Grandstanding's not a good look in this line of work. Besides, getting anything done in an environment like this is a collective effort. So, the focus needs to be on that. And there's no guarantee the Department will even agree to this. I'll ask, but you've got to promise you won't publish anything until everyone's on board."

"Hundred percent," Hank said, and the two of them headed for

Leslie's car, an ungainly, heavily armored late-model Cadillac. Once they were settled in the back, a bodyguard climbed into the right front seat and, on his cue, the limousine and a small SUV carrying more security personnel and the embassy nurse exited the compound. As they made their way to the street through the serpentine exit, an open-top jeep with four Yemeni police officers brandishing automatic weapons pulled in front, and the three vehicles moved quickly through the early-afternoon traffic.

Without looking at Hank, Leslie said: "Shortly after the ambassador arrived, she put a stop to our Yemeni police escort's use of the siren every time either one of us left the compound. That, and their regrettable habit of pointing their long guns at passing cars. Believe me, it was a struggle. Much less fun for them now, I'm sure."

They covered the distance to the girls' school in a matter of minutes, arriving at a shabby, three-story concrete block building with exterior corridors. The school was literally adjacent to the twelve-foot high, razor-wire-topped wall that surrounded the embassy. The plot of land on which it stood was just packed dirt, and the cars sent small clouds of dust into the air as they approached.

"This is close enough, Hussein," Leslie said to the lead bodyguard in the front seat. The cars stopped, the security detail opened the heavy doors, and the two of them got out. The only emergency vehicle in sight was an aging pumper truck belonging to the Sana'a fire department. Several firefighters were moving about, ushering students from the building. To the rear, on a small basketball court, a half dozen girls were lying on blankets. Some were crying, others weren't moving at all.

Leslie waited for the embassy nurse to join him, and the two moved quickly toward a woman speaking with one of the firefighters. She wore a black *chador*, which covered her from head to foot. Only her face was visible.

She seemed to recognize Leslie, and the two of them spoke briefly in Arabic. Leslie drew the embassy nurse into the small huddle, and the woman, who Hank concluded must be the school director, walked with them over to where the injured girls had been taken. The nurse, a sturdy-looking American woman carrying a small satchel of what appeared to be emergency medical supplies, didn't seem to speak any Arabic, so the school director stayed with her, translating as needed, reassuring her students that the *ajnabia*, the foreign woman, was there to help.

As the pair moved from child to child, sirens could be heard in the distance, and in a matter of minutes, two ambulances drove up to the school entrance, one following closely behind the other. Hank realized that he had lost track of Leslie. He looked to his right, to the spot where the girls who had been escorted from the building were now sitting on the ground in small groups, and there he was, moving quietly among the students, down on one knee, then up again, a tall American in a dark suit among a sea of young Yemeni girls wearing identical school uniforms.

The ambulance personnel spread out across the schoolyard. The American nurse walked with them for a few minutes, pointing out the most severe injuries. Then she peeled away and headed back in Leslie's direction.

"They've got this under control now," she said. "There's nothing more for me to do here."

"How badly are they hurt?" Leslie asked.

"One's got a nasty cut on her head from a falling ceiling tile, and several have bits of glass in their hands and legs from windows that shattered with the explosions, but I think they'll all be okay. The director would like a word."

Leslie approached her, and the two fell into a deep conversation that Hank couldn't hear. As their discussion concluded, Leslie brought his right hand up to his heart, bowed slightly, and turned away.

"What did she say?" Hank asked as they returned to Leslie's car and it slowly pulled away from the school.

"That she was grateful we had come. She said some people will blame the Americans for the girls being injured because the embassy is so close to the school, but she will tell them to blame those who are responsible for the attack. That the Americans had the decency to come immediately to care for her students, while the criminals who launched the bombs slinked away in shame."

"How does that make you feel?" Hank asked.

Leslie didn't respond immediately, then he said: "I feel like we're barely scratching the surface. Like we don't have enough traction to move things forward in a meaningful way. I wanted to reassure the school director that there won't be any more incidents like the one today, but I can't. There's so much to do in this country, and I've got an embassy full of capable people who want to make a difference: Reinvigorate the agricultural sector. Develop school curricula. Support electoral reform. Train police officers, judges."

He looked out the window at the city that, for the moment anyway, was his home. "But how do we send people out knowing they might not come back at the end of the day? Already, everyone travels with a full security detail, but it ties us in knots. We can only support so many movements in a day, and even our best contacts are sometimes reluctant to meet with us because it becomes such a big production. It takes a toll on everybody, but we persist. Why? Because we believe if we make a difference out here we'll all be safer back home." The car slowly came to a stop. "Okay, that's the end of my homily. And here you are back at your hotel, courtesy of the US government."

"Well, this sure beats the taxi I came over in. Thanks for the ride. And for letting me tag along."

"You're welcome. Stay in touch. Especially if you decide to go ahead with a story. I'll alert our press office to what we did today so they can start to run the traps with the Department."

One of the bodyguards swung open the car door, and Hank slid out. He stepped onto the curb and watched the vehicle drive away.

He walked into the hotel, his head still spinning from everything he had just witnessed. He went to his room and wrote pages of notes. Over dinner that evening he described the experience to Kit.

"I thought I understood how the world works. But not this world. Not a place where explosive devices drop from the sky onto a school playground. A place where American diplomats are targeted by terrorists and then help triage young girls who end up becoming the victims." He laughed ruefully. "I feel like Dorothy when she realized she wasn't in Kansas anymore."

CHAPTER FORTY-EIGHT

Sana'a, Yemen

The following morning, Hank stowed the heavy cloth sack full of Moishe Azani's jewelry into his backpack, slung it over his shoulder, and walked alone to the furniture shop in the Old City where he and Haitham first met Yahya Habib. He had texted Yahya to say he was leaving Yemen, hoping to bid farewell and leave a small gift behind before he did.

The shop was empty as Hank entered, but he could hear noise at the rear, so he continued past the stacks of milled lumber and dismantled tables and chairs until Yahya came into view.

"*Shalom*," Yahya said as Hank approached. "So, you've come to say goodbye?"

"Yes, Yahya. To say goodbye and to leave something with you." He took the backpack from his shoulders, opened it, and removed the bag. "This is what I would like you to have. It is for you and your family and all the Jews of Yemen who have worked proudly and honorably over many generations. I told you about Moishe Azani, the silversmith who was among the Jews my grandfather flew to Israel in 1949. This is the jewelry he was forced to leave behind, jewelry he asked my grandfather to retrieve and keep safe. That never happened because my grandfather never managed to return to Yemen, so I have come on his behalf, and I have been fortunate enough to find what Moishe left behind."

He handed the bag to Yahya, who sat down, made a small well in the heavy apron he wore, and emptied the contents onto his lap.

He looked at the pieces carefully, one by one, holding them up and turning them in the light.

"How did you ever . . . ?"

Hank interrupted Yahya before he finished his question. "It was simply good fortune. But I promise you no one is going to come looking for any of this and cause you any trouble. Moishe made sure of that."

"*Mash'allah*," Yahya said quietly as he continued to examine the individual pieces. "I am a simple furniture maker. This is the work of a master craftsman."

"I think you're not all that different from one another," Hank said. "You may not be in his bloodline but in every other respect you are a direct descendant of Moishe Azani. If he could be here with us, I am sure he would be very happy to see that the jewelry he loved so much is now in good hands. Do what you think is best with all this. Use it to make your life, and that of your sons, better."

Yahya seemed moved by Hank's words. He slowly shook his head as he continued to examine the jewelry

"There is one other thing, Yahya, and I hope you won't think I have overstepped my bounds. You told me that the Alloush family always dealt fairly with Jewish craftsmen. I called them, Yahya. I spoke with Hassan Alloush, the grandson of Abdullah. He runs the family business in Dubai now. I said that a valuable collection of silver jewelry has just come into the possession of a family in Sana'a, and it might be available for purchase. He was quite excited when he heard the news. He comes to Sana'a three or four times a year and said he would be very happy to examine the jewelry on his next visit. He gave me his cell phone number. You can call him if you wish. That's up to you. As I say, the jewelry is yours to do with as you please. Now I must go."

Hank stood and waited as Yahya returned the silver pieces to the cloth bag. They embraced, and Hank departed, leaving a trail of footprints through the sawdust covering the floor.

CHAPTER FORTY-NINE

Sana'a, Yemen

"Do you have anything more to do here, Hank?" Kit rolled over onto her left side so she could see his face clearly. He was sitting next to her on the bed, a pad of yellow lined paper on his lap. He was writing a letter to his grandfather.

"No, I'm done," he said. "Yahya has the jewelry, and he will care for it. Or maybe he'll sell it, but what he does with it is up to him. It was all created by Yemeni Jews and now, more than a half century later, it's in the hands of another. I feel somehow as though this story has come full circle. How about you?"

"I'm ready to leave," Kit said. "London has my story, and they're happy with the way it came out. They said it will run in a couple of days. Let's go find that beach you promised." She rolled closer, laid her head on his chest, and closed her eyes. He put his arm over her and kissed the top of her head.

"That's the best idea you've had since you invited me to come to Yemen with you." Hank reached his hand down to the left pocket of his jeans. He felt the ring he had purchased from the old man the day he visited Bayt Baws. He didn't know if it was worth anything, but it would forever connect him to this place, to its history and to its people, to their faith, their pride, their wisdom, and their struggle to come to peace with the world, and with each other. He wanted Kit to have it, to remind them both of this time they had together in a land that was at once deeply troubled and stunningly beautiful. He was going to give it to her when he asked her to marry him. Not now. Not tonight. But soon, *insh'allah*.

EPILOGUE

In the end, it wasn't just one beach, it was a string of beaches, sprinkled along the coast of Yemen from Aden to Salalah, Oman, eight hundred miles to the east.

Hank and Kit had flown from Sana'a to Aden on a Tuesday morning. Haitham took them to the airport.

"My uncle will be waiting for you when you land in Aden," Haitham said as they bid farewell to each other in the terminal. "He'll take you to your hotel and you can plan your trip from there." Haitham's uncle was a cab driver who at one time had made a decent living serving the modest flow of adventure tourists, mostly Europeans, who turned up in Aden. That traffic had all but dried up in recent years as terrorism incidents spiked, and he happily accepted the offer to drive two Americans to Oman and escape the drudgery of scouring Aden's streets looking for fares. "You'll like him, Hank. He taught me how to drive," Haitham said, a smile on his face.

"As long as he doesn't meet us at the airport in a dodgem," Hank replied, putting his bag on the floor so he had both arms free to embrace Haitham. Kit promised to be back in a couple of months. Hank said he probably would not be, but he hoped to catch up with Haitham somewhere down the road.

Their Yemenia Airways flight to Aden took forty-five minutes. As they walked from the plane to the terminal, Hank told Kit that Aden Airport was built on the same site once occupied by Royal Air Force Khormaksar, where his grandfather picked up Moishe Azani on a sultry summer day in 1949. "Who knows," he said as they crossed the tarmac, "he might have walked right here at one time." He paused in front of the terminal so Kit could take a photo and he could show Dewey how the air station had grown in the six decades since he taxied along its runways.

They spent two nights in Aden, in a quiet hotel that backed onto a half-moon beach they had pretty much to themselves each day. They ate spiny lobster from the Gulf of Aden and drank cold beer the hotel's owner kept in a separate refrigerator, away from the prying eyes of those who frowned on the consumption of alcohol.

On the third day, Haitham's uncle Rashid pulled up in front of the hotel in his Hyundai sedan, just as they had agreed on the day they arrived in Aden. He loaded their bags into the trunk, and they drove away, heading for the small port town of Bir Ali, six hours east. "Very beautiful beaches," Rashid promised, and indeed, they were. So beautiful they spent three nights there, in a small deserted beachfront hostel that was perfectly situated to catch the breezes blowing in from the gulf. Each night Hank and Kit carried the thin mattress from their room up to the roof and slept under the stars.

The hotel owner was ecstatic to have guests again. "We used to be busy, before all this trouble started. The German ambassador and his family used to come here. He was an amateur pilot and he would rent a small plane at the airport in Sana'a and fly it himself to a landing strip about twenty minutes from here. We'd pick them up and they would stay for two or three days. They had a son who said he wanted to become a pilot when he grew up. They were a nice family."

They stopped again and again at nearly every beach that caught their eye as they continued eastward, sometimes just long enough to take a quick walk along the shoreline. They spent their final night in Yemen in Shihr, at the home of a childhood friend of Rashid's who operated a small trucking company. He drove them to a secluded cove with a white sand beach just west of the Omani border. Hank and Kit swam and sunned themselves while their host built a small wood fire on the beach and cooked fresh-caught fish that he filleted, and they ate with their hands, along with small potatoes that were skewered and roasted on the coals.

They crossed into Oman and arrived in Salalah early the following afternoon. Kit had reserved a room at a small beachfront hotel she found on the internet before they departed Aden, one that offered a full breakfast each morning and the assurance of a Wi-Fi signal. Her editor had told her to take some time off, but she was itchy to reconnect after a week of being without email. More than anything, she wanted to see if her piece on Abdulwahab, which had run on page one of the *FT* while they were still in Aden, had stirred any sort of reaction.

They bid farewell to Rashid, checked into the hotel, and took the elevator to the fourth floor. Their room was clean and bright and the sheets on the bed were crisp. Hank walked to the windows that looked out onto the Gulf of Oman and threw open each one. He was enjoying the offshore breeze blowing in warm and inviting when he heard Kit gasp.

"Kit, are you all right?" he asked, scarcely able to conceal the alarm he was feeling.

Kit's hand covered her mouth, and Hank could see tears welling in her eyes. Surely, he thought, someone has died.

"What is it?" he asked again as he approached the bed where she sat, hoping this time she would reply.

"Hank, I got an email from Carole Ann McAfee. The French government has informed Washington that it will accept Ashraf al-Akli as part of the Guantanamo resettlement program. He's going to France, Hank. He's going to be free." She was weeping now, tears of relief and gratitude for a small miracle that she had never allowed herself to believe might happen.

Kit composed herself long enough to read the rest of the email to Hank: *I had a long conversation with the French ambassador, and he told me it was a gesture of thanks to Abdulwahab for the information he provided that led to the arrest of Jubaili and the others, which prevented a second attack in Paris. The ambassador said that the recommendation came from a most unusual source within his government—the domestic intelligence service. He said he couldn't remember another case like this.*

Kit looked up from her laptop, her eyes glistening. "It was Bernard, Hank. He did this. Bernard and his stupid brown shoes." Hank handed her a box of tissues and she wiped her eyes.

"He did it, but you made it possible, Kit. Are you going to let Abdulwahab know?"

She thought for a moment and then shook her head. "No, that's not for me to do. Carole Ann has earned that privilege for all the years she worked on Ashraf's behalf. But someday, perhaps, we'll speak again, and I hope when we do, he'll have his son by his side. That would make me very happy."

Hank leaned over and kissed her. For the umpteenth time he made sure the ring was still in the pocket of his jeans. "Come on," he said. "Close the computer. Let's go outside. We have something to celebrate."

ACKNOWLEDGMENTS

The idea for *The Silversmith's Secret* slowly germinated over the dozen or so years I spent working on Yemen, including the three I spent living there. While the experience allowed me to imagine the story I wanted to tell, it didn't provide sufficient insight into crucial elements of that story, so I relied on the work of others to add authenticity and detail.

The "Magic Carpet" Exodus of Yemenite Jewry: An Israeli Formative Myth, by Esther Meir-Glitzenstein, is a meticulously researched chronicle of the lives of the Yemeni Jews who chose to immigrate to Israel in the years immediately following the state's creation. Not only does it describe in vivid detail the arduous journey thousands undertook to make their way from their homeland, it also reveals the external pressures at play that exacerbated the suffering of these émigrés.

On Eagles' Wings: An Untold Story of the Magic Carpet, by Captain Elgen M. Long provided an invaluable firsthand account of the emigration of Yemen's Jews from the perspective of a crew member of one of the airplanes that ferried them from Aden to Tel Aviv. Long served as navigator on those flights and many others before qualifying as a pilot and rising to the rank of captain. His account of his seventy-year flying career reads like an adventure story in its own right.

To understand Yemen's silver trade and the unique contributions made by generations of Yemeni Jews, I relied on *Silver Treasures from the Land of Sheba: Regional Styles of Yemeni Jewelry*, a remarkably thorough examination of the subject written by Marjorie Ransom. An accomplished American diplomat, Marjorie Ransom traveled throughout the country with her husband, David, documenting the cultural and economic importance of jewelry to Yemeni women. Her affection for Yemen and its people is palpable in her lavishly illustrated book.

Finally, to the people of Yemen who continue to struggle against enormous odds and at great personal risk to build a just and peaceful society, *Allah yatikum al afiya*. May God give you health, strength, and all good things.

www.ingramcontent.com/pod-product-compliance
Lightning Source LLC
LaVergne TN
LVHW041911070526
838199LV00051BA/2579